Also by Auralee Wallace

Skinny Dipping with Murder
Pumpkin Picking with Murder
Snowed In with Murder

RING IN THE YEAR

With

MURDER

Auralee Wallace

St. Martin's Paperbacks

This is a work of fiction. All of the characters, organizations, and events portrayed in this novel are either products of the author's imagination or are used fictitiously.

RING IN THE YEAR WITH MURDER

Copyright © 2017 by Auralee Wallace.

All rights reserved.

For information address St. Martin's Press, 175 Fifth Avenue, New York, NY 10010.

ISBN: 978-1-250-15145-2

Our books may be purchased in bulk for promotional, educational or business use. Please contact your local bookseller or the Macmillan Corporate and Premium Sales Department at 1-800-221-7945, extension 5442, or by e-mail at MacmillanSpecialMarkets@macmillan.com.

Printed in the United States of America

St. Martin's Paperbacks edition / November 2017

St. Martin's Paperbacks are published by St. Martin's Press, 175 Fifth Avenue, New York, NY 10010.

10 9 8 7 6 5 4 3 2 1

The Morning After

My head. My head. My head!

I untangled one of my arms from the mess of sheets that had me wrapped like a mummy, then dug the heel of my palm into my temple.

Ow.

Why . . . ? How . . . ? What happened?

I mean, clearly, I was dying. It felt like someone had buried their hatchet in my head for safekeeping, but . . .

. . . wait a minute . . .

New Year's.

That's right. It was New Year's Eve . . . or maybe New Year's Day judging by the sunlight burning through my eyelids.

I pushed off the duvet and sheets still covering me and blinked my swollen eyelids open.

Huh.

While we were on the topic of unusual things, this . . . this was not my room.

It was way too nice to be my room.

Exposed wood beams held up a white-painted ceiling. An artsy miniature sailboat sat on top of a bookshelf.

There was even a rich-people rocking chair. Don't ask me how you can tell the difference between a rich person's rocking chair and every other rocking chair. You just can.

But the room was elegant in a distant kind of way. No personal photos. No clothes. No books lying around half read. This had to be a guest room.

How much did I drink?

Wait . . . why did I drink?

I wasn't supposed to be drinking!

I pressed my hands harder into the sides of my head. There was a lot I was having trouble remembering, but the one thing I did know for sure was that I had explicitly vowed not to drink this New Year's. We were on duty. Not to mention the fact that drinking while in the presence of one's ex and one's ex's new girlfriend was a high-risk activity for humiliation. Everybody knew that.

So what the heck was going on?

I jolted against the bed when I heard what sounded like a chain saw start up next to me.

Okay, so let me rephrase that earlier question.

What the heck was going on and *who was snoring beside me?*

It only took a second to place that deviated septum. And it only took that long because I had obviously suffered brain damage. I gave the air a sniff. Champagne-induced brain damage by the smell of it. Maybe with some tequila? Oh boy, things must have gone really, really wrong if I drank tequila. I rolled over in the unknown bed, which may have been the most painful thing I had ever done in my entire life, and whacked the fur-covered shoulder of my sleeping companion. His snore cut off with a snort. He coughed. Then groaned.

"Freddie," I croaked.

Nothing.

I cleared my throat and went for something a little louder, but not so loud as to rupture a blood vessel. "Freddie."

The fur-clad figure rolled on his back, and blinked a few times. "Where am I?"

"I think . . ." I had to pause a moment. The act of talking caused a slight increase in blood pressure, which made the back of my eyeballs feel like they were being stabbed with a million tiny knives. "Matthew's. We're still at Matthew's."

It was the most likely option. The New Year's party was at Hemlock Estate, and this room screamed money.

"Why are we in bed together? And why did you dress me in a fur?"

I closed my eyes and shook my head, instantly realizing that all movement was very, very bad. I made a noncommittal noise in the back of my throat—which was also bad. I nearly threw up. I would have argued against taking responsibility for dressing Freddie in anything, let alone a fur, but it wasn't worth the effort.

He struggled up onto his elbow to look over at me. Horror spread across his face.

"What?" I asked.

"You're wearing a turban."

"A what?" I reached up and pulled the gold satin monstrosity off my head. It had dangling strings of fake pearls sewn to the front. Pearls!

"Wait . . ." Freddie's eyes darted around the room before landing back on me. Oh wow. He'd slept in his contacts. The capillaries in the whites of his eyes pulsed a bright red. That had to hurt. He might need surgery to get those puppies off. "Something's coming back to me."

"What?"

Freddie almost sat up but thought better of it real

quick. "Didn't we . . . ? Wasn't there . . . ?" Suddenly he gasped and sat up for real this time. "My dog!"

My dog? Oh right . . . Stanley, I think his name was. Freddie had brought a dog to the party. At least one of us had a date. I watched Freddie roll out of bed, falling hard onto his knees. With the gigantic fur coat he was wearing, he looked a lot like a hungover bear . . . if bears actually got hungover. He then crawled over to the small furry creature sleeping by the cold fireplace. The French bulldog lifted his head, totally encased with a plastic cone, and swiveled it toward him.

"Are you all right, puppy?" Freddie crooned in a baby voice—which was just wrong. Freddie didn't like the dog. Freddie had a history with dogs. In fact, he was just watching the dog until the pound reopened after the holidays. Seriously, what was going on? How long had I been asleep? Not that it felt like sleep. It felt more like I had been in a coma. And why was the dog wearing a cone of shame? And did I need to borrow the cone of shame for the snowmobile ride home? Oh God, I couldn't handle a snowmobile . . .

Freddie rolled to his side on the floor, his one hand still on Stanley's back, and pulled out his phone. The strangest look came over his face as he swiped at the screen. "What the . . . ?"

"What? What is it?"

"I have . . . wait." He poked at his phone a few more times. "In the last twenty-four hours, I got sixty thousand new followers on Twitter."

"What? Why? What did you do?"

"I don't know," Freddie said, looking both bewildered and nauseous. He collapsed back onto the floor, letting his hand flop to the side. "Wait . . . something else is coming back to me."

"What?"

"Did you . . . ?"

My stomach dropped then bounced right back up. *"Did I what?"*

"Did you . . . kill someone?"

"What?!" Ow. Ow. Ow. *Yelling was bad. Very bad. "No, I didn't kill anyone."* I sounded pretty certain, even though some strange images were coalescing into memories. But given the way my body felt, I was thinking a more likely scenario was that someone had tried to kill me. And it wasn't just the epic hangover. My elbows hurt. A lot. Like the skin had peeled off them. And my knees. My fingers and toes too. Not to mention the fact that my ankle felt funny. Almost like . . .

I struggled to get my one foot out from under the sheets, but it kept catching. My shoe maybe? It didn't feel like I was wearing a shoe. I peeked over the side of the bed. No shoes. One boot, though. I finally managed to kick my foot free. Holy . . .

"Hey! Somebody cuffed you!" Freddie nearly sat all the way up before dropping back to the floor with a groan.

"These can't be real," I said, curling myself in a ball to bring my ankle to my face. I squinted at the shiny metal. *Huh.* Otter Lake Police Department. *Well, that wasn't reassuring.*

"Are you sure you didn't kill anyone?" Freddie asked. *"A call girl maybe? From a bachelor party?"*

"That's a movie, Freddie."

"Then why is there police tape outside?"

I tilted up and peeked one eye open at the glaring light coming from the window. Hmm, Freddie was right. Those fluttering strips of yellow and black plastic probably weren't New Year's streamers. Man, it looked like the whole yard was marked off. I suddenly had a really, really terrible feeling that somehow this was our fault. Why was it always our fault?

"Freddie," I said as calmly as I could. "What did you make us do last night?"

"Me? What did I make us do last night? You're the one who killed the call girl!"

"Nobody killed a call girl!" I couldn't help but shout. I didn't care anymore if it killed me. In fact, a big part of me welcomed death. "You knew I wanted to lay low at this party! And you double dog knew I didn't want to do anything embarrassing in front of Grady and Candace! So help me if you made me kill someone, and Grady saw it . . ." About halfway through that speech I realized I wasn't making a whole lot of sense.

"Double dog knew?" Freddie snickered. "That's a lot of knew."

"Oh my God! Shut up!" I closed my eyes again. "My brain. It hurts so much." It was then I noticed a big glass of water and a bottle of pain pills on the nightstand beside the bed. "We need to get up. We need to find somebody who knows what happened last night. We need to find a key for these handcuffs."

"Oh relax," Freddie groaned. "I need a minute. Besides, I don't think you killed anyone. The police would have nabbed you by now. It doesn't look like we made a run for it. Plus . . . I think you'd be bloodier."

I groaned. My body didn't want to get up either.

"That being said, I do feel that something murdery happened last night."

We fell into silence.

"Oh my God!" Freddie suddenly shouted.

"What? Who murdered who? Is somebody dead?"

"Forget the murder."

"Forget the murder?"

"We need to talk about the kiss!"

I froze. "The kiss? What kiss? I don't remember any

kiss." I brought my fingers to my lips. They felt kind of kissed. Or maybe just swollen. With evil, evil champagne.

"How could you forget the kiss? It was epic."

I squinted again against the harsh sunlight.

Think, Erica. Think.

My brain had forgotten how to do that.

Hmm, let's see. Kiss. Kissing. Kissed.

A tidal wave of hot and cold emotion rushed over me.

I did kiss someone.

Freddie was right. There was no way I could have forgotten that kiss. All the champagne in the world wouldn't stop me from remembering that kiss.

But who did I kiss?

"So . . . ?"

I shook my head. So much confusion. "Okay, we need to back way, way up here."

"Right."

"Let's start from the beginning. So we pulled up to the estate on your snowmobile—"

"And you came up with that weird resolution."

Chapter One

"The Year of the Adult?"

"Yeah," I said, carefully navigating my way up the stone steps of the stately home. They were well salted, but my low strappy heels weren't great climbing shoes. "And it's not so much a resolution as a theme."

"A theme?" Freddie asked, stopping to look at me. He was having his own trouble with the steps given the furry bundle in his arms.

"For the New Year."

"Right."

Once I got safely to the top, I took a moment to look around. It was so pretty out here tonight. Floodlights, half buried in snow, lit up the house while twinkly lights sparkled in the trees. Hemlock Estate was always impressive, but tonight, all lit up, it was magical. Well, except for maybe the ice carvings left over from the winter carnival that took place here last week. They were looking a little worse for wear. The temperature had gone up and down quite a bit in the past few days. In fact, the moose carving kind of looked like it needed to be put out of its misery. The ice slide for the kids was looking a little warped too.

"So what exactly does this *theme* entail?"

"I think the title is pretty self-explanatory. This is going to be the year I get myself together. You know, practice adulting." I smiled at the little French bulldog in Freddie's arms. He was much easier to talk to with his nonjudgey dog face. "I'm going to make good decisions. I'm going to take that contract court-reporting job in—"

Freddie swatted me on the arm. "What about Otter Lake Security?"

"Um, ow," I said, rubbing the spot where he'd smacked me. Otter Lake Security. Our fledgling company. Our fledgling company that we were having a really hard time getting off the ground. The main problem was that we weren't legally allowed to do much more than watch over farmer's markets, and, really, farmer's markets didn't need a whole lot of security. We wanted to get into more private investigation—cheating spouses and insurance fraud, that's where the money was—but our other partner, Rhonda Cooke, was the only one of us who qualified for a license. She had applied for it a while back, but it still hadn't come through. Once it did, though, we'd be taking pictures of people in motel rooms and picking through garbage like nobody's business. "If you're worried about this job taking away from all the time we spend discussing the business while eating pizza and drinking beer, I'm pretty sure we can still fit that in."

"No, I don't like this idea," Freddie said. "I've got big plans for us."

"Hey, I do too," I said. "But in the meantime, I'm almost out of savings, and I need to find a place of my own. I really can't live at the retreat anymore." Currently I was living with my mother in my childhood home, which also doubled as her business—an island getaway for spiritual healing. And while I was really grateful to be home, let's just say my mother and I were on much better terms when we had more space. The other day she accidentally jammed her baby finger up my nose while breaking into a spontaneous tree pose. "Then after I find my own place, I'll start exercising, eating healthy—"

"Boring."

"Oh! And I'm going to start taking care of myself. You know, be one of those women who never forgets to shave her legs and uses hand cream and always has those small packages of tissues ready to go. Those women really have it together."

Freddie frowned at me a moment before finally saying, "That sounds awful. You're terrible at resolutions."

"Hey! No I'm not. And it's not a resolution. It's a *theme.*" A pretty awesome theme. "In fact, I think you should do the Year of the Adult with me." I stamped my feet lightly. My toes were going numb.

"No, thank you. I don't want to shave my legs, and I'd actually like to have fun this year." Freddie thrust the dog in his arms toward me. "Here, hold this thing for a second. My tux is all twisted from the ride over."

I reached out for the pup. "Come here, you." He was such a wee little furry piglet with the most adorable white and brown patches. "Hey," I said, looking back up, "you never told me his name."

Freddie reached under one of the cuffs of his overcoat and tugged at the sleeves of his suit jacket before straightening the white silk scarf that fell over his lapels. "Stanley? Sully? Steve? I don't remember."

I blinked at him. "You don't remember?"

"Why would I remember the name of a dog that's going to the pound asap?"

Freddie Ng. Best friend. Business partner. One-time

online fortune-teller. Also temporary dog owner, which, I guess, made him a likely candidate for the next Disney cartoon villain. In all seriousness, though, Freddie had a painful history with dogs, so I was willing to cut him some slack. In fact, it was that painful history that got him into his current temporary dog ownership predicament. "Okay, but in the meantime, we have to call him something." I brought my nose closer to the dog's button one. "I think we should call you Killer. Because you're so cute."

"Killer? Really?" Freddie shuddered. "Don't ever have children." He brushed some nonexistent dirt from his arm. "Let's just go with Stanley."

I peered into the dog's big round eyes. "Is that your name? Stanley?"

The dog licked my face. Unfortunately it was one of those dog licks that catches you right under your top lip and ends up at your nostrils.

"*And* that's how you get flesh-eating disease," Freddie said, reaching for the door. He suddenly stopped mid-motion and squinted at me. "You're oddly cheery tonight. What's going on with you?"

"What do you mean, *what's going on with me*? It's New Year's Eve! Time for new beginnings. Fresh starts. Of course I'm cheery."

"You weren't this cheery a couple of days ago," Freddie said, raising a suspicious eyebrow. "In fact, I'm pretty sure you said something about New Year's always being a letdown. That it was a whole bunch of hype for something that lasts ten seconds. I remember because it got me worried about your sex life."

I frowned.

"What's more," Freddie went on, "you were the one who originally suggested we skip this party and spend the night watching Japanese game shows where people get knocked off of inflatable gauntlets into lakes."

"That was before we got hired to keep an eye on things here. And by the way, I stand by my original idea. Game shows are an awesome way to spend New Year's." I blew some warm air into my hands, Stanley still huddled in my arms. "But, you know, this is good too."

"No. No." Freddie's eyebrow was still cocked. "I think you might have even said that you hated New Year's."

"I did not. That's ridiculous."

"And I suppose you're not the least bit worried about seeing Grady and Candace ring in the New Year? With their lips?"

I frowned again. "Well, I could have done without the image," I said, scratching Stanley behind the ear, "but no, I am not."

Grady Forrester. Sheriff. Most handsome man in the universe. My ex-*something*. Now half of the cutest couple in Otter Lake. The other half? Candace Carmichael. Blond. Sweet. Dimpled-cheeked Candace Carmichael. Who would have thought that Candace, the woman I had once accused of murder—in fairness, I wasn't the only one—would now be Grady's girlfriend? Well, actually a lot of people might have thought that. But I was pretty sure nobody thought that they would still be together. I certainly didn't.

I could see why Freddie might be concerned. Okay, yes, a week ago I was a little anti-New Year's. After all, this time last year Grady and I were pretty rock solid. While we hadn't actually spent New Year's together because he had to be in Otter Lake for work, we had spent an amazing Christmas with one another as a couple in Chicago. But that was last year. This year I'd spent Christmas eating tofu turkey with my mother. So there was that. But I'd made it through. The worst was over now. It was time to move on.

Freddie threw his hands in the air. "Just like that? You're over it."

"Yes. Just like that. Can we please go inside now?" Stanley was giving off a little body heat, but my nose was still starting to run.

Freddie pinched his lips and shook his head. "Yeah, I'm not buying it."

I groaned.

"Look, you and I both know that you've never really talked about how things ended between you and Grady, probably because at first we all thought that this thing with Candace wouldn't last, and then you were pretty distracted with the move home, but now—"

"There's nothing to talk about, Freddie," I said with a shrug. "I've accepted that sometimes relationships just don't work out."

"Really?"

"Yes, really." I ignored the super skeptical look he was giving me and instead ran my hand over the bumps of my finger-waved, 1920s-styled tresses. It had been my greatest hair achievement to date, but I was concerned the snowmobile helmet I had worn on the way over had given it a mermaid silhouette—you know, skinny at the top, flared at the bottom. We hadn't had a choice though. Freddie's Jimmy was in the shop, and I didn't have a car.

"Okay," Freddie said. "Well, I'm willing to go along with your whole delusion du jour, but remember, we're representing the company tonight. Who knows what rich, security-needing friends of Matthew's might be here?"

"I won't forget."

Matthew Masterson, of course, owned Hemlock Estate, and yes, he did have rich friends. He had done pretty well for himself as an architect in New York before moving back to New Hampshire, but I couldn't help but think Freddie was overstating the importance of this night as a business opportunity. That being said, I wasn't going to argue with him. Again, the whole Stanley situation had him a little on edge.

"We need to be professional tonight," Freddie went on. "It's already bad enough that I had to bring the dog."

Speak of the furry devil. "Why did you bring him?"

"Because he's like eight thousand years old and sleeps all the time, but if I leave him alone for even two minutes"—Freddie jabbed two fingers into the air—"he pees all over the place. Every time."

I looked down again into the dog's big, sweet, bulbous eyes. "Don't you listen to him, Stanley. Freddie can be super mean sometimes. I'd take you home with me, but right now, I'm living with my mother who has the most evil cat in the whole entire world." I made some big scary eyes. "And he'd eat you right up. Yes, he would."

"Okay, you're really freaking me out right now."

I blinked. "Why?"

"You don't talk baby talk with animals, and—"

"Yes, I do," I whispered down at Stanley.

"And I'm really concerned that you are overcompensating with all this sunshine because you're actually really upset. And we both know that when you get upset, and put too tight a lid on your emotions, things tend to get a little crazy."

"I have no idea what you are talk—"

"Hey, guys!"

Freddie and I turned to see Rhonda hurrying down the path toward us, hand up in greeting. Excellent. I didn't like where Freddie was headed just then. Okay, so fine, back when we were teenagers, I may have had a bit of a reputation for losing it once or twice when my emotions got the better of me, but that was a long time ago. I was a kid. I was much better at handling my feelings now. I'd only slipped up once or twice in the past couple of years, and those had been in pretty extreme circumstances. Besides, I knew how important the business was to Freddie. It was important to me too. I didn't want to go back to court reporting full-time. I wasn't going to mess this night up.

"Hey, look who it is," Freddie called out. "The captain of the *Good Ship Lollipop.*"

Rhonda shot him a look as she climbed the steps to join us on the veranda.

"Rhonda! Happy New Year!" I ignored the slightly startled look she gave in response to my greeting and subsequent one-armed, dog-holding hug. I'd never been much of a hugger in the past, but I was working on that too. "You look great!"

She pulled back, giving Stanley a scratch behind the ear. She must have already heard all about him from Freddie. "Do you really think so? It was the only thing the costume shop over in Honey Harbor had left."

I took in her sailor's outfit. With her red curly hair she *did* kind of look like a grown-up Shirley Temple. "Yeah, sorry, I think I got their last flapper dress. But I mean it. You look great. It's super fun."

"Thanks," Rhonda said uncertainly. She exchanged a look with Freddie. "And how are you doing tonight, Erica? You okay?"

"I'm fine."

She gave me a sympathetic nod like a nurse might give to a terminal patient. "Really? I know this can't be an easy night for you what with Grady and—"

"Oh my God. What is with you guys?" I asked, eyes darting back and forth between them. "Okay, yes, I will admit Grady and I never really had any closure. One minute we were together then *poof*!" I exploded my fingers in the air. "We weren't. But it's been almost a year now.

And you know what? I'm young, I'm single, and I am working security at a fancy New Year's Eve party. With all that going for me, how sad would it be if I were the type of person who was still all hung up on her ex-boyfriend after nearly a year had passed?"

Rhonda suddenly looked like she might cry. "It would be really, really sad, Erica. Especially if that type of person didn't feel like she could talk about her feelings with her closest friends."

"Oh for the love of—" I threw my free hand up in the air as she and Freddie exchanged another look.

"Would you two stop looking at each other! What do you think is going to happen tonight? I'm going to burst into tears when Grady and Candace kiss at midnight? Knock a few glasses out of people's hands as they pretend to know the words to "Auld Lang Syne"? Maybe flip a table filled with champagne bottles?"

"That was scarily specific," Freddie said.

Stanley groaned in my arms. Perhaps I was holding him a little tight. "For the last time," I said, taking a breath. "Thank you, but I'm fine. Really. Just freezing to death."

"Okay, well . . . good," Rhonda said.

"Great," Freddie added.

"Perfect," I finished.

"You two should go on ahead," Rhonda said. "I saw you when I was parking the car. I just wanted to say hi."

"Where are you going?" I asked.

"I'm, uh, just going to meet my cousin," Rhonda said, her eyes darting away from mine. "She's almost here."

Rhonda's cousin.

Rhonda's infamous cousin.

The cousin she was always threatening to set up with every eligible bachelor in town—including Grady when he was eligible. My guess was that she had her match-

making sights set on Matthew now. Which was totally
fine. Because Matthew and I were just friends. I mean,
yes, we did have some sort of connection. But with everything that had happened with Grady, the timing never
felt right. And while I may have been thinking that we
were getting closer to the right time—what with Grady
and Candace coming up on a year—I wasn't ready to
make a move yet. And it certainly wasn't fair to ask Matthew to wait any longer. If that's even what he was doing. So yeah, it was fine. Totally fine. "I didn't know she
was coming," I said with a smile. "Aren't we working?"

"Rhonda's not," Freddie said, jumping in. "She was
already coming to the party as a guest before we got the
call, so it's just you and me keeping an eye on things.
Besides," he said to me under his breath, "they're only
giving us two free meals at the Dawg, so—" He made a
quick "cut it out" gesture with his hand.

That's right. We were getting paid in gift certificates.
But it wasn't actually a bad deal given that we weren't
expected to do anything tonight but keep an *eye on
things*. Whatever that meant. The whole situation was
kind of strange though. Freddie and I had both found it
weird that the historical society had made a point of asking us to come last-minute. Otter Lake didn't exactly
have a lot of crime . . . well, aside from the recent spate
of murders. Three to be exact. Over the period of like a
year and a half. But that was crazy high. "Hey, did you
ever find out what made them ask us to come?"

"Possibly," Freddie said with a knowing twinkle in his
eye. "I tried asking a few more members of the society,
but they just kept saying stuff like, *It wouldn't be a party
without Otter Lake Security,* so I started asking some
questions around town and—" He leaned toward us and
gave a completely unnecessary side-to-side look. "Rumor
has it that someone in town received a threatening letter."

He then leaned back and folded his arms across his chest.

"What?" Rhonda and I both asked at the same time.

"What kind of threatening letter?" I went on. "To who? Why would somebody do that?"

Freddie shook his head. "I couldn't find out any more details. But I figured we'd ask around tonight."

Huh, I wasn't sure exactly how I felt about all this. I mean, until we had more details, there wasn't any reason to get all freaked out. Otter Lake thrived on gossip—the more outrageous the better. Facts sometimes got lost in the mix. But, even so, I didn't like the idea of someone sending threatening letters. That was just not cool. Otter Lake wasn't like that . . . again, murders aside.

"Well, if anything exciting happens tonight," Rhonda said. "You'd better tell me. Jessica will understand if I have to work. She'll be fine on her own. She's really good at making friends."

I found myself rolling my eyes again for some unknown reason.

"I should probably go find her," Rhonda said, looking out to the driveway. "She's coming on her own. She had a work emergency. A mare went into early labor."

Oh yeah, that's right. Rhonda's cousin was a vet. And Matthew was an architect. That was a cute professional match. They could live in a fabulous house with lots of healthy animals . . . and nice doghouses. Probably end up on the cover of a magazine.

"Okay, well, we'll see you inside," Freddie said.

Rhonda waved and hustled back down the front steps.

"You still good?" Freddie asked.

"Yeah. Totally. Why wouldn't I be?"

"No reason." Freddie held open the front door for me. I ignored the explosion sound he made as I passed by.

Chapter Two

Walking into a warm home after taking a cold snow-mobile ride had to be one of the best sensations life had to offer—especially when the home was as beautiful as this one.

I mean, yes, again, Hemlock Estate was a gorgeous house any time of the year, but tonight, she was spectacular. The main entrance hall in which we were now standing had a classic black-and-white tile floor and two wrought-iron staircases that curved up either side of the foyer to the second floor. Dropped down in between was an enormous mirrored glass chandelier that did a pretty fantastic job of setting off the white poinsettias and giant freestanding candelabras that filled the room.

I only had a second to enjoy it, though, before I was torn from the view by Freddie's fingers snapping in the air.

"What are you doing?"

"Summoning Tyler."

I spotted the teenage boy hurrying across the foyer.

"By snapping at him?"

"He likes it," Freddie said sharply, while clipping a

bedazzled leash onto Stanley's collar. "Makes him feel important."

"Right."

Tyler and two of his buddies had crashed Freddie's boat about a year and a half ago during a joyride. After much pleading from the boys' parents, Freddie had opted not to press charges—*if* the boys agreed to an informal community-service agreement. Now, when anybody in town needed anything—driveway shoveled, rain gutters cleaned, dogs walked—the boys were called up to bat. I guess Freddie had volunteered them to help out at the party tonight.

Turned out, they were all pretty nice kids. They just didn't have the best judgment, as evidenced by the joyride that got them into their indentured servitude in the first place. And even though they had crashed Freddie's *baby,* he had formed a strange bond with the teens. I think they found his constant insults entertaining. Tyler was my favorite of them all. He was a little shy, but a total sweetheart.

"Sorry, Miss Erica," Tyler said, hurrying to take my coat then Freddie's. "They needed me in the kitchen."

"Miss Erica?" I repeated, looking pointedly at Freddie.

"What? I'm teaching him some manners and respect." He then lowered Stanley to the floor and pointed at him. "Don't pee."

Stanley just groaned and closed his eyes.

Freddie sighed then frowned at Tyler. "What's that?" he asked, pointing at the boy's throat.

Tyler tilted his chin down in a vain attempt to get a look at his own neck.

"Straighten your tie. That is a two-thousand-dollar tuxedo jacket you're wearing. Show some respect."

I looked back and forth between the two of them. Two-thousand-dollar . . . ?

"Better?" Tyler asked, tugging at the ends of his bow tie—our jackets still hanging over his arm.

Freddie sniffed. "Passable."

"Do you think Chloe will like it?"

"Don't know. Don't care. Off with you."

Tyler smiled and shot Freddie a thumbs-up. "Your dog's awesome, by the way."

"He's not my—"

But Tyler had already taken off in what I was guessing must be the direction of the coat room.

I waved a hand after him. "What was that all about?"

Freddie rolled his eyes. "He wants to impress this girl Chloe, so I lent him some clothes. She's helping out tonight too."

"Oh yeah, I know Chloe," I said. "I mean, not well, but, whatever, that is so sweet of you."

Freddie let out a disgusted sigh. "I'm regretting it already. I'll never get all the body spray out of that shirt."

I nodded. The kid did like his spray. "So, about this whole threatening-letter business—"

"I'll be right back," Freddie suddenly said, walking away. "Restroom break."

Well, that had been abrupt. But if I wasn't mistaken, Freddie had been looking down at Stanley right before he walked away. The dog had already fallen asleep on the floor. Judging by the drool puddling on the tile, he was really tired. This whole dog thing was obviously more traumatizing than I'd thought. I really needed to find a way to cheer Freddie up. And even though it wasn't my business—actually, it was totally my business, we were best friends—I couldn't help but think that if Freddie could just open his heart up a little bit, Stanley would be really good for him. Maybe help him heal some old wounds. The only problem was, I couldn't even get him to talk about Daisy and what had happened to h—

Just then I felt a tap on my shoulder.

"Erica, thank goodness I was able to get you alone."

Well, that wasn't a promising start to a conversation.

I turned to see Mrs. Watson, president of the historical society. People sometimes referred to her as the dragon because even though she came off as a very sweet, community-minded, God-fearing woman—and for the most part, she totally was—she wouldn't hesitate to take you down with a well-placed word if you crossed her.

She looked awesome tonight. Her pixie-cut white hair and red-rimmed glasses set off the crimson Nehru jacket she was sporting. Sure, it wasn't exactly flapper gear, but the embroidery on the satin made me wonder if it was a legit piece from the period.

"Hi, Mrs. Watson," I said with a smile. "Happy New Year. Is there something—"

She cut me off with a wave of her hand. "Yes, your mother was hoping to have a word with you, and *only* you, in the other room."

This conversation was becoming more alarming by the second.

"My mother?" I said it like I had never heard of the woman before—which was strange. I mean, I knew she was coming to the party. But what I didn't know was why she would want to have a word with me. Alone. Or why she'd send Mrs. Watson and not just come herself. I sidestepped out of the way of a group of newly arrived guests. I didn't recognize them. Must be Matthew's friends from New York. A shuttle bus was apparently bringing people back and forth from a resort in the White Mountains. "Is something wrong?"

"I certainly don't think so. Not yet at least."

I cocked my head. That wasn't *exactly* the reassurance I was hoping for.

"Follow me. She's in the old smoking room getting ready."

"Getting ready? Getting ready for what?"

"It's nothing really," she said, patting my arm. "Better if you see for yourself."

I scooped up Stanley and followed Mrs. Watson through the early crowd of party-goers. I nodded at a few people I knew as we came to a set of sliding pocket doors which she opened just a foot or so. "I'll close this after you. We don't want to spoil the surprise for everyone."

"What surprise?" I asked, still repeating everything she said in the form of a question.

"Your mother will explain everything."

"Oh, okay." I didn't move though. It had just occurred to me that Mrs. Watson might be the best person to ask about all the rumors floating around town. She had hired us after all. Maybe I could get a little further than Freddie had to the truth about why. "Uh, before I go in," to see God knows what behind door number one, "I wanted to ask you . . ."

Mrs. Watson raised an eyebrow.

"You haven't . . ." I stopped a moment, choosing my words. "This may sound a little crazy, but seeing as Freddie and I are keeping an eye on things tonight, I thought I'd ask you about some strange rumors we heard around town?"

"What kind of strange rumors?"

"Well, you haven't heard anything about a threatening letter?"

"Oh dear, that wasn't supposed to get out," Mrs. Watson said, shaking her head. "You see, I know about it because my nephew, Amos, works at the sheriff's department. Did you know Amos worked there?"

Of course I knew. Everyone knew. Mrs. Watson was

very proud of her nephew. And Amos was very sweet, but . . . well, let's just leave it at *Amos was very sweet*.

"He told me about the letters because he thought we might want to be a little more vigilant at the party tonight, but we weren't supposed to spread it around town." She leaned in close and whispered, "But I'm glad you know. And it's been more than just one letter. There's actually been quite a few."

I frowned. "Exactly what kind of letters are we talking about?"

"Well, I won't go into the details, but let's just say somebody wants Candace to leave town," she whispered, "or else."

"Candace!"

She covered her mouth with her hand. "I probably shouldn't have let that slip either. And it's not about Candace. It's about MRG."

MRG was the company responsible for turning Otter Lake's small quaint cottages into luxury summer homes. Not everybody was happy with all the changes, but pretty much everyone liked Candace. My ex-boyfriend's new girlfriend was very likable. Like baby bunny likable. It took a lot of work not liking her . . . not that I'd know anything about that. I'd moved on.

"Grady's been working round the clock to find out who's been sending the letters, but no luck so far," she said, shaking her head. "He's so protective." Her eyes widened a touch. "I'm sorry. Was that awkward of me to say?"

"Not at all," I said. Although Stanley was groaning again. I relaxed my grip. "But . . . you don't have any reason to believe that something will happen tonight?"

"Oh no. In fact, Amos tells me these poison-pen types are usually all bark and no bite."

I nodded. "Well, I suppose that's something."

"And I'm sure Grady won't be taking his eyes off of Candace, so you don't have to worry," she said. "But if you do see something strange . . ."

I nodded. "Of course."

Mrs. Watson patted my arm. "Now you go see your mother before Freddie sees you."

I blinked. "Before Freddie sees me? What?"

But Mrs. Watson had already turned to leave.

Well, this night was becoming more complicated by the second.

I took a deep breath and stepped into the cozy lamp-lit room to find my mother sitting at a round wooden table. An array of what I could only assume were props lay spread out in front of her.

"Erica!" my mother said, jangling her braceleted arms into the air. "What do you think?"

I had so many questions to choose from, but I decided to go with, "Mom, why are you wearing a turban?"

Chapter Three

"And why do you have a crystal ball?" I said, pointing to the glass monstrosity mounted on a pewter base smack-dab in the middle of the table. "And a plastic skull?"

My mother closed her eyes and placed her fingertips on her temples. "I'm sensing that you are a little grumpy." She then peeked one eye open to see if I had gotten her joke.

I frowned.

"What?" she asked, getting up and twirling around. She was wearing a gold hip scarf with coins dangling from the seams. She had been really into belly dancing for a while. I was pretty thankful I had missed that stage. "You don't like it?"

"Mom, stop moving. You know I can't talk to you while you're dancing."

She dropped her arms. "I think the room is perfect."

"Every room in this house is perfect." I had to admit, though, with the fireplace going and lamplight, it *was* pretty cozy in a wealthy Victorian kind of way. It also had nice dark wood paneling, some leather armchairs, and an audibly ticking clock on the mantelpiece. "And it's hard to say whether I like this or not given that I don't know exactly what *this* is."

"I think it's pretty obvious."

I waited.

"I'm tonight's entertainment."

"No. No," I said, pointing at the door. "There's a jazz band in the other room. I heard them warming up. They're the enter—"

"They're the *background* entertainment," she said, once again spinning in a circle and letting the many folds of her skirt fly. "I'm the main event."

I took a deep breath. My mother and I had always had somewhat of a reverse parent-child relationship. She flung herself headlong into things without really giving much thought about how they might affect her, her business, or other people, and I basically just worried. But I had been trying to let a lot of that go because my worrying never really stopped her from doing anything. Ever. "Mom, seriously, stop spinning. Does Matthew know you're the main event? Did he agree to this?"

"Well, it's not just his party. It's the Otter Lake Historical Society's party, of which I'm a member." She placed a hand on her chest and curtsied. God knows why.

That was true. The event tonight wasn't just a New Year's party, it was a thank-you party put on by the Historical Society to show their appreciation to all of the volunteers who had helped put on the Winter Carnival.

I gently lowered Stanley to the floor then slid him toward the fireplace with my foot. He looked like he might be cold. "Since when have you been a member of the Historical Society?"

"Since Mrs. Watson asked if I would be interested in telling people's fortunes for the New Year. That woman

makes wonderful fruit cordials." She leaned over the table
and smiled. "And yes, Matthew agreed to this. He thought
it would be cute."

"Let me guess," I said. "He was drinking the cordials
too?" It wouldn't be the first time Mrs. Watson had ma-
nipulated Matthew with her sweet liquors.

"Darling," she said with a big smile, "we were all
drinking the cordials."

I sighed.

"You should try one. I think she's got some samples
at the martini bar."

"Mom, since when are you a fortune-teller?"

"Oh, don't worry. It's all in good fun," she said, half
twirling around a chair before she caught herself mid-
spin. "And you know I've always considered myself to
be a little bit psychic."

I took a long, deep breath. In the past, this was exactly
the type of thing that would have had me really worried.
I mean, my mother ran a spiritual retreat for women. Her
wheelhouse was probing into her guest's deepest fears
and insecurities. She'd probably have half the room in
tears by midnight with her predictions . . . probably di-
agnose a few with adrenal fatigue too—she was also
really into naturopathy . . . but that was none of my concern. Healthy boundaries. That's what adults practiced.
"Well, it's not my party. I mean, you can do whatever
you want. Just maybe keep things light and fun. And
don't fake any accents, okay?"

"*Vat* accent should I *vake*?"

"Oh God." I put my hand over my eyes. "Please stop."

"I'm kidding! Of course I'm not going to fake an accent. That is so insensitive."

Not sure what that made the turban.

"And I didn't ask you in here to get your permission."

"Okay," I said, trying to anticipate what possible turn

this conversation would take next . . . and coming up empty. "Why did you ask me in here?"

"To get *you* to ask Freddie for *his* blessing." She sat back in her chair and folded her hands on the table. "I don't want to hurt his feelings."

"Why would he be offended?" Oh wait . . . *uh-oh*. I couldn't believe I hadn't seen the issue the minute I walked in here. For a while, Freddie had worked as an online psychic. In fact, I was pretty sure he prided himself on being Otter Lake's one and only psychic. And while I was also pretty sure that he wouldn't have wanted to spend tonight doling out fortunes—pretty sure, not entirely sure—he would have expected to have at least been asked. "Why didn't Mrs. Watson go to Freddie first?"

"Well . . . there was that *unpleasantness* between them a couple of years back."

The next logical question would have been, *What unpleasantness?* But I just didn't have it in me.

I sighed. "You couldn't have chosen a worse night for this. Freddie's already in a mood because of Stanley."

"So this is him?" my mother said, looking at the floor. "He's adorable." She didn't come over to pet him though. She saved all her love for evil cats. "It's so strange to think of Freddie with another dog."

"Yeah, and it's bringing up a lot of stuff for him."

"All the more reason for you to talk to him about this." She swirled her hand around the room.

"You know what? I'm really sorry," I said, "but I think I'm staying out of this one. You guys made this decision. You have to own it."

"I understand, darling," she said, nodding and then adjusting her turban. "I really do. But Mrs. Watson just asked me to talk to you because, well, so many people have worked so hard to make tonight happen." She sighed heavily as she stroked her crystal ball. "And she was worried that Freddie might make a scene."

"Come on, when has Freddie ever made a—" I couldn't say it. Some lies are too big to come back from. "I'm really sorry, but you should know by now that I can't stop Freddie from doing anything."

"Fine. Okay," my mother said, arranging her bracelets. "Then maybe you could just steer him away from this side of the house?"

I shook my head. "I'll see what I can do, but I'm not promising anything," I said, scooping up Stanley.

She sighed. "Well, I'm sorry we felt we needed to bring this up. I know this is already such a difficult night for you."

"Why does everyone keep saying that?" I asked. "This is not a difficult night." Well, maybe it was a little more difficult than it had been just moments ago, but still, I wouldn't say *difficult*. "I love New Year's and—"

"And Grady Forrester is coming."

She always said his full name like he was still an eleven-year-old boy.

"No, Mom, it's—" It was too late. That's what it was. My mother had flown across the room in an instant and had me clutched in a bear hug. Stanley grumbled as I spat out the strands of curly brown lemon-grass-scented hair covering my face. "Mom, seriously," I said, pulling back from her. "I'm fine with Grady being here."

The absolute last thing I needed tonight was my mother getting all worked up about Grady. Because, really, nothing tells your ex-boyfriend that you are totally cool postbreakup better than your mom yelling at him in front of the entire town. "Things just didn't work out between us. It happens. He's allowed to date other people." Sounded reasonable in my mind.

"I hate him."

Guess not in hers. This was my fault. I had shared too many of the details from when Grady and I broke up last spring. She took great exception to the fact that Grady had refused to talk our issues through and had just started dating Candace. Come to think of it, I took a bit of an exception to that too.

"He has caused nothing but heartache in your life—"

"Whoa. Whoa. Whoa," I said, stepping back. "Let me stop you right there."

Her eyes narrowed.

"I'm fine."

She just kept on staring at me.

"Really. I am. You don't need to worry. I'm looking forward to the new year."

Huh. Funny. Her look was the exact same one Rhonda and Freddie had given me earlier.

"Really?" she asked.

"Really."

Suddenly she smiled. "It was that retreat I gave a few weeks ago, wasn't it? Be Your Own Best Boyfriend?"

"Sure," I said, trying to nod, but it came out a little wobbly. "That was a big help."

"Well, good. I'm proud of you."

"Me too," I said, readjusting Stanley in my arms. "Okay, so I'm going to go." I jerked a thumb back at the door. "But, good luck with all this."

"Thank you, Erica," my mother said, eyes twinkling.

I slid the door on its track and walked out into the party.

Maybe there was still time to go back to Freddie's and find some game shows on TV.

I sighed and scratched Stanley's ear. No. No. While all these new developments were a little stressful, I was going to have a good time tonight. And really, I had handled that situation with my mother pretty well. I mean, yes, I was a little worried about how Freddie might take the fortune-telling news given his current mood, but I couldn't take that on. I wasn't responsible for his feelings. My job was to simply support him *through* all those feelings. I frowned. Where had I heard that? Maybe it had been from the Be Your Own Best Boyfriend retreat. Whatever. It felt right. Mature. Adult.

I was still perturbed about the whole threatening-letters thing though. I really needed to talk to Freddie about it. If nothing else, it might distract him from all of his dog troubles.

"What do you think, Stanley?" I said, looking down at the furry monster in my arms. "Should we go talk to your daddy? Oh, there he is. I see him."

I hustled across the marble floor as quickly as I could clutching a dog and wearing strappy heels. Freddie was in the middle of talking to a group of people, but I figured it was worth interrupting. "Fred—"

I suddenly cut myself short.

And much to my surprise, spun on my heel in a full one eighty, and hurried back in the opposite direction.

Mrs. Watson's information could wait for a little bit.

Freddie was busy talking to people.

People I wasn't necessarily ready to see.

Candace and Grady–type people.

Chapter Four

"Erica?"

I was pretty sure that was Freddie calling after me. But not certain. Who could hear anything over all this jazz music and party noise? Not me. Besides, I couldn't answer him anyway. I was busy too. Running away. Well, maybe not running . . . speed walking. I was speed walking toward the ballroom with a dog clutched in my arms. Nothing weird about that.

Okay, so maybe hiding from one's ex and one's ex's new girlfriend wasn't the most mature thing in the world to do. But I needed to start my adulting adventures slowly. I'd have more success that way. And in all fairness to me, it was really hard to be fine when everyone was telling you you're not fine.

I hustled my way through the crowd smiling and nodding at the early guests, being careful not to make eye contact long enough for anyone to waylay me with talk. A moment later I spotted the perfect safe haven by a small bit of wall that separated the foyer from the ballroom. There was a seating area with a coffee table, a large potted frond-type plant, and three heavy leather club chairs—one of them unoccupied.

I laid Stanley on the floor and quickly scissored my way over the armrest of the open chair, landing my butt awkwardly in the seat. I nodded at the identical faces seated across from me. "Hey," I said, probably too quickly to achieve the level of casualness I was going for. "I like your outfits."

The twins across from me exchanged identical looks.

"Really," I went on, darting a quick glance behind me. "The matching tuxes are cool."

They were cool. Then again, the twins were cool.

I turned back to them. "You kind of look like hit men for Al Capone. Very gangster."

Kit Kat and Tweety were my pseudoaunts and the only other inhabitants living on my mother's island. Currently their friend Alma was putting them up in town while the lake was frozen over. It was tricky business living on an island in winter. In the past, the twins just bulked up on supplies until the lake was safe enough to cross by snow-mobile, but their place had burned down last spring and the new one wasn't ready yet. They had been staying with my mother and me at the retreat, but this year none of us wanted to be stuck on the island, so we were all staying on the mainland until we could get back and forth.

The twins were in their seventies and completely identical in both appearance and dress tonight—right down to the thick black bow ties hanging loose around their necks, collars slightly open. It was a good look for them. I couldn't really see them in flapper dresses. They were also holding identical glasses of what I was guessing was Scotch. They looked right at home.

"Erica," Tweety began. "What the h—"

"Oh!" I said, jumping to my feet. "Just one second." I shuffled the half step over to the large fern and grabbed the pot. Hmm, this sucker was heavy. I pushed it against the hardwood floor but that made an awful scraping sound—and these floors had to be a hundred years old. I then tried rocking it side to side a few inches away from the wall to give us some more cover. After that I dropped back into my seat, with its back against the small partition wall, and smiled. "Sorry, what were you saying?"

"What the hell are you doing?"

I nodded. "I'm, uh . . ."

"Hiding," Kit Kat said, leaning back in her chair to see into the foyer. "She's hiding. Grady and Candace have arrived."

"Ah," Tweety said knowingly.

"Well, I wouldn't say that I'm hiding exactly. They surprised me. That's all." I started chewing the corner of my mouth before I remembered I was wearing lipstick. I gave my teeth a quick rub with the side of my finger. "I just needed a second to compose myself. I'll go and say hi in a bit."

I got an identical "Uh-huh."

"No, really. It's kind of like spiders," I went on.

"Spiders," Tweety repeated, tapping the side of her glass.

"Like I'm fine with spiders in theory. And I don't squash them with tissue when I see them in the house. In fact, I take them outside by trapping them in a glass and sliding a piece of paper underneath." I made the gesture with my hands. "But it's not like I want to be surprised by one running across my pillow when I'm half asleep. 'Cause that's terrifying. Like Candace and Grady suddenly appearing when you're not expecting them. You know what I mean?"

"Nope," Kit Kat said.

I nodded. "Can you see them?"

She leaned heavily over the armrest of her chair to peer out into the front hall. "Yup. They're talking to Rhonda and some beautiful redhead."

Tweety had to get up to lean over her sister to see. "Oh yeah. She is beautiful." She looked over to me. "Nice dress. Kind of looks like yours. But, you know . . . what's the word I'm looking for?"

"Nicer," Kit Kat replied. "Much nicer."

"What?" I leaned over to get a peek. Huh, Grady and Candace had their backs to me, but I could see Rhonda and her cousin. Wow, she was gorgeous. And yes, she was wearing a dress near identical to mine except hers was white and silver, not red, and was probably the dress that my dress wanted to be when it grew up. She also had finger-waved hair—perfectly done finger-waved hair by the looks of it—that wasn't in the shape of a mermaid. How had she found time to do that and deliver a baby horse? They must teach that in grad school.

I sat back down. "That's Rhonda's cousin Jessica," I said. "She's a vet."

"Oh that's good," Tweety said, sitting back down. "Maybe she can take a look at Freddie's dog. I think it might be dead."

"Stanley's not dead," I said, leaning over to pat his belly . . . and maybe check to see if he was still breathing. "Just really old."

"We're really old," Kit Kat said, smiling at her sister. "And you don't see us passed out on the floor of a New Year's party."

"Not yet anyway."

They clinked glasses and laughed, arms crossed over their bellies—probably to prevent any laughing hernias.

We fell into silence.

"So . . ." Tweety said with a slow nod. "You want to talk about it?"

"No. No. You guys just carry on with whatever you were talking about. Don't mind me."

"Okay," Kit Kat answered. "Hey, Erica, did you hear Burt Young died yesterday? He went to five different family Christmas dinners. Doctor said no heart could take that many marshmallow-topped sweet potatoes."

"Interesting," I said, looking over my shoulder.

"Although," Tweety went on. "I think it would take more than just sweet potatoes. I'm going to ask Joyce what kind of desserts he had. She knows Betty, Burt's wife, pretty well. She'll find out the real deal. Eggnog cheesecake," she said with a knowing wag of her finger. "Now that's a killer."

"Sounds nice," I said, stretching up a little farther in my seat.

Kit Kat slapped my knee. "Burt Young dying sounds nice?"

"Sorry. Sorry," I said, sinking back down. "I was just . . . nothing." I shook my head. This was ridiculous. I was being ridiculous. I needed to focus. I was here to do a job tonight, and despite what Amos had said about this letter writer being all bark and no bite, I couldn't help but think finding out as much as I could about the threats to Candace was an important part of doing that job. Now might be a good time to do a little intel gathering. "Hey, have you guys heard about anything weird at all happening around town lately?" I was purposely avoiding any details. Amos was a sweet kid. I didn't want to get him in trouble for being loose-lipped about police business.

"You're going to have to be way more specific than that," Tweety said. "Do you mean weird like Mr. Carlise mowing the church's lawn at five in the morning?"

"Or weird like Mrs. Coulter stealing her neighbor's cat and trying to pass it off as her own," Kit Kat finished.

"Neither. Weird like illegal maybe?"

"Nothing that jumps to mind. Why do you ask?"

"No reason really," I said, trying to look like I meant that. "I just heard something about Candace that—"

"Candace! Oh we've got news about Candace," Kit Kat said, hauling herself up excitedly in her seat.

"I can't believe we've been sitting here talking about a dead man and his sweet potatoes when we could've been talking about what we heard at euchre last night."

Kit Kat nodded and leaned in too.

I thought about resisting the group huddle. I was pretty sure, judging by the excitement on their faces, that this was some pretty salacious gossip, and I *was* trying to be a better person, but who was I kidding? Sure, I had moved on, but I was still human. And it was totally normal for me to be interested in what my ex was up to. I mean, would social media even exist if people weren't interested in what their exes were up to?

"Well," Tweety said, leaning in even closer—which made me lean back. I didn't want to get drunk on the fumes of her breath. "It seems there was a new man in town yesterday looking for Candace."

"Big guy," Kit Kat added with a double pop of her eyebrows. "Really handsome."

I frowned. "How do you know he was looking for Candace?"

"He was sniffing around MRG." MRG Properties had bought an old Victorian house on Main Street and had converted it into a temporary base of operations.

"That could be anyone," I said. While my interest was definitely piqued, given the letters, I didn't see what was so exciting about this. "It was probably work related."

"No. No. No," Tweety said with a devilish smile. "That's not what it looked like at all."

Kit Kat nodded. "Word has it, he was nervous. Like he couldn't quite work up the guts to go up to the door."

"At least one source had him carrying flowers."

I cocked my head. "What exactly are you two getting at?"

They exchanged looks before Kit Kat said, "You put it together."

I sighed. "Candace isn't cheating on Grady." I believed that too. In many ways, Candace and I didn't have a lot in common. As a person, she was warm and welcoming and sweet. And not that I wasn't those things, but . . . well, she was much better at them. And even though I couldn't see us having sleepovers anytime soon so we could braid each other's hair, I did believe she was a good person. "She's not the type."

"We never said she was *cheating*," Kit Kat said deadpan. "What a thing to say!"

"Although," Tweety added, pointing her Scotch glass at me, "it would make sense given all the other rumors that have been floating around."

I looked from one twin to the other. "What other rumors?"

"You know. All the ones about Grady and Candace—"

Suddenly Kit Kat slapped my knee. "Whoop! Whoop! Red alert! Red alert! The eagles are flying."

"Who's flying? Grady and Candace?"

"How many other people are you hiding from tonight?"

I popped to my feet and lunged to the far side of the wall. "I'm not hiding. I'm just taking a moment to get myself to—"

"Erica! Not that . . ."

And ran right into Candace and Grady.

". . . way."

Chapter Five

"Grady! Candace! Hi!" I practically shouted. "Happy New Year!"

Oh wow, Grady looked nice in his tux. Then again with his model build, chiseled good looks, and soul-piercing blue eyes, Grady looked nice in just about anything . . . and nothing. He really looked good in nothing . . .

I gave my head a shake. Candace looked great, too, in her black sequined dress. It contrasted nicely with her bouncy blond hair and dimples. Well, maybe her dimples didn't contrast with the dress, but . . . whatever.

They both smiled at me, looking just a little taken aback by my enthusiastic greeting, then in a startling gesture Grady leaned toward me. Oh my God. What was he doing? Kissing my cheek? I wasn't ready for that kind of contact! And I couldn't help but think Candace wouldn't appreciate it either!

Before I realized what I was doing my hand had flown up into a stop gesture right in front of Grady's face. Yup, that's right, this year I was single-handedly bringing back *talk to the hand*.

He froze.

I chuckled. "Uh . . . New Year's high five!"

He lightly slapped my palm with his.

Well, that had gone well. Almost exactly how I had pictured it in my head.

I took a breath then turned to Candace. Oh jeez, it looked like she was coming in for a hug. She always had been a hugger. Okay. No problem. I could do this. I could hug my ex's girlfriend. No big deal.

Candace and I both lifted our hands at the same time for the embrace, knocking each other's knuckles.

"Oops," she said sweetly.

"Fist bump," I said, chuckling and rubbing my knuckles. That had hurt.

We leaned toward each other again . . . and I don't know exactly what happened. I think she thought I was going for the fake cheek kisses when I thought we were doing a straight hug, but whatever happened, somehow my lips ended up smearing across her cheek.

"Oh," she said, leaning back. "I think you got me there."

I stared at the horror of what I had done. "Oh . . . I did. You've got just a bit of lipstick on you . . . there." I pointed at her cheek. It kind of looked like I had slashed her with a razor.

She rubbed the spot. "Well . . . Happy New Year."

"Happy New Year to you too!" I smiled big and nodded. They smiled back. Then we all looked away . . . at nothing.

"Oh Erica, I wanted to introduce you all to someone," Candace said, stepping to the side to reveal a pretty but dour-looking girl wearing a long black dress. "My sister, Bethanny."

I shot the girl a quick wave. "Hi!" I didn't know Candace had an adopted sister. At least I was guessing she was adopted given that she was Asian. Freddie would be excited. He thought it was really funny to take pictures of himself and every minority that came to town and then offer the photos to the library for the archive. Freddie was a master at awkwardness.

"She's doing her first year at Dartmouth. We're so proud of her," Candace said, giving the girl's shoulders a squeeze. She then leaned toward me and said in a quiet voice, "We were hoping to cheer her up tonight. She's going through a bad breakup."

"I am standing right here," Bethanny said dryly. "Where's the bathroom?"

Candace looked around the room. "Oh, I'm not sure . . ."

"Never mind, I'll find it." And with that the girl left.

"Don't mind her," Candace said quickly. "You know how brutal breakups can be."

I nodded. Yes, yes, I did.

She blushed and exchanged a quick look with Grady.

This was going great. Now how did I make it stop? What was the minimum acceptable time for small talk with one's ex?

"So, Erica, how's the house hunting going?" Grady asked.

I shot him a look that said, *Really, Grady? Really?* A moment later I saw the realization dawn in his eyes. Real estate wasn't exactly a neutral subject in Otter Lake. "Um . . . it's been tricky."

Candace nodded.

Part of Candace's job at MRG these days included getting a jump on any property that went up for sale in Otter Lake. There was no way I, or any other mere mortal who wanted to live in town, could outbid MRG.

Silence fell over us again for a good long moment.

"I heard Freddie got a dog," Grady suddenly said. "I

was kind of surprised after . . . what was his other dog's name?"

"Daisy," I said with a small nod.

"Yeah, Daisy." Grady's face broke out into a smile. "That's right. After Daisy, I didn't think he'd ever love again."

"Who's Daisy?" Candace asked.

Grady frowned. "It's a long story."

"A sad one too," I threw in.

"Oh," she said with a nod.

Okay, fine, that had felt a little rude. It's not like we were purposely trying to leave her out. Grady and I shared a lot of Otter Lake history. But I guess he was feeling the same guilt because he added, "I can tell you later."

"Sure."

"He says he's not keeping him, though," I threw in quickly.

"What?" Grady asked.

"Well, he only has him because Stanley's original owner is going into a nursing home. She was the breeder for Daisy. She remembered how much Freddie loved Daisy, and asked him to take Stanley. He couldn't say no, but now he swears he's taking him to the pound once—"

Suddenly the sound of a glass shattering came from behind me. I whipped my head around. Mrs. Robinson, town librarian, had dropped her champagne. When I turned back, though, I saw Candace clutching Grady's arm, face white as a sheet.

"Are you okay?" I asked.

She shook her head, making her blond bob shudder. "I'm fine. I was just startled. It's been a long day. Week, actually."

"Can I get you a glass of water or something?" I asked,

reaching to touch her elbow, but she stepped back with a nervous chuckle.

"I think I might need something stronger."

Okay, that was new. Candace wasn't a drinker. My eyes flashed to Grady's. His jaw flexed.

"Erica," Grady said, shaking his head. "Candace is . . ."

My breath caught as I waited for him to finish that sentence.

It could be anything.

Maybe something to do with our earlier conversation . . .

Candace is just doing her job.

Or . . .

Candace is going through a tough time. Someone's been threatening her.

Or maybe something unexpected like . . .

Candace is allergic to gluten.

Or maybe . . .

Candace is no longer my girlfriend, so she's turned to the bottle.

"Grady," Candace interrupted. "Can I talk to you for a second?"

The couple exchanged an intense look. There was a lot going on in that look. I couldn't help but wonder if it had anything to do with the rumors the twins had been going on about. 'Cause right before I had run off, I almost thought they were about to tell me that Grady and Candace were breaking up. Not that I was swirling overhead like some starving vulture.

"Erica," Candace said, turning to me. "Would you excuse us?"

Caw! Caw!

"Oh sure. I'll just . . ." I put up my skedaddling thumbs and jerked them to the side.

"Actually, we'll go. If you see Bethanny, tell her we'll be right back."

I nodded. "Sure. No problem."

"Oh, but before we do," she said. "I wanted to tell you something."

Uh-oh, I did not like the seriousness of her expression at all.

"I just wanted to give you a heads-up that Bryson is coming tonight."

"Oh," I said, straightening. Then I repeated my "oh" with a lot more disgust. "Your boss, Bryson?"

"He's not my boss anymore," Candace said. "He's actually my assistant now. The company didn't know what to do with him after all those accusations of bribery and blackmail two summers ago."

Bryson had been accused of paying some town locals to cause trouble around the lake to incentivize some of the older property owners to sell their land to MRG. The charges never went anywhere. MRG could afford some pretty fancy lawyers.

"Okay, but I don't get what this really has to do with me?"

She winced. "I think he's got it in his head that you are going to be his New Year's Eve . . . conquest."

"Ew," I said, meaning every last bit of it. "Seriously?"

"I just thought you'd appreciate having some warning."

"I do. I mean, thank you."

She nodded and walked toward a hallway on the opposite side of the foyer. Grady hesitated, meeting my eye. There was a lot going on in that look too . . . but I had no idea what any of it meant! Then he was gone.

A strange powerful feeling thudded in my veins. Nope. That could not possibly be what I thought it was. Not again. I mean, couples did fight . . . and I had moved on.

For the most part. So there was no way I was feeling just the tiniest flicker of hope right now . . .

I chewed the side of my thumbnail, but stopped when I felt a bit of polish chip off into my mouth. Gross. I brushed it off my lip.

No. No. Hope was not a good thing. Hope meant opening doors. Opening doors that I had been working so hard to shut.

I had spent *a lot* of time over the last nine months trying to process what had happened between Grady and me. And it wasn't just about how things had ended. There were other sticking points that I had trouble moving past. The main one being that the major obstacle that had been standing in our way was now removed. Grady had never really believed that I was going to move home. And now that I had spent months and months thinking about it, it made total sense that that was such a big deal for him. You see, Grady's father had left when he was a teenager. It was a big shock for everyone—especially Grady. It had seemed like they'd had the perfect family, but, apparently, his father had fallen in love with someone else and just left. Grady had told me how much it had hurt him, but I didn't realize at the time that my inability to jump into a relationship with both feet had probably triggered a lot of that pain. Stupid, I know. But I was dealing with my own commitment stuff, and now I was home, and . . . Gah!

See? This was exactly what I did not want to do anymore. Go over the same stuff again and again. It got me nowhere. So what if I had figured all this out now? Grady was with Candace. End of story.

"Hey," Freddie said, suddenly appearing at my shoulder.

I jumped.

"Did you know that Candace has an Asian sister? I was going to ask her to take a picture with me, but—Why do you look so funny?"

"I, uh, just said hello to Candace and Grady."

"Really? And how did that go?" Freddie asked. "Did you and Candace start pulling each other's hair and crash into the table with the ice swan?"

"There is no table with an ice swan."

"You know what I mean," he said. "I want to hear all about it, but before you start . . ."

I noticed Freddie looking around.

"Where is Stanley?"

The Morning After

"I can't believe you lost my dog."

"I didn't lose him. He's right there." I gestured to the floor. "He's fine." Cone of shame notwithstanding. I took a few shallow breaths. Deep ones felt a little rough on the stomach. "And besides, I thought he wasn't your dog. I thought he was going back to the pound."

"Don't listen, Stanley, and don't worry, I'll never leave you with her again." Freddie looked up at me. "You know what else I can't believe?"

"I'm sure you're going to tell me."

"I can't believe you all thought I'd freak out that your mother was fortune-telling."

"I didn't know for sure that you would freak out. Mrs. Watson was the one who—"

"Mrs. Watson," Freddie said, lying back down. "You know she's just mad because I once predicted someone else's granddaughter would win the Most Beautiful Baby contest at the fair."

"Oh, that's the unpleasantness my mother was talking about."

"And I wasn't as grumpy as you're making it sound,"

Freddie said, staring up at the ceiling. "Although you were a hot mess."

"I will admit the night got off to a bumpy start," I said, running both hands over my face. "But from what we have pieced together so far, nothing that murdery had happened at this party. Threatening letters, yes. Murder, no."

"Oh, that part's coming," Freddie said.

"Are you sure?"

"It will go down as a dark, dark time in Otter Lake history."

Chapter Six

"What do you mean where's Stanley?"

I looked down at the empty floor.

Uh-oh.

"Erica, where is my dog?"

"Kit Kat and Tweety! I left him with them." I hurried around the partition to where I had been sitting with the twins. No twins. No Stanley.

"You left my dog with the twins? I wouldn't let the twins watch a goldfish," Freddie said, looking around at the empty chairs and floor. "So where is he?"

"He was here a second ago. He can't have gone far."

"I can't believe you lost my dog!"

I held up my hands and took a breath. "I didn't lose your dog . . . like permanently. He's here somewhere. I'm sorry. I was distracted. You're never going to believe what just h—"

"Remind me to never let you babysit again." Freddie's gaze whipped around the crowd. Then he pulled out his phone. "I'll get Tyler on it. He'd better have his phone on." Once his thumbs stopped jumping he looked up at me. "So what am I never going to believe happened?"

"Oh," I said, grabbing his elbow and giving it an excited little shake. "I think Grady and Candace might be having relationship trouble."

Freddie had gone from angry flutter-blinking at me just a moment ago to the slow blink. It was hard to say which one was worse.

"I mean, we were talking—just the three of us—and then Candace gave him the ol' *Can I speak to you in the kitchen, honey?* but, you know, not in those words."

"That's it?"

My hands fell to my sides. "What do you mean, that's it? That's huge. They even went to another room to *talk*."

Freddie scratched his chin. "So what you're telling me is that you lost my dog because—"

"Wait! There's more." I was in big trouble here. Freddie's right eyelid was twitching a bit now.

"Okay," he said, folding his arms across his chest, but quickly unfolded them when he saw that he was creasing his silk scarf. "Let's hear it."

"Mrs. Robinson dropped her champagne glass just now and Candace totally freaked out."

No reaction.

Oh wait, that was because he didn't know what Mrs. Watson had told me. "I realize that doesn't sound like much, but Candace is the one who has been receiving the threatening letters in town. Multiple letters."

"What?"

I held up my hands. "Okay, so Mrs. Watson was taking me to see my mother in her fortune-telling room, and—"

"Fortune-telling room?" Freddie asked, suddenly looking even more dangerous. His eyebrows were pointed down now like two thin lightning bolts. "Your mother is fortune-telling? And nobody thought to tell me?"

"Let me back up for just a moment here. Or maybe I

should just fast-forward over that part to—dog!" I suddenly shouted, pointing toward the hallway that Candace and Grady had headed for. "I see tail!"

The tiniest of smiles touched the corner of Freddie's mouth.

I smiled big back at him and nodded. "It was the *I see tail,* wasn't it?"

He whacked my arm. "Let's just go get my dog."

Freddie and I navigated our way through the rapidly thickening crowd to the far side of the foyer.

"He must have gone in that door at the end," Freddie said, pointing down the hallway.

We had only walked a few steps down the wood-paneled passage when Freddie stopped short. So short that I stumbled into his back. It was my fault. This was a pretty nice corridor, and I wasn't paying attention. I was too busy running my fingers along the glossy wood. "What's the matter?" I asked. "Why are we stop—"

"Shush!" Freddie hissed.

"What?" I whispered.

"Don't you hear it?"

"Hear what?"

"Voices."

"We're at a party," I said. I kept my voice to a whisper though.

"Not just voices. *Angry* voices."

I stopped talking to try to hear what Freddie was going on about, but all I could hear was the jazz music and din of conversation from the party at our backs. "I don't hear any—"

"Shush!" Freddie hissed again, waving me forward.

Suddenly I *did* hear a voice. It was coming from the far room.

"And we're right back to where we started, aren't we?"

My breath caught. That voice had sounded an awful lot like Candace's . . .

Silence.

Then . . .

"I don't think I can do this anymore."

Chapter Seven

I don't think I can do this anymore.

That was definitely Candace!

Freddie and I exchanged wide eyes.

"What do you want me to say?"

I gripped Freddie's wrist. No mistaking that voice.

Grady.

Grady and Candace. They were the ones with the angry voices.

My heart thudded in my chest. "I don't think we should be listen—"

"We're doing our job," Freddie shout-whispered, clutching my arm. "People are angry. We are security. We need to"—he snapped his fingers—"keep an eye on things. Besides, my dog's in there. He is going to pee everywhere."

I shook my head and took a step back. "We can't. Eavesdropping is not what we were hired for and you know it."

Freddie stamped his foot. "The only thing I know is that we are both dying to know what Grady and Candace are fighting about in there, but you're too worried about being a good person." He put some air quotes around that last part. "So, here's what's going to happen. I'm going to drag you down there now, so we can hear, and then it won't be your fault. Consider it a late Christmas present."

I chewed the corner of my lip.

"We both know there's no way we're not doing this."

I didn't move.

"Okay, fine," Freddie said, throwing his hands up in the air. "We'll be good people. We won't—"

I held out my wrist for Freddie to grab.

"There's my girl." He pulled me down the hall, so we could sneak right up to the edge of the door.

"I can't talk about this right now," Candace said. "I can't. Not with everything that's going on."

"Wow. She does not sound happy," Freddie whispered. "At least you managed to ruin her night."

I leaned in close to his ear and hissed, "I didn't want to ruin Candace's night. I—"

"Shush. Grady's talking."

We leaned as close as we could to the doorjamb without being seen, our backs pressed against the wall. I pushed Freddie down a little so I could slide my head closer to the threshold over his.

"It could be anyone," Candace said. "This entire town hates me."

"Nobody hates *you*. It's not about you."

Grady sounded tired. I wouldn't go so far as to say *frustrated*. But definitely tired. They'd had this conversation before.

"Grady, I know you're trying to make me feel better, but what do you think that so-called invitation I got to leave town was? A kind suggestion from a concerned neighbor?"

"I told you. We'll find out who sent that note."

Hmm, note. Not multiple letters. Amos must have

exaggerated things to his aunt. Or she exaggerated the details for me. Or—

"Grady, we both know if you could have figured that out, you would have already. We might as well go ask Summer's crystal ball."

Freddie shot me a look and mouthed, *She has a crystal ball?*

Thankfully just then Candace went on. "Otter Lake will never accept me," she said. "This town doesn't accept anybody who wasn't born here."

"That's not true," Grady said . . . again. "Everybody likes you."

"But nobody wants me here."

"They don't want MRG here. There's a difference."

I couldn't help but think Candace's statement was the kind a girlfriend makes when she wants her boyfriend to say *I want you here.* And I couldn't help but notice that Grady hadn't said that. And there it was again. That tiny thrill of hope shooting through my veins. Followed quickly by guilt. I was the last person on the planet Candace would be wanting to hear this conversation. I grabbed Freddie's elbow and took a step back just as I heard Grady say, "Candace, It's going to be okay. We'll figure everything out."

Then I heard a funny sound like someone colliding with a heavy piece of furniture.

"Candace, I—"

"I mean it. Don't touch me. No—"

Suddenly we heard something clatter to the floor. Freddie jolted so hard he nearly lost his footing. He then took a super quick peek into the room. "She just dropped her drink."

"Did it break?" Grady asked.

"No," Candace answered. "I'll go find a cloth or something."

"I can do it."

"I'll do it. I need a moment," Candace said. "Why don't you just go back to the party and take Freddie's dog with you before he licks this all up. You and Erica can share more Otter Lake stories."

Freddie shot me another look. At least this time it was of the *Oh no she didn't!* variety.

I took a step back as my eyes darted around. We needed to get out of here. Hide. There was a shut door on the opposite side of the hall. I tugged at Freddie's elbow.

He waved me off.

I did not like this. I was officially a bad person. The sweat popping up under my armpits told me so.

"I'm sorry," she said. "It's the stress. I didn't mean—"

"Candace, I don't know how many times I have to say it. I think it's pretty clear to just about everyone, except you, that Erica and I were never meant to be."

I let out a breath like I had been punched in the stomach.

"Ouch." Freddie hissed some air through his teeth. "Okay, time to go. We stayed just a moment too long."

I couldn't seem to move.

"Come on," Freddie said, pushing my back. "Go! Go! Go!"

Footsteps came toward us. We darted across the hallway and ducked into the room I was eyeing earlier, quietly, shutting the door behind us.

It's pretty clear to everybody that Erica and I were never meant to be.

Hot pricks stung my eyes.

Nope. Nope. Nope.

I blinked furiously. I was fine. This is exactly why I had moved on . . . so I wouldn't be completely devastated hearing Grady say something like that.

Yup. I was fine.

Just fine.

Actually, I'd be even finer maybe if I folded up that particular little incident like a piece of paper and shoved it in the back pocket of my consciousness. Forever.

"Whoa," Freddie said, yanking me back to the fact that we were somewhere that we had no right to be.

It was a big room with a fireplace across from the bed. I had always wanted a fireplace across from the bed. The linens and furnishings were all dark neutrals. Very masculine. And the spicy scent of male deodorant, cologne, and other products hung in the air—which may not sound that sexy, but mixed with the undercurrent of just the right pheromones it was pretty overpowering. All things considered, this bedroom looked kind of like the setting for a Ralph Lauren photo shoot. All it was missing was the hot man.

"Great Gatsby," Freddie said. "We must be in—"

Just then a man walked out from an adjoining room.

"Hi, Matthew," I said with a small wave. "Happy New Year."

Chapter Eight

"Hey guys," he said, hands frozen mid-buttoning on his shirt. "Happy New Year to you too."

"Me three," Freddie said. "I mean, Happy New Year from me too. Additionally. Um . . . changing shirts?"

"Oh," Matthew said, looking down at his hands. "Yeah, I got an overly enthusiastic hug from Ms. Applebaum and her red wine."

"Nice," Freddie replied. "The shirt, I mean."

I nodded in agreement. "And the house looks fantastic."

"There are still a lot of renovations going on upstairs." He cocked his head as a bemused smile spread across his face. "But I don't think you're here to talk design . . ."

I broke first. "We were eavesdropping on Grady and Candace having a fight, and we were about to get caught, so we ducked into the first available room, which, I guess, just happened to be yours."

Matthew nodded slowly. "Makes sense."

We all just stared at each other before Freddie said, "We just need to wait here a few minutes until the coast is clear."

"Of course."

"Oh crap," I said, looking at Freddie. "But Candace told me earlier she was going to look for Matthew!"

"Relax. I doubt she'd just barge into his bedroom," he said. "I mean, that would be pretty rude. Somebody will find her a paper towel or something."

"Paper towel?" Matthew asked, adjusting his black silk bow tie around his neck.

"She spilled her drink," I said. "But don't worry. Freddie's dog is licking it up."

"Yeah." Freddie chuckled. "My dog is getting hammered tonight." Then his face dropped. "You don't think he'll throw up, do you?"

"When did you last feed him?" I asked.

His eyes darted side to side. "Um . . ."

"You are feeding him, right?"

"Of course I'm feeding him. It's just . . ."

"Just what?"

"I may have forgotten to give him supper."

"Freddie!"

"I do not appreciate you taking that tone with me. You're the one who lost him."

"That's it," I said. "You're doing the Year of the Adult with me."

"Oh no, I'm n—"

"Year of the Adult?" Matthew asked.

Freddie and I looked back over to Matthew. We had momentarily forgotten he was there—which was almost crazy impossible given how he looked in his natural bedroom setting.

"Sorry," I said.

"It's a long story," Freddie added. "And we'd better get going. We need to find Stanley. I don't want him puking all over the snowmobile on the way home." He reached for the door. "No telling where it might end up."

I took a step away from him. "I'm not going out there." It's not like I was still thinking about what Grady had said about us and was worried that I might start crying if I saw him—because the excitement of nearly getting caught and the visions I had of Matthew doing a half-naked photo shoot were totally distracting me—but yeah, I was thinking that. And crying would really be a setback to my having achieved *moved on* status.

"Well, you can't stay in here all night." A smile spread across Freddie's face. "Or can you?" He double-popped his eyebrows.

I felt my cheeks burn.

"Or if you want, we can just walk around the terrace?" Matthew pointed to the glass door behind him. "It leads all the way around to the back. No one will even know you were in my bedroom."

"Perfect," Freddie said, sliding out the door. "Meet ya back at the party."

"Wait. Why don't you come with . . ."

Freddie had already shut the door.

". . . us."

I turned back around.

"Hey."

"Hey."

Chapter Nine

"You okay?"

"Totally fine," I said with my best casual nod. "It's a great party." I nodded some more. "Really . . . great."

"Good," he said. "I mean, good that you think it's great." He smiled that friendly warm smile of his that seemed to say everything was going to be okay. "I'm glad you came."

I raised an eyebrow. "You are?"

"Well, I've got something you might be interested in."

Wow. That remark could be taken in all sorts of ways.

"The Arthurs," he said. "They're here already. I told them you wanted to talk to them."

Oh! Okay, well, that was good too.

Matthew had heard that the Arthurs were looking to sell their cottage. It had everything I could ever want in a place. It was on the water, right in the nook of a private inlet. It wasn't too big, and rumor had it that the Arthurs had done a whole bunch of upgrades. Even better, according to Matthew, there was a good chance they'd sell to me. They were off-the-gridders. Very anticorporation. And I probably wouldn't have a lot of other competition because the place was so small. Not great for a family, but perfect for me. "Thank you so much for doing that. I really appreciate it."

"It's no problem," he said, adjusting his shirt sleeves. "Really. I know how badly you want to find your own place."

And, not for the first time, I couldn't help but think how awesome it would be to date a guy like Matthew. Easy. Drama-free. So unlike what I had with Grady. But . . . no, that wasn't fair. Things hadn't always been difficult between Grady and me. In fact, a year ago I had been the happiest I have ever been. Even if it had only been for a little while. In fact, I'd had that feeling everyone dreams about—that overwhelming sense of rightness in my soul. That what we had was it. We were it. That was a pretty hard feeling to get over.

Of course, there was still that bit about Grady thinking we weren't meant to be.

Yup, even when I was thinking about other things, his words were still right there . . . strangling my heart in their icy grip.

"Shall we?" Matthew asked, slipping on his jacket and gesturing toward the door. "Let me get you a coat."

"Don't worry about it. It's a short distance."

"Yeah," he said with a bit of a twinkle in his eye. "But I kind of wanted to show you something on the way."

Chapter Ten

"Wow."

"Spectacular, isn't it?"

Matthew couldn't find a coat that would work for me, so he had offered the gray chenille throw from his bed to drape around my shoulders. And yes, it smelled like him. I couldn't remember the last time I had done so much breathing through my nose. Then he had led me out onto the oversized porch around toward the side of the estate to show me his surprise.

And what a surprise it was.

"I thought the lights you had out front were nice," I said, shaking my head. "But this . . . how did you even . . . ?"

"Mrs. Watson got the fire department to come out."

The front line of the trees leading to the forest had been covered top to bottom with twinkly lights. The effect was magical. It kind of made you believe there could be some winter wonderland or castle hiding in the woods.

"I've never seen anything like it. At least not in Otter Lake."

"Yeah, I've got to say the historical society is a force

to be reckoned with. Not that twinkly lights are a historical thing, but as Mrs. Watson put it, *we are not just
responsible for preserving Otter Lake history, we are
also responsible for creating it.*"

"She's intense," I said. "And a little scary."

"You're telling me. Never accept a fruit cordial from
that woman. That's how she gets you."

I walked to the railing to take in more of the sight.
"Well, the effort was worth it."

"I'm glad you think so," Matthew said, coming to my
side so we were standing shoulder to shoulder.

I met his smile and somehow got myself stuck in his
eyes. Matthew had really pretty green eyes.

Thankfully he was able to think of something to say.
"So, is . . . was everything okay back there?"

And . . . I take back the *thankfully*. Talking to Matthew about Grady always left me feeling kind of guilty.
Like I was somehow betraying Grady *and* being unfair
to Matthew. "Yup."

"I see." He chuckled. "Isn't there some warning about
eavesdropping?"

"That you might not like what you hear?" I nodded.
"I think there's some truth to that. But you know what?
It's fine. I'm fine. Whatever happens . . . I'm fine."

"That's a lot of fines," Matthew said with a smile.

"It kind of goes with my theme for the new year. You
know, even if things are not fine, I will be fine." Huh, that
sounded pretty good. I should give that to my mom for
one of her retreats. It was a little too early to say for certain that it worked, but, hey, fake it till you make it. She
could have that too. It wasn't mine.

"You know, I've been thinking about making some
resolutions of my own." Matthew said, tilting his head
side to side. "Or maybe just . . . changes."

"Oh yeah? Like what?"

He leaned his elbows on the railing. "Like I'm thinking I'm going to go back to New York for a couple of months. Maybe longer."

"What? How come? I thought you really liked being home."

"I do." He met my eye for just a moment before looking back at the trees. "But most of my work is based in New York. I have a lot of friends there that I've missed, and this place," he said, looking back at the house. "It's just heavy with memories. A lot of them not very good."

"But you're not thinking of selling?" I mean, I knew Matthew's parents hadn't exactly had a happy marriage, but this house was his family's legacy.

"I don't know. It's just so big for one person," he said, gripping the railing before leaning back to take a deep breath. "It should be filled with people . . . kids."

We were getting into some sticky territory here. I wanted to choose my words carefully . . . mainly because there was a tiny voice in the back of my head screaming something about having a whole bunch of babies with Matthew. "I . . ." I swallowed hard. "It's not my business, but can I just say . . ."

He met my eyes again.

"I think that's a terrible idea."

Matthew laughed.

"Seriously, Otter Lake wouldn't feel right without you. We'd all miss you so much."

He looked at me with some pretty serious eyes. I wanted to follow that last bit up with how much I would miss him. But I couldn't.

After a moment, we both looked back out at the trees. "Well, I haven't decided on anything. I'm just thinking about it."

"Yeah, well, maybe don't jump into anything." I shivered as the cold seeped through the blanket wrapped around my shoulders. "Rhonda brought her cousin to-night to meet you."

He laughed again. It was such a nice sound. "I heard. That may be part of the reason why I'm in no hurry to get back to the party."

I wrapped the Matthew-smelling throw more tightly around my shoulders. "No. No. She's gorgeous. She's smart. And she's a hero to all horse-kind. You should go meet her and have like a million babies and then stand out on this porch every New Year's Eve as a happy couple and talk about how lucky you are that you found each other." I rolled my eyes. I still had a ways to go with the whole grown-up thing.

"So that means you'll come to the wedding?"

I laughed and looked at him again. Wow, on top of being nice and funny, he really *was* handsome. In fact, he kind of looked like a young Robert Redford tonight. When we got the call to this party, Freddie made a joke about me kissing Matthew at midnight. He seemed to think Mr. Masterson—as he put it—would really be able to bring the fireworks. I mean, I wouldn't know one way or the other. We'd certainly never kissed. Not even once. Huh, come to think of it, he'd probably kiss Jessica before he'd kiss me. Maybe even tonight. At midnight. A fact I was totally completely comfortable with because Matthew was a good man who deserved to be happy. Yup, happy . . . just like me, who'd be kissing no one at midnight because he'd be kissing Jessica and Grady and I weren't meant to be. But I was still happy because I was going to grow as a person this year. Figure out what I really wanted out of life. Start the new year off right. With a mature mind-set. Yup, still happy.

Happy. Happy. Happy.

"Hey? You okay?" He bumped me with his shoulder. "Should we go back in?"

"Oh yeah, I'm fine. Great actually," I said brightly, turning to resume our walk. "Oh, do you want me to run and put this blanket back in?"

"No, leave it out here on the railing," he said, taking it from me. "You're going to want it for the surprise later."

"Another surprise? What is it?"

Matthew just smiled.

We headed around to the back of the estate. Again, wow. Evenly spaced outdoor fireplaces lined the entire length of the back porch. Nice touch for the guests who might need a moment outside. We walked in silence, stopping just a few steps back from the oversized glass doors. Muffled jazz found its way outside.

Matthew touched my elbow. "Erica, I just wanted to say—"

I raised my eyes to his, but he wasn't looking at me. He was looking inside.

I followed his gaze.

There was definitely some sort of commotion going on. Well, maybe not a commotion, but a small group of people clustered in a circle.

I touched Matthew's arm. "Is someone hurt?"

"I don't know. We'd better—"

Suddenly the glass door banged open a little ways down from where Matthew and I were standing on the terrace.

"Erica! Come quick."

Rhonda.

"Something's wrong with Freddie's dog."

Chapter Eleven

About ten minutes later, Freddie and I were keeping watch over Matthew's bed as Rhonda's cousin Jessica examined Stanley, her stethoscope moving over his furry little rib cage. A moment later she leaned back, concerned-doctor expression on her face.

Freddie chewed his thumbnail. "Just tell me what's wrong with my dog."

"Well, it's hard to say without blood tests, but my guess is that he got into something he shouldn't have." She frowned. "You said he threw up?"

"Yeah, I just thought he was drunk because he licked up a bit of a spilled drink, but could a little alcohol have done all this?"

Jessica didn't say anything for a minute. I did not like the way she was considering her answer.

When Matthew and I had got inside, a little group had formed around Stanley. Freddie was freaking out—like one step away from hand-wringing and wailing—but to be honest, Stanley didn't seem all that different to me. Granted, he had thrown up—which was pretty exciting, you know, given Stanley's general lack of movement—

but it was the tiniest little barf ever. My mom's cat Caesar had once managed to get my duvet, pants, and sweater all in one shot. So at first I'd figured this was nothing, but now, with that look on Jessica's face, I wasn't so sure.

"When you say he was acting drunk," she began, "do you mean he was having trouble walking?"

Freddie nodded again.

"He hasn't been spending any time in your garage, has he?"

"What? No," Freddie snapped. "Why would I do that? It's cold and lonely in there."

"I'm just trying to narrow down some possibilities," she said, shaking her head. "It could have been the drink, but it also could have been the poinsettias."

"The poinsettias?" Freddie clutched his shirtfront, I guess at the horror of the poinsettias.

"They're toxic for animals," she said. "Dogs sometimes nibble on the leaves when they're hungry."

I gasped. I couldn't help it. Freddie hadn't fed him dinner!

He whirled around to face me and hissed under his breath, "Not one word, Bloom. Not one."

"Well, the poinsettias would actually be good news. Compared to some of the things dogs can get into, they're not that bad." She scratched Stanley's ear. "But I don't like how lethargic he is."

"He's always like that," I said quickly.

"Quiet," Freddie snapped. "You're not his mother."

Jessica took a step toward the door. "I think I should get my bag from the van. I'd like to give him something that blocks toxins from being absorbed into the bloodstream just in case. As luck would have it, I've been in process of moving offices. I should have everything I need."

"Do it," Freddie said. "Spare no expense. Just save him, Doctor."

Jessica gave Freddie a sympathetic smile. "Let's not worry overmuch just yet—although, if you agree, I think I'll give him some fluids too. See if that perks him up."

Freddie nodded quickly.

She took her stethoscope from her neck and turned to Matthew. "Given that it's New Year's, is it okay if I treat him here?"

"Of course," he replied, giving her a warm smile.

She smiled back.

Wow, they were halfway to the altar.

It was just so easy for some people.

"I think I have everything I need in the van. I'll just go—"

Matthew took a step to the door. "I'll come with you."

"I'll get Tyler to help," Freddie said, whipping out his phone.

"Oh, I'm sure we can manage," Jessica said. "There's not really that much—"

"Already done," Freddie said, texting like mad. "He'll meet you out there. Anything you need, Doctor."

As Jessica passed by Freddie, she gave his arm a squeeze. "I know. They're family."

He nodded.

After they were gone, Freddie and I stood in silence watching Stanley's rib cage rise and fall.

Finally I said, "Freddie—"

"I know I was acting like I didn't care about the dog, but I care about the dog, okay?" His face was tight, like he was holding on to his emotions for dear life. "I didn't want to care about the dog. But I care about the dog."

"Of course you do."

"But that doesn't mean I'm keeping him."

"Okay," I said carefully.

"And I did feed him dinner. Steak. I prepared it myself. I was just trying to be funny earlier."

I nodded. "Sure."

"I'm not heartless, you know?"

"I know you're not heartless," I said. "I caught you crying watching *Elf* just last week."

Freddie gasped. "We agreed we would never speak of that."

"It's not a big deal, Freddie. Lots of people cry watching movies. I mean, I doubt it's the first film people think of when asked for a Christmas tearjerker—"

"The misfit elf is a classic archetype! You'd have to have a heart of stone not to—"

"Freddie," I said as gently as I could. The time had come. We needed to address the elephant in the room. Or golden retriever as the case may be. "Do you . . . want to talk about Daisy?"

"Oh my God, no!" he shouted, eyes going terribly wide.

I shrugged. "It might help."

"I hate you!"

I nodded. "I don't think you hate me. I think it's—"

He stomped on my toe.

"Ow!" I mean, he didn't stomp so hard as to do any damage, but enough to cause a good amount of pain. "Fine! We won't talk about Daisy."

"Good," he said tightly. "Besides, we don't have time for this."

"We don't?"

"Of course we don't. What is the matter with you?"

"What exactly is it you think we should be doing? I mean, I am fine hanging out in Matthew's bedroom playing nursemaid to the dog all night if you want to—"

Freddie whacked me.

"Again, ow!"

"We're not staying here either."

I rubbed my arm. "Well, if we're not staying then—"

Freddie moved to hit me again.

I whipped a finger up. "Okay, you need to stop that now."

He dropped his whacking hand. "We're going back to the party."

"Why? I think the historical society will understand if—"

"Not to work! Although I guess it is kind of related . . ."

Uh-oh. I had a feeling I knew where this was going. I shot him a sideways look. "Why do we need to go back to the party, Freddie?"

"Because we have to figure out who did this to my dog."

Oh boy. I met Freddie's super intense gaze. Things never turned out well when he was showing that much white around his irises. "Freddie, you heard what Jessica said. Nobody did anything to your dog. He just got into something he shouldn't have."

"Um, I beg to differ," he said, gesturing to Stanley. "Someone has clearly poisoned him."

I let out a frustrated sigh. "What possible motive would anyone have to poison your dog?"

"They weren't trying to poison my dog, Erica."

"Oh God." I put my hands over my face.

"They were trying to poison Candace."

Chapter Twelve

"I knew you were going to stay that," I said from underneath my hands. "As soon as I said the thing about the motive—" I cut myself off and dropped my arms to my sides. "Freddie, you are just upset and—"

"Don't you just upset me Freddie anything!"

I cocked my head. "What?"

"You know what I mean."

"I get that you feel responsible, but—"

"I don't feel responsible for anything!" Freddie shouted. "Because I didn't do anything except bring that poor innocent dog into this murderous town!"

"Freddie . . ."

"So help me, if you say my name one more time like you're about to offer me a tissue to wipe my tears I will . . ." His face twitched as he struggled to find the right words. "Cut off all of your hair!"

I blinked a few times as my hand rose of its own accord to pat what was left of the bumps of my finger waves.

"Would you please just think about it for a minute?" Freddie asked.

I stared off into the flames flickering in the fireplace. "What is there to think about?"

"Well, for one thing, we've been with Stanley the entire time. Except for when *you* lost him. We would have noticed if he was chewing on the decorations."

"Fr—" I caught myself just in time. I liked my hair. Most days. "I don't think I would have noticed." I looked over my shoulder. "Sorry, Stanley." The dog groaned. "You were right. His name's definitely Stanley."

"That reminds me," Freddie said, pulling something shiny from his breast pocket.

"What is that?"

He didn't answer, just walked over to Stanley on the bed, sat and gently swapped out one collar for another.

"Is that . . . does that collar have *Stanley* engraved on it?"

Freddie didn't answer.

"But . . . I thought you weren't keeping him?"

"I'm not. But every dog should have a collar. And besides, when I take him to the pound, they should know he already has a name, so no one calls him anything stupid like *Killer*."

"Okay, let's look at what we know for sure," I said, holding out some placating hands that I lowered once I realized they would probably just anger him. "One, you are very upset right now, so I'm not sure you are thinking str—"

"My thinking is just fine."

"Two, I think because the town has had an unprecedented amount of murders in a short period of time . . ." Again. Three to be exact. Over a period of a year and half. But still, that was crazy high for Otter Lake. ". . . I think maybe you are just jumping to murderous conclusions."

"Oh really?" Freddie raised an eyebrow. "Because I think you just proved my point."

"How?"

"It's a proven fact that when you have murders, people then have murder on the brain, so hence, they are more likely to murder in a stressful situation—a situation that in the past would have, say, just resulted in a mean tweet."

I squinted at him. "That is not proven fact. In fact, I think that is the complete opposite of a proven fact."

"Haven't you ever heard of copycats? Same thing."

"No. No, it's not. And back to my arguments, three—"

"Oh great. There's a three," Freddie said, bobbling his head around. "No, you know what? Forget three. You heard Candace say everyone in this town hates her!"

I frowned. I had heard that. I had indeed. "I think she was just upset . . . and she's drinking! You know she doesn't drink, and—"

"And what about the threatening letters? Multiple threatening letters."

"I'm actually thinking Mrs. Watson was exaggerating. Candace said note—"

"You know what? Discussion over. We are investigating Stanley's attempted murder and that is that."

"No, that is not that." I felt kind of beastly for saying it. Mainly because I knew Stanley being sick brought up a whole lot of memories for Freddie, but I couldn't help but think being a good friend meant not letting one's friend run off half-cocked solving attempted murders that never happened.

Freddie spun around, putting his back to me.

Okay, well, if we were going to be mature about the whole situation.

"Can we please just talk about this?"

"No, you're doing this for me."

"Freddie . . ."

"Again! Stop saying my name!" He spun back around. "Besides, you owe Candace."

Okay, that gave me pause. "I'm sorry, what now?"

"I said, you owe Candace."

"How do I owe Candace? She stole my boyfriend."

"Oh yeah. Right," Freddie said with a scoff. "That's how it happened, *Miss I've Moved On*."

"Okay, maybe I haven't entirely moved on, but—"

"You broke her. Now you gotta fix her. Well, maybe not fix her, but protect her from whoever's trying to poison her."

"I did not break Candace. And nobody is trying to poison her."

"You heard her arguing with Grady. She used to be a cute, happy ball of pink, sunshiney things before she met you, Erica Bloom. And now she's like the mean ex-wife who arches her eyebrow and makes snide comments over her martini glass at everyone. That's what you did. You made the world a less happy place."

My jaw dropped.

"Okay, you know what?" Freddie said, "Let's compromise. We won't launch an official investigation or anything. But let's just see if we can get the cloth or paper towels that mopped up the drink, and I'll send it to a lab. It's for my peace of mind."

"I really think—"

"I need to know for sure this isn't my fault," he said, voice dropping.

We both looked down at Stanley.

I felt my shoulders sink. "It's not your f—"

"I never should have left him with you."

"Hey!"

"Erica, when you were suspected of murder, who helped you prove your innocence?"

I cleared my throat.

"Sorry, what was that?" he asked.

"You did."

"And when your crazy pseudoaunt was being accused of murder, who helped you then?"

"That was you too."

"And when you were trapped on an island with a freaking serial killer, who helped you th—"

"You, Freddie. It was you. But those were very different circumstances."

Freddie didn't answer though, and when I caught a look at his downturned face, I could have sworn . . .

"Oh my God. You're not . . . going to cry, are you?"

He looked up at me, eyes glistening. "Say you'll help me, Erica. Or I swear to God I will."

I took a horrified step back, bumping into a dresser.

"Tears are going to spill right down my face."

I braced myself against the drawers. "You wouldn't!"

He sniffed. "Oh . . . oh boy, here they come."

I looked at him sideways. "You . . . you are evil."

"So you'll help me?"

"Gah!"

"Yes!" Freddie shouted.

"But you have to promise me one thing."

"What's that?"

"That this little investigation of ours will be as low-key as possible," I said. "I do not want us making fools of ourselves tonight."

"Really, you're telling me that," Freddie said right as Jessica opened the door for her and Matthew. "I'm not the one who once paraded a beaver around town topless."

"Oh," Jessica said, half turning to leave. "Sorry, did we come back at a bad time?"

I sighed. "And so it begins."

The Morning After

"I can't believe I let you emotionally blackmail me into an investigation of a dog poisoning that didn't happen."

Freddie patted Stanley on the belly. "It's what friends do, Erica."

I started to shake my head, but then clutched it with both hands just to be sure it didn't fall off. "And I'm going to go out on a limb here and say that given where we're at right now, I don't think we were able to keep the investigation low-key."

Freddie nodded. "Not looking that way, is it?"

Chapter Thirteen

"Okay, let's do this." Freddie yanked down his cummerbund and strode down the hall with startling purpose.

"Do what exactly?" I called after him. Low heels or not, these were not speed-walking shoes. I'd be hobbled by the end of the night. "And where are you going? The conservatory is back this way." I jerked my thumb behind me, but Freddie was paying zero attention.

"I think our first step is pretty obvious, don't you?"

I screwed my lips to one side. "First step? I only agreed to one step and that was to look for poison samples that don't exist."

"Just come on."

Freddie resumed his stride, and I chased after him once again. He was cutting through the crowd like a hot knife through soft butter . . . until a woman sidestepped into his path.

Tyler's mom.

And she looked upset.

This could take a while.

You see, Nancy was a bit of a helicopter parent. She was always worried about everything, like Tyler using sunscreen, or staying hydrated, or having an undetected peanut allergy that he didn't actually have—seriously, the kid loved peanut butter. And ever since Freddie agreed not to press charges, Nancy had been bringing all of these worries to Freddie for some reason. It was kind of like that belief where if you save someone's life, you're responsible for them. That or maybe she had just worn out all of her family members. Either way, she was driving Freddie nuts.

"Freddie, thank God I found you. You're not going to believe what's happened." She darted a look over his shoulder. "Where's Tyler? Have you seen him?" Her short hair was shellacked tight to her skull in little curls, and she had a black feather boa wrapped around her neck. Both the hair and the boa really set off the crazy in her eyes.

Freddie frowned. "I sent him to bring in some supplies from outside. Is this about the peanut allergy again because—"

"No. No. This isn't about the nuts. It's about your suit."

Freddie froze. "What happened to my tux? Tell me nothing happened to my tux. I don't think I can take much more."

She held up her palms. "No. No. The tux is fine. It's just . . ."

Freddie raised an eyebrow.

She clutched her hands together at her chest. "The whole thing's backfired."

"Backfired? How could it possibly backfire?"

"Well, I don't think Tyler wants you to know, and I tried to talk to his father about it, but you know how fathers can be—"

"Cut to the chase, woman!"

"Well," she said, face twitching. "I just knew something was wrong with him, so I texted some of his friends and . . ."

"And?"

She pinched her lips together before saying, "Apparently, Chloe laughed and asked who he was trying to be dressing up in that cheap tux."

I froze. It was the only thing to do because for just a second it felt like a crack had split open in the earth's crust right underneath Hemlock Estate.

Cheap.

I had heard Freddie called many things over the years. I, myself, had called Freddie many things over the years. But I had never once heard anyone use the word *cheap*. I mean, sure, Freddie might complain about being pigeon-holed as the rich kid in town—a title he had stolen from Matthew who had been sent off to prep school during his teenage years—but just because he didn't necessarily want that title foisted upon him, from what I could gather, he didn't exactly want it taken away either.

"That little—"

"Freddie!" I snapped.

"I knew you'd understand," Tyler's mom said. "We can't let her get away with this, right?"

"Of course not. Why would you even think of going to his father with this first? He's a pastor! He can't help us."

"I know," she said, nodding too big. "He thinks I'm crazy, but this . . . this cannot stand."

I didn't know Tyler's dad, but it was good to hear that there were some levelheaded types in town. "Okay," I said, putting my hands up in *whoa* position. "Let's just calm—"

"You know what else I heard she said?" Nancy went on, ignoring me completely.

"What?"

She stepped in and clutched Freddie's forearm. "That Chloe thinks she is out of Tyler's league."

His eyes flashed madly around the room. "Where is she? No. Better yet. Where is her mother?"

All right, that was my cue. I grabbed Freddie by the elbow and yanked him back. He held up a finger to Tyler's mom to wait then said, "Erica, what do you want? We're kind of busy here."

"Um, okay," I said, scratching at my hairline. "Weren't you the one telling me earlier that Tyler's mom was a . . . helicopter mom?"

"Yeah, so?"

"Well, *whuppa whuppa*."

Freddie cocked his head. "*Whuppa whuppa?* What the hell is that?"

"A helicopter sound."

He angry-squinted at me.

"Fine! I'm not good at sounds, but the point is *you* were the one telling *me* not too long ago that Tyler needed to handle this stuff on his own. That with Nancy interfering all the time it was stopping Tyler from becoming a man." At least I was pretty sure that had been what he'd said. Sometimes I tuned out Freddie when he was ranting. "Well?"

No response. Just fire. Deadly fire in the eyes.

"And let's not forget that you are supposed to be a respected business leader in this town. How's it going to look if you and Tyler's mom go off seeking revenge on a sixteen-year-old girl because she can't appreciate fine tailoring?"

A tense moment passed. Freddie wasn't one to let perceived slights pass—and this seemed like a maybe real, secondhand, gossipy-type slight. That being said, he was very concerned about his role as a business leader in this town even though our business had yet to actually make any money.

Finally Freddie took a slow breath and turned back to

Tyler's mom. "All right, I know this is upsetting, but I need to give this some more thought before we do anything about it. I have a lot on the go at the moment."

"What did you say to him?" she yelled, looking at me over Freddie's shoulder.

I half ducked.

She looked back at Freddie. "Whose side are you on?"

He swivelled some pleading eyes back in my direction.

I shook my head firmly no.

"Just promise me you won't do anything yet," he said, patting her hand. Hard. He had gone back to looking like he wanted to fight the entire room—me definitely included. "One way or another. We'll make this right." He leaned in toward her, and I could have sworn he added in a whisper, "Once I get rid of Erica."

"Freddie!"

He leaned back. "Just don't do anything."

Nancy stomped away.

Freddie stomped off too, but in the opposite direction. I scampered after him as best I could. These heels were getting more wobbly by the second.

"Out of his league," I heard Freddie mumble. "Out of his league!"

Uh-oh.

"I'll tell you one thing," he snapped, suddenly whipping around to point at me. "She may be out of his league, but she is nowhere *near* being in the league of my tuxedo."

I nodded quickly. It seemed the safest course of action. I was actually a little surprised, and more than a little grateful, that I had been able to pull Freddie away from this fight in the first place. I could be agreeable.

He whipped back around and resumed his march headed straight for . . . Rhonda? She was busy talking to a group of people, with her back to us. Freddie tapped her on the shoulder.

She whirled around. "Hey!" She looked super happy to see us . . . then suddenly super sad. "How's your dog?"

"Stanley is in dire straits, Rhonda."

I let my chin fall into my chest.

"Oh no, that's awful," she said, dropping a heavy arm around Freddie's neck and pulling him in for a hug. Freddie kept his body ramrod straight, but I could see him puffing her red frizzy hair from his mouth kind of like I had earlier with my mom. "Is there anything I can do?"

"Yes," Freddie choked out. "There is."

I think Freddie was having trouble breathing what with the death grip she had on his neck. Someone had obviously been into the champagne.

"Rhonda," Freddie said, voice muffled through her hair. "Rhonda!" But she just kept on hugging. He whacked her on the arm. "We need your help."

Rhonda finally let Freddie go, face dropping into her most authoritative ex-cop expression. "What do you need, boss?"

"I have a job for you."

"Got it."

"Right." Freddie leaned in closer to Rhonda, but not before darting his eyes side to side again. I don't know why. No one was listening. "I need you to find Candace and make sure she doesn't eat or drink anything for the rest of the night."

Rhonda nearly jumped to attention. "Done." I was a little surprised she didn't salute.

Freddie turned back to me. "I love the way that woman takes orders."

I pressed a finger into the spot between my eyebrows and closed my eyes. "Rhonda?"

"What's up, Erica?"

"We've talked about this."

Since the three of us had started our business together, we'd had some trouble working out the power dynamics. I considered us all equals. Freddie considered himself boss. Rhonda, having been used to being Grady's deputy, was having a little trouble not showing belly when Freddie barked. I had been trying to explain to her the importance of asking questions when Freddie ordered her to do something, because if she wasn't careful she'd be pumicing the calluses off his feet and making him martinis before anyone could put a stop to it.

"Oh right," Rhonda said with a slow nod. She then squinted at Freddie suspiciously. "Why do I have to stop Candace from eating or drinking anything?"

"Because someone is trying to kill her. With poison."

"Right. Got it."

She had just spun on her heel to leave when I again said, "Rhonda."

"Wait," she said, slowly turning back around. "Someone is trying to kill Candace?"

"We don't know that," I said.

"Yes we do." Freddie turned back to face me, yanking his cummerbund down. "Stop playing God," he hissed. "Rhonda doesn't want free will. You're just confusing her." I thought he was going to end it there, but at the last second he tagged on, "It's cruel," before turning back around. He then filled Rhonda in on everything that had happened so far.

"Should we call the police?" Rhonda asked me over Freddie's head. She was quite a bit taller than him in her nautical-looking heels. "Grady's here somewhere. He'd want to know."

"Well, I don't know about that," Freddie said with an

unpleasant snicker. "He and Candace were having quite the brouhaha in the conservatory. You missed it."

I whacked him. "It wasn't a brouhaha. It was just one of those conversations couples have when they're experiencing issues." And maybe breaking up.

Rhonda eyed me suspiciously. At one time, Rhonda had been Grady's and my biggest supporter, but she had taken his side when things started to go downhill and I couldn't make a decision whether or not to move home. We had gotten beyond everything, but the subject was still a little touchy. "And you just happened to stumble across this discussion of issues, huh?"

"We were looking for Stanley! And he was ambling his way down the hall and—you know what?" I felt my cheeks go red. "It's a long story. And I've moved on. Mostly." I waved my hands out. "We're all missing the point h—"

"The point is there's no need to tell Grady," Freddie said, jumping in.

"So nobody is trying to kill Candace after all?" Rhonda asked.

"No, someone definitely is," Freddie said at the very same time I said, "Exactly."

Rhonda looked down at the teacup of champagne in her hand. "Does everyone have a headache, or is it just me?"

"Listen," Freddie said with quite the dramatic hard-done-by sigh. "We could tell Grady, but you know he won't believe us."

"I don't know if I believe us!" I said, slapping my chest. This was all happening so fast. "And you said—"

"Besides," Freddie said, ignoring me. "He'll probably just end up arresting us again."

"Oh please," I drawled. "On what charges?"

"I don't know," Freddie snapped back, barely controlling the volume on his voice. "For being awesome in the face of the law? Does it matter?"

"But say on the off, off chance you are right," Rhonda said with a slow nod, "and we don't tell him"—she threw on a point—"then he'll arrest us for sure."

Freddie opened his mouth to argue, but quickly closed it again. "You may be right."

"That's my job," Rhonda said, trying to hook her free thumb into her gun belt. A momentary look of confusion crossed her face as she realized she wasn't wearing one. She really missed being a cop.

"Okay, so new plan. We need to split up. I doubt Grady and Candace are hanging out together after their brouhaha"—he threw me a pointed look—"so Rhonda, you find Candace and don't let her die."

"Why am I on babysitting duty?"

"Because you haven't ever accused her of murder. We have."

It was a long time ago, but still.

"True. True," Rhonda answered.

"Erica and I will look for Grady and find out what has become of the glass Candace was drinking from earlier. There might be poison residue or something on it. If not, there has to be damp cloth or paper towel."

"Good plan," Rhonda said. "I know a retired medical examiner who does lab tests for a fee in his basement. I can hook you up."

I frowned. "That sounds wrong on all sorts of levels."

She smiled. "I know, right?"

"Okay," Freddie said, clapping his hands together. "We should get moving. Candace could already be dead."

"No, she's not," I said, looking over Rhonda's shoulder. "She's standing right over there with her sister in line at that minibar."

"What the—" I swear if Freddie was wearing a hat, he would have taken it off and swatted me with it.

"Rhonda! Go! Go! Go!"

"Right," she said, before quickly adding, "What reason am I supposed to give her for not letting her eat or drink?"

"Tell her the truth," I said. "Freddie is crazy."

"No, not the truth! We can't tell her that someone really is trying to kill her on New Year's," Freddie said. "That's so mean. What's wrong with you?"

I frowned. "But aren't we trying to save her life? Isn't that why we're doing this?" I was really having trouble remembering why we were doing this. I think Freddie was losing sight too. It wouldn't be the first time we had gotten carried away, and we usually had more to go on.

"It is too early in the investigation to make any conclusions."

"So did we decide what I'm going to say to Candace?" Rhonda asked.

"I don't know!" Freddie said. "I can't do everything. Just go. You'll think of something."

Freddie and I watched Rhonda hurry off in her sailor's uniform. She reached Candace just as she was accepting a drink from the bartender. Rhonda slapped it out of her hand, sending it crashing to the floor.

"Okay, well, I guess that will work," I said.

"Now, where's Grady?" Freddie asked. "Use your Gray-dar."

I rolled my eyes. "I don't have any Gray-dar. It's not like I just instinctually know at any given moment where—Oh! There he is!" I said, pointing over at the other side of the ballroom. "By the grand piano."

"Okay, let's go."

"Erica," a voice called out from behind me.

What now?

Oh.

"Freddie, you go on ahead. I'll be right there."

"What?"

I pushed him on. "I'll catch up. This is important."

Chapter Fourteen

"Important?" Freddie asked. "What could possibly be more important than this?"

Mrs. Arthur was waving at me. The same Mrs. Arthur who might be selling the property I wanted to buy. Mr. Arthur was there too. I waved back. "This will just take a second."

"But we've got an attempted-murder investigation on the go."

"That's debatable."

"Oh crap! Grady's on the move."

"You go," I said, waving him on again. Truth was, I was grateful for the opportunity to avoid Grady for a little longer. I wasn't ready to see him what with the whole "we were not meant to be" thing still rattling around in my head.

"Fine, but hurry up!"

Freddie rushed away as I maneuvered around a group of short, older men wearing fezzes. The Shriners were in Otter Lake? This party sure had a weird mix of guests.

Now I had to play this just right. I didn't really know Nanette and Gerald Arthur. In fact, I don't think I had even spoken to them directly. I knew of them though. They had left the rat race in New York to live a minimalist existence off the grid in New Hampshire, and they were friendly with my mother—similar philosophies toward life. If I had to guess, they were probably in their mid to late forties, but both were in great shape. Nanette had her hair styled into a cute glossy bob that made a V-shape on her forehead, and Gerald had his hair slicked back and was sporting quite the dapper monocle. They were really going for it.

Nanette held out her gloved hand. "Erica, hello. Sorry to interrupt, but Matthew said you wanted to speak to us, and there are so many people here tonight"—she gave her head a bewildered little shake—"it's difficult to find anyone in this crowd."

"No, absolutely. Thank you for calling me over. I did want to speak to you. Matthew mentioned that you two might be thinking of selling—"

"Let me stop you right there," Gerald said, fiddling with his monocle. "We know what it is you're hoping for, but I'm afraid we can't help you."

"Oh," I said, shoulders slumping. "So you're not moving after all?"

Nanette smiled sympathetically. "Well, we are, but . . ."

I sighed. "MRG has already made you an offer."

"Candace is very persuasive," she said, looking to her husband. "Gerald and I just wanted you to know that we really are sorry. We'd much rather sell to you, it's just . . ."

"It's okay. Really," I said, not *really* meaning that at all.

She tucked the sides of her V-shaped bob behind her ears with her gloved fingers. "It's not. We know everybody hates what MRG is doing to this town, and yet . . ."

"They haven't really left anybody any other choice," I offered. Deep pockets could do that.

She gave me another pained smile. "Besides, despite the work we've put into it, our place still needs a lot of upgrading. Living off the grid isn't for everyone."

"It's exhausting really. You have to be really resource-ful," Gerald added with a nod. "Up for anything. You know, be able to think on your feet."

Obviously he had never had a best friend like Fred-die. "Well, thank you for letting me know," I said, trying really hard not to look quite so much like I was five, and they had just popped my balloon. "I wouldn't have wanted to get my hopes up." I didn't carry that line off at all. "I have to go meet up with my friend," I said, pointing in the direction Freddie had scurried off to. "So thanks again."

The couple exchanged another concerned look, before Nanette added, "There's just one more thing we wanted to talk to you about, Erica."

Gerald jumped in. "It's really none of our business, but—"

"We think very highly of your mother," Nanette con-tinued, "and . . ."

They both fell silent.

I frowned as a cold feeling crept over me. Why were these people I barely knew looking at me like my dog had just died. *Oh! Bad thought. Sorry, Stanley.* "And what?"

"You know what?" Gerald said, patting his wife's arm. "It really isn't our business. You know how rumors get spread in this town. Have a nice night, Erica."

His wife nodded. "Sorry we couldn't have given you better news."

I opened my mouth to say something, I guess to stop them, but they had made a beeline away from me.

Well, what the heck was that all about?

I blinked a few times then looked around the room.

Okay, call me paranoid. But suddenly it seemed like a lot of people were looking in my direction. Far more than would be possible by chance. Something was going on here. Over the years I had developed a special talent for knowing when I was at the center of town gossip.

My eyes trailed around the room again.

No, I wasn't imagining it. A number of people were giving me sideways looks and whispering.

I did not like this at all.

Okay, yes, I had promised Freddie I'd meet him ASAP. And I would. In a minute. But I needed to find out what was going on first.

And I knew just who to ask.

I looked over to the club chairs by the ferns. Still empty. Hmm, maybe these looks had something to do with Grady and Candace breaking up? But that didn't explain the Arthurs' nervousness. It was almost like they wanted to warn me about something.

Yup, the case of the poisoned dog would have to wait.

I scanned the crowd some more.

Aha! Got 'em.

Blackjack table three o'clock.

Chapter Fifteen

"Hit me."

I poked the shoulder of one of my pseudoaunts.

"Erica! Finally," Tweety said, whacking her sister's arm.

Kit Kat grabbed me by the wrist, pulling me closer to the table. "We've been looking for you everywhere. We lost Freddie's dog. We've looked for him everywhere."

"Really?" I asked, eyeing the drinks and cards on the table in front of them, and the handsome dealer standing behind it. "Because it kind of looks like you've been busy playing blackjack."

"Hey, this is a great spot," Tweety said. "You can see the entire room from here. We knew you'd turn up. And we've got information you're going to want to hear." Her eyes snapped away from me to the dealer. "I said hit me, Carl."

Carl flipped the king of hearts onto Tweety's nine and three.

"Aw, busted." She looked back to me. "Now what was I saying?"

"You've got information for me? Maybe what you were trying to tell me earlier about Candace and Grady?"

"Oh, we are way beyond that now," she said. "You tell her, Kit."

"Hang on. Hang on," Kit Kat said, eyes glued to the cards on the green felt table. "Hit me."

"Hit me?" her sister yelled. "You've got sixteen. You don't hit on—"

"Twenty-one! Blackjack!" Carl called out.

"Boom!" Kit Kat yelled, smacking the table.

"She's counting cards again," Tweety said. "I knew it. She's—"

"Relax," I said. "You know the money you spent on chips is going to charity, right? Children's hospital?" Or maybe it was the new roof for the rec center.

"Who told you that?" Kit Kat asked, pointing at me with her cigar.

"I don't know," I said with a shrug. "I think it's just like known."

The twins looked at Carl. The handsome young dealer arranging chips peeked up at them.

"Is this true?" Kit Kat asked, turning her cigar on him.

He shrugged apologetically.

"Well, son of a—"

I waved my hands out. "All right. All right. Never mind all that. We need to talk."

"Take five, kid," Tweety said, cigar pinned in the corner of her mouth. They'd better be careful not to let my mother catch them smoking those things. She had taken on as her personal mission to cure the sisters of their diabetes and improve their health in general.

Once Carl was gone, I said, "So what's going on? Please tell me you know what, uh—" I looked behind me back out over the room. Yup, people were still looking at me while trying to look like they weren't looking at me. "Why is everybody looking at me?"

"She doesn't know."

"Told ya she didn't know."

"Don't tell me word has already gotten around that Freddie thinks someone poisoned his dog?"

The twins exchanged looks and asked an identical, "What?"

I sighed. "Freddie's got it in his head that someone is trying to poison Candace and got his dog instead," I answered. "It's crazy. It's—"

"Well, you'd better quash that rumor real quick," Kit Kat said.

"Yeah," Tweety added. "Otherwise people might start to think . . ."

They exchanged another look.

"What will be people be thinking?"

"Well, that Grady is trying—" Kit Kat cut herself off by chewing her lip. They were both eyeing me carefully like I might blow.

"Trying to what?"

They both winced, features nearly disappearing in the folds of their wrinkles.

"Trying to what?"

"Well, there's this crazy rumor that—"

"Grady might be trying to kill his girlfriend."

Chapter Sixteen

"What? That's ridiculous. Why would anyone think that?"

Kit Kat scratched the side of her forehead with the pinkie finger of her cigar hand. "Well, we tried to tell you earlier about all the scuttlebutt around town this week. And it seems there's been a development."

"What scuttlebutt?" I asked, looking back and forth between them. "What development?"

The twins looked nervous. "Well, you know all the gossip about Grady and Candace?"

"No, I really don't know."

"I thought you of all people would know what's going on," Kit Kat said.

"Just tell me!" Then a horrible thought occurred to me. What if they said Grady and Candace were getting married? No . . . surely I would have noticed a ring on Candace's finger. And what about their brouhaha earlier? Not that it was any of my business, because we weren't meant to be. But what if they—

"They're breaking up."

"Oh, thank God," I said before I could help myself.

The twins chuckled.

"Tell us how you really feel," Tweety said, picking up her tumbler and taking a sip.

"I can't believe you didn't know," Kit Kat said again.

"Well, I can't believe you two didn't tell me!"

Tweety shrugged. "You're always over at Freddie's."

"You could have texted me. I know you know how to text." The twins had somehow discovered adult emojis and thought it was hilarious to send me barrages of them at weird hours of the day.

"Yeah," Tweety said, shooting her sister a look. "Truth was, we didn't know how you would react."

"How I would react?" I asked, really confused. It's not exactly like my feelings for Grady were a secret in this town. Nothing was a secret in this town . . . unless you were me! "Are people blaming me?" I gasped. "Are they saying Grady's still in love with me? Is that why he's breaking up with her?" In all honesty, I would have never been so happy to be hated in my life . . . or at least that's how I would have felt if I hadn't moved on.

"Yeah, no," Tweety said. "That's not it."

Dammit.

"And for the record, it's Candace who's breaking up with Grady."

"Tonight," Kit Kat jumped in. "If you believe the rumors."

"What? That doesn't make any sense. Why would she do that? At a party of all places?"

"Yeah, that's the crazy part."

I waited. I was getting pretty tired of prodding these two for information.

"Apparently." Kit Kat paused to take a deep breath. "It's because she's afraid of how he's going to react. She wants lots of people around. Everybody to know. In case he's thinking of doing something crazy."

I blinked. "Come on."

They just looked at me.

"You can't be serious."

Kit Kat shrugged.

I once again looked back and forth between the two of them. They weren't kidding. "Nobody's going to believe that. I mean, Grady's . . . Grady."

"Hey, you don't have to tell us," Kit Kat said. "I'm just saying it's the rumor."

Tweety frowned. "And now you're saying someone is trying to poison Candace. People will have a field day with that."

"I'm not saying that. Freddie's saying that because he's upset about his dog." I did not like this at all. Okay, I mean, fine, Freddie and I were occasionally prone to flights of fancy, but this could not be one of those times. I needed to shut this down now.

"Well then, you had better stop him from spreading it around," Tweety said. "You of all people know how rumors can get out of control in this town."

Kit Kat nodded. "And let us know if there's anything we can do to help."

"Okay, I gotta go. You two behave yourselves," I said, pointing at them both.

Tweety snorted. "Yeah, 'cause we're the duo that's going to get out of control."

I hurried back to the hallway that led to the conservatory. I got a text from Freddie saying to meet him there. I almost texted Grady to join us, but I needed to think on how to tell him about all of this. He'd be really hurt if he knew what people were saying. But maybe it was better if he got a heads-up from me? No, I couldn't do it. I'd talk to Candace first. That seemed like a better idea. Maybe she could kill all this gossip before it reached Grady. I couldn't help but think that all the rumors about the threatening letter had somehow morphed into this accusation against Grady—kind of like a game of broken telephone. Candace could clear this all up. Yeah, I'd talk to her—once I got Freddie back on the leash.

The door to Matthew's bedroom was open just a smidge as I passed by. Stanley was still asleep in the middle of the bed like the princess and the pea. Oh, and wasn't that sweet. Matthew and Jessica were chatting by the fireplace across from his bed. They looked so cozy. Not that I cared. Much. I had way bigger fish to fry.

I was actually kind of angry that the people of this town would let the rumors get this far. Everyone knew that Candace doted on Grady. She put every picture of him she could up on social media. Just the other day she had posted a photo of him drinking coffee on his snowy porch. Not that I was anonymously stalking her pages or anything. She had blocked me from her social media a while back. And everybody knew that Grady was definitely not the type of guy you needed to be concerned about when it came to breakups. I mean, we had certainly done it enough. It was really easy. We hadn't even had a real conversation about our last split. Just bam! Broken up. I probably should have asked the twins who was spreading all of this talk in the first place.

I spotted Freddie walking by the wall of stained-glass windows at the far end of the conservatory with his fingers pyramided under his chin. At the sound of my footsteps he whirled around. "Where have you been? Grady got away from me. I've tried texting him, but he's not answering. And the glass is gone. Maybe we can find whoever cleaned it up. Hopefully it hasn't been washed yet, or we can get the cloth that—"

"No. No. No." I sliced my hands in the air. "There has been a change of plans."

Freddie arched an eyebrow.

"The investigation's off." I filled him in on everything the twins had told me. When I finished, he didn't say anything right away. I prepared myself for the onslaught of protest. I was holding firm though. We couldn't make things worse for Grady. I mean, that was kind of like a hobby for us given that we were always investigating crimes we shouldn't be and he was sheriff. But this was personal.

Finally, Freddie nodded and said, "I can see where you are coming from."

"You can?"

"Well, yeah."

I shot him a sideways look. "Really?"

"Of course," he said. "I mean, I'm still pretty upset about Stanley, but given this new development, it would be extremely reckless to spread unfounded rumors."

Relief washed over me. "Exactly."

"I think we should still tell Grady what happened, though, just in case someone really is trying to kill Candace, but otherwise we need to shut this entire operation down."

"Great, I—"

"Well, well, well," a voice said from behind me. "Erica Bloom."

Freddie brushed by me. "We shut everything down just as soon as we talk to him."

My stomach dropped as my skeevy meter went through the roof.

Nuts.

Chapter Seventeen

"Finally," Bryson said, pushing himself off the frame of the door he was making a show of casually leaning against. Somehow he always managed to look like the good-looking rich douchebag holding a tennis racket from every eighties high school movie ever made—except, oh wow, now he had grown quite the blond beard. An extensively groomed blond beard. Very hipster. "I have been looking for you everywhere."

Bryson. Candace's ex-boss, now assistant, I guess. He was also one of those guys who always seemed to be asking every female in his path for a hug, pelvis thrust out first.

"Well, that's funny, Bryson," Freddie said walking toward him. "Because it just so happens that we wanted to have a word with you. Glorious beard by the way."

"Thanks." Bryson squinted at Freddie. "Have we . . . ?"

"Met?" Freddie's face hardened. "Several times, Bryson. Several times."

"Really?" Bryson said with an easy smile. "Help me out here. I'm pulling nothing."

I wasn't the only person that Bryson aggravated to no

end. He was terrible at remembering the name or face of anyone he didn't want something from.

"It's Freddie. Freddie Ng."

"Freddie . . . ?" Bryson asked, still squinting.

"We were partners at the chambers of commerce golf tournament?"

Bryson shook his head. "Still nothing."

"I pulled your BMW out of the ditch that one time with my Jimmy?"

Bryson's brow contracted. "Sorry, man, I remember going into the ditch. There was a scratch on the passenger door."

"Then there was that time—Actually, never mind." Freddie spun away from him and walked toward me. "I'm out. You're going to have to sleep with him to see if he knows anything."

"What?" I snapped under my breath. "No!"

"And you say *I* never want to do what *you* want to do."

I whacked him.

He smiled then frowned. "You're right. It's funny. But it's not. We are in a very complicated space in history when it comes to men like Bryson."

I shot a look over Freddie's shoulder. Bryson had made himself extremely comfortable on a rattan settee. His arms were spread wide across the top of the seat and his legs . . . well, he was really taking man-spreading to a whole new level. "And what information are you even talking about?"

"Candace information?" Freddie said in his *isn't it obvious?* voice. "He does work for her."

"No," I said firmly. And when that didn't seem to have any effect, I tried another, "No."

Freddie just stared at me.

"No!" I shout-whispered. "We are not doing this."

"I'm not saying you have to ask him about any poison. Just find out what's going on with Candace these days. Has he taken any calls for her of a threatening nature? That kind of thing."

I sighed.

"Maybe he can clear up some of these outrageous rumors about Grady."

I growled. "Fine. But after this, we go straight to Grady. Or Candace." I couldn't keep straight what the heck it was we were supposed to be doing.

"Fine."

"Fine."

"Fine." Freddie grabbed my shoulders and spun me around to face Bryson while he whispered in my ear. "Remember to stay calm though. He's useless to us dead."

"Whatever," I said from the corner of my mouth. "Bryson can't get to me. He's not worth it. I'm totally in control."

"You're adorable. I see why he likes you." He pushed me lightly on the shoulder blades. "Now go. Make Stanley proud."

I stumbled toward Bryson.

"Erica," he said in an overly deep voice that seemed to have all sorts of implications.

"Bryson," I said in a corrective tone.

"I have been looking forward to seeing you."

Oh God. Candace's words about my being Bryson's conquest for the evening rang in my ears. I looked up at the ceiling. "Okay, well—"

"I know what you're thinking," Bryson said.

I lowered my eyes to his.

"You're thinking that I am going to proposition you for a night that we both know you would never forget but would ultimately be meaningless in the grand scheme of our lives."

"I . . ."

Freddie made a retching noise.

"But that's not what I have in mind at all," Bryson said.

I studied his handsome but douchey face. There was something about him that just looked . . . pampered, despite the beard, or maybe because of the beard? It was quite disturbing.

"You see," he began. "I've learned a lot this past year with everything I've been through."

I cleared my throat. "By everything you've been through, are you referring to the fact that you paid locals to cause trouble around Otter Lake to soften up seniors and make them more likely to sell their properties to MRG?" I just wanted to be sure.

"Not so much," he said as though he were giving it considerable thought. "More what happened after." His index finger made a little jump in the air to get to the end of the story.

Freddie and I exchanged confused glances.

"The part where I nearly got fired?"

"Oh yeah, that is a terrible thing to happen to a person," I said with a nod. "To almost be fired for doing something illegal."

"Well," he said, frowning like my words had given him stomach troubles. "Unproven illegal. There is a difference."

I tipped my chin at him. "Speaking of which, why didn't you get fired?"

Freddie piped up. "His uncle is Bill MacDonnel. The M in MRG?"

"You never told me that," I said to Freddie with a surprised smile. That just seemed like the kind of thing we would discuss in passing. We spent a lot of time together.

"Oh yeah, totally."

"The point is," Bryson said really loudly, "I've come

to appreciate what's truly important in life. I've seen the light."

"Oh boy," Freddie said, throwing his hands in the air. "Clear a path, everybody. He's coming to Jesus."

Bryson smiled. "You are an odd little duck, aren't you? What did you say your name was?"

Freddie took a deep breath, spun on his heel, and walked toward the windows. It was probably for the best.

"Okay, Bryson," I said, sitting in another rattan chair opposite him. I was perched right on the edge. It never seemed wise to get too relaxed around Bryson. "I'm glad you've had this spiritual awakening, but we were just curious—"

"There I was, just sitting there at my brah's place in Maine, drinking bourbon, when it hit me. I want something more out of life." He clenched his fist. "A deeper connection. With someone real. I'm so tired of gorgeous socialites and models. I want someone . . . normal."

I closed my eyes. Oh no.

"And I think that someone is you."

Chapter Eighteen

"Oh . . . wow."

I heard Freddie snicker behind me.

Me? Why me—*Oh,* I think I knew. Maybe it wasn't the reason Bryson had in his head, but if I had to put money on it, I would guess this had a lot to do with Grady. Otter Lake was a small town. Certainly not big enough for two cocks of the walk . . . *and,* that sounded and *looked* very wrong in my head. Anyway, it really bothered Bryson that there was another equally handsome man in town—with a uniform no less. He was always making jokes about Grady winning the coveted most beautiful baby title three years in a row back in the day. Nobody really laughed with him though. Grady truly was a beautiful baby. And Bryson knew that Grady and I had a history, so if he could claim me, it would be like marking his territory. Huh, that was a disturbing image too. I suddenly felt the urge to take a shower.

"You can say something now," Bryson said.

"Um . . . no, thank you?"

He laughed. "You are adorable."

"Hey, that's what I just said," Freddie called out with a chuckle.

I shot him a look over my shoulder before turning back around to face Bryson. "Now that we've got that out of the way, Freddie and I were wondering if you could—"

"What? That's it? Just no?"

"I said *thank you* too."

"I pour my heart out to you, and that's all I get?"

"Yes . . . thank you." Not sure why I threw on that second *thank you*.

"Wow," Bryson said. "I knew you could be mean, but I didn't think you were such a b—"

I screamed. I couldn't help it.

Freddie rushed over.

I shook my head in disbelief at him. "Did he just call me a . . . ?"

"Maybe we should switch again. It's your turn for a break," he said reassuringly. "Just maybe give me the sculpture." Freddie took a heavy abstract sculpture from my gripped hands. Huh, how did that get there? It had been on the coffee table just a moment ago. "You don't want to break it."

"If you weren't interested," Bryson said, "you shouldn't have followed me in here."

"We were in here first!" I threw my hands in the air. "I'm going to lose my mind, Freddie." If I had to guess, I think I was starting to look like one of those crazy Muppets whose arms flail around like wet noodles.

"Maybe we should just go," Freddie said, nodding quickly. "Bryson looks like the type to press charges."

"I don't believe this," I heard Bryson mutter as we headed for the door. "Here I am stuck in this backwater town on New Year's answering e-mails for Candace and updating her social media, cleaning up her spilled drinks, and I can't even get Boobsie Bloom to—"

I screamed again.

"Wait . . . what?" Freddie asked, whirling around. Then he remembered me and said, "Stay," before moving me away from a fireplace poker. "Actually stay here. Don't move. I'll be right back." He hustled back over to Bryson. "What drink? Where?"

"In here," Bryson said, throwing his hand out. "Can you believe that? I should ask that fortune-teller out there if Candace ran a sweatshop in a previous life."

"So what did you do with it?"

Bryson frowned. "Do with what?"

"The glass. The cloths! What did you do with the glass and the cloths?"

Bryson frowned. "I didn't actually clean it myself."

"Who did?"

"I don't know," he said. "One of the servers."

"Which one? Man? Woman? What did they look like?"

"I don't know. It was guy. I wasn't paying attention. He had a nice watch for a server though. Probably stole it."

Freddie looked at me with that twinkle in his eye that meant this situation was about to be taken to a whole other level.

"Freddie, I know what you're thinking right now," I said, recovered enough to think straight, "but we discussed this and—"

He rushed toward me and grabbed my elbow. "Come on. Let's go."

"You're just leaving?" Bryson asked. "I was just telling you how crappy my life is and that's it? I thought we were friends, Eddie."

Freddie swirled on his heel. "Nope."

"Erica?"

"Oh my God, no!" I shouted.

Once we were in the hall, I yanked my elbow away. "No. No, we are not doing this. Not with all these crazy rumors flying. You agreed that we should let this go."

"Exactly, I did agree with that until I realized that it's a much better idea to prove nobody is trying to poison Candace. That way everyone's collective mind can be put at ease."

"Nobody's mind is uneasy but yours!"

"Said Ms. Bloom who was about to do it in the conservatory with a mini-statue," Freddie said knowingly.

"That was temporary insanity. I'm fine now."

"But what about the twins?"

"What about the twins?"

"You don't think they're going to tell anybody what you told them about the poison? I mean, you told me what they said about the rumors."

"That is totally different. Of course I'm going to tell you. Best friends don't count."

"Yeah, you're right. Totally. I mean, I doubt the twins have friends," Freddie said, nodding. "Oh wait . . . they're friends with all the old ladies in this town!"

Oh wow, he was right. A vision of an old-timey phone operator popped into my head frantically connecting calls like nobody's business.

"Besides," I said, "they're the ones who told me to make sure I quashed this rumor."

"Yes, and I'm sure they will include that detail when they retell this story to all of their friends. I mean, they're not bad people."

"They wouldn't," I said, but a sinking feeling fell over me. I mean, they wouldn't mean to, but they might tell one friend something—everybody was worried about Freddie's dog—and then that person might—

Freddie must have known what I was thinking because

he said, "And then she tells two friends. And then they tell two friends. And—"

I whacked him. "All right. I get it."

"You sold Grady down the creek, sweetheart. Now we have to clear him."

I closed my eyes, put my hands over my face, and shook my head. "Why didn't I just stay home?" I mean, I could ring in the New Year quite happily from home. "Why—"

"There's no time for all that," Freddie said, yanking my elbow again. "We've got a server to find."

"I can't help but think," I said, letting Freddie drag me down the hall, "that even though I'm agreeing to do this to help Grady, Grady wouldn't want us doing this. And he would probably be right."

"Well, I hate to break it to you, but this isn't just about Grady," Freddie said, thumb of his free hand bouncing around his phone. "It's about Stanley. Hashtag, justice for Stanley."

"Wait . . . are you tweeting about this?"

"Oh yeah," Freddie said. "Who knew if you tweeted *Someone tried to poison my dog,* you'd go viral?"

The Morning After

"Oh, so that's how you got . . ." My brain hurt too much to finish the thought.

"Oh yeah," Freddie said.

"Justice for Stanley."

He swiped at his phone. "Somebody has already made T-shirts."

"Huh."

"I am an Internet sensation." He snapped a quick picture of the little dog lying on the floor. "Good boy."

Chapter Nineteen

Freddie and I maneuvered our way through the crowd of partygoers about as subtly as one might expect. If you stop every male waiter you come across and ask to see his wrist, people, unsurprisingly perhaps, start to wonder what exactly it is that you are doing. When asked, Freddie had taken to saying, "Mind your business," while I silently mouthed behind his back something to the effect of *It's the stress.* I may have even done the universal cuckoo-bird swirling with my finger a couple of times. Not appropriate, I know, but apparently neither was my life. Finally, we decided we might have better luck finding the bee in the hive, so we headed for the kitchen.

And what a kitchen it was. Man, if I hadn't wanted to marry Matthew before . . . wait, what? Who said that? It was a really nice kitchen. The kind of kitchen that made you think you could cook really fancy, delicious things based solely on the inspiration of your surroundings. At least that was what it did for me. In fact, I am pretty sure I had never once thought about making artisan jam previous to this very moment, and probably never would again. The room had such a nice combination of tan wood, brushed chrome finishings, and stone countertops. It also had small chandeliers running the length of the room over an oversized harvest table. The tin ceiling tiles was probably the best touch though. They defused warm light throughout the entire space.

Despite the calm design of the room, the kitchen was bustling. Even though this was supposedly the Otter Lake Historical Society's party, there was no way they could have forked out the dough to hire this many people. This had to be Matthew's doing. Again, the architectural business must be really paying off.

"How the heck are we supposed to find this—"

"There he is," Freddie said with a point. "That is a really nice watch."

Freddie was pointing at a server with his back to us arranging champagne flutes on a silver tray.

"Okay," Freddie said. "Let's go talk to him."

"Fine, but please, *please,* Freddie. Let's at least *try* to do this subtly."

Freddie stopped and flashed me an annoyed look. "We don't have time for subtle. Do you want to clear Grady or not? I'd say that enough time has passed that the villagers will be thinking about getting their torches and pitchforks to go after him."

"Oh, stop it," I said. "Nobody is—"

"And it will be all your fault." Freddie suddenly gasped. "It's just like that scene in *Beauty and the Beast.* You're the magic mirror that sets all the townspeople off to storm the castle and kill the beast!"

I blinked.

Freddie wagged a finger in the air. "Or maybe you're more like the jerk guy with the thick neck who wants to marry—Wait, I'm confused. No, I think I was right the first time. You're the magic mirror that—"

"Can't I just be Belle?"

"No," he said with a high degree of certainty. "I can't see it. But Grady as the beast? That's perfect! He's always so grumpy and—"

"Fine. Forget the cover story," I said. "Let's just get the glass. Then tomorrow you can turn it over to the police or a secret lab in some guy's basement and we will put this entire thing to rest." I looked back at the server who was just getting ready to leave with his tray. "Okay, we'd better hurry. I'm guessing you want to take the lead with the questioning?"

Freddie didn't answer. When I looked at him to see what the holdup was, I noticed he seemed almost mesmerized by our target, who had finally turned around. The server *was* pretty hot. Tousled brown hair. Big, warm eyes. He almost would have been intimidatingly hot had it not been for the round lenses on the glasses he was wearing. They were nerdy and fashionable—and definitely managed to make him look more approachable.

"You know," Freddie said slowly, "I think you should question him." He pushed me toward the waiter. "It's time for you to take the training wheels off. I'll . . . I'll wait here."

I felt a smile spread across my face. Well, well, well, maybe finally Freddie's love life could be put in the spotlight instead of mine. That would certainly be nice for a change. I put on my best Southern accent and said, "Why, Freddie, I do declare. You seem quite taken with that there handsome young man."

Freddie didn't return my smile. "Don't do that."

"Yeah, it didn't feel right."

He pushed me forward. "Would you just go?"

"Fine, I'll do the talking," I said. "But you're staying." I grabbed his arm, and before Freddie could protest any more, I waved the server down.

He spotted me and walked toward us.

"I swear, you'd better not embarrass me," Freddie muttered, "or, forget Candace, the only murder tonight will be me killing y—"

"Hi," I said as the man approached. I looked at the gold plastic nametag pinned to his vest. "Sean?"

"That's me," he said. "Can I get you two anything?"

"Oh no, I'm fine," I said. "Freddie?"

Freddie shot me a threatening look.

"No? Are you sure?"

The look he gave me this time was so terrifying it made me question my life choices. And truth be told, I didn't want to push him too hard. Freddie and I talked about pretty much everything *but* his love life. Being gay in a town like Otter Lake hadn't been easy, and while everyone was getting used to the idea, it still wasn't exactly the best place to meet people.

I looked back at a very confused Sean and rebrightened my smile. "I don't suppose you were the server who cleaned up the small accident a little while ago?"

"You mean the drink that spilled? Or the dog accident out in the ballroom?"

"My dog is very sick!" Freddie snapped. "He didn't know what he was doing."

"Oh no," Sean said, putting his hand to his chest. "That's your dog? He's adorable."

Freddie just stared at him.

The server gestured around the room. "We've all been wondering how he's doing." None of the other servers looked particularly concerned, except for . . . was that Chloe? The girl that Tyler had tried to impress with Freddie's tux? She was standing by herself, sniffling, in the back corner of the kitchen. She was either crying . . . or had allergies. My guess was the former. I quickly looked away. Alerting Freddie to her presence couldn't lead anywhere good.

"Stanley's stable," Freddie said. I guess he was letting go of some of his indignation because he tagged on, "Thank you for asking."

"Stanley," Sean said with a sad smile. "I love that name. Do you know what's wrong with him?"

"We have our suspicions."

Sean's brow furrowed.

"He means ideas," I said quickly. "We have some *ideas*. Poinsettias. Keep them away from your dogs."

"Oh," Sean said with a careful nod. "Sure. And I really am sorry. I didn't realize when you waved me over that he was your dog." He made eye contact with both of us.

"Oh no," I said, waving my hands out in front of me. "We're not—"

"Now I think I'm the one who's going to be sick," Freddie said, bringing a hand to his forehead.

"So you're not . . ." Sean looked back and forth between the two of us, hesitating just a moment longer on Freddie. "I love your tux, by the way."

Freddie pointed at his wrist. "I could tell you have good taste by your watch."

"Oh yeah," Sean said excitedly, holding out his arm. "I got it—"

Freddie suddenly spun on his heel. "I've got to go. I just remembered—you got this, Erica." He hurried off before either Sean or I could blink.

Okay then. I hadn't seen that coming. I mean, I knew Freddie was nervous, but . . . but it had been going so well! They had been doing the flirty *I like what you're wearing. No, I like what you're wearing* talk. I thought Freddie was afraid of being shot down, not picked up. This was not good. He was so going to kill me later. "I'm sorry," I said with an awkward chuckle. "Freddie has a thing . . . he wasn't supposed to forget."

"Right," Sean said, smile dropping. He actually looked kind of disappointed. Maybe even hurt.

This was terrible. I had to do something. Cute gay men like this didn't just show up in Otter Lake every day. "The vet! He was supposed to meet back with the vet to get an update on his dog. He's just upset about Stanley being sick."

Sean nodded and a bit of his former smile returned. "Yeah, it's a pretty helpless feeling waiting for information about a sick pet."

"That is so true," I said with a big nod. "I like you." I hadn't meant to say it in a voice that spoke to the fact that I could already see him fitting in nicely with our bizarre little family. But I could totally see it.

"Um . . . thank you?"

"You're welcome." Yup, Sean could teach me how to make cocktails in Freddie's kitchen while wearing his very nice watch. Okay, fine, it wasn't a full-fledged vision, given that all I knew about Sean was that he served drinks and had a nice watch, but it was a start. "Now back to the whole mess thing," I said, shaking my head. "I wasn't actually talking about the dog. I meant the drink in the conservatory. Was that you who cleaned it up?"

He nodded.

"What exactly did you do with the glass? You didn't wash it, did you?"

Man, I was terrible at this. You could tell by the suspicious side-eye Sean was giving me.

"No, it had a little chip in it, so I threw it out."

"Oh good. Good." I clutched my hands to my chest and tilted my head. "Which garbage can?"

He half smiled, half looked at me like I was crazy. "Can I ask why?"

"Why? Oh, of course you can ask that." Do not start

any more poison rumors, Erica. Do not start any more poison rumors.

"Okay," Sean said in that slow way that meant he was questioning my sanity, but totally willing to have a laugh about it if I had a reasonable explanation. "Why do you want to know where I put the glass?"

"Oh right." I chuckled. "I did say you could ask. It's, uh . . ."

He waited as I looked around the kitchen.

"Poison."

Dammit.

"Poison?"

"Yeah, well at least poison for the dog. You see, it might not have been the poinsettias. Stanley is allergic to nuts, and Freddie was worried that the spilled drink might have actually contained nuts, and Stanley got into it . . ." So, so bad at this.

"What kind of drink has nuts in it?"

"Oh well, I didn't mean it was like a peanut martini or that kind of thing. Just the factory it was made in may have contained nuts. You know how like they never want to guarantee that sort of thing. Or coconut water," I said, waving my hands out like *Of course!* "Everybody's drinking coconut water these days. And a coconut is still a nut." At least I thought it was.

"I . . . I guess."

"Yup. Coconuts." I gave the air a little *Go team!* punch for some inexplicable reason.

"Right."

"Listen, truth is I know it's a little crazy, but Freddie really loves that dog. And I would like to be able to put his mind at ease. You're a dog lover. You know how it is." I slapped his arm lightly. "I'm not a dog person. Not really a cat person either. My fur-brother is my mom's favorite.

It left me with some issues." Oh, so now I babble when I lie. Good to know.

He nodded. "If Freddie needs to talk to someone—dog lover to dog lover—I'd be more than happy to meet up with him on my break."

I was smiling and nodding again, but at least I stopped myself from saying another *I like you*. "I'll tell him that you said that. I'm sure he would appreciate the offer. Now that garbage?"

"Oh, I already took it to the bin outside," he said, pointing to a door at the far end of the kitchen. "I didn't want anyone to get hurt with the glass."

"Outside?"

"Yeah, sorry." He smiled at me apologetically. "I wrapped the glass in the paper towel I used to clean up the mess then put it in a little food box, so it might be tricky to find."

"Great. You've totally helped. Thank you." I turned to leave.

"Oh, and tell Freddie that I really am sorry about his dog."

I shot him a thumbs-up. "Sure thing."

Yup, we were all very sorry about Freddie and his dog issues.

Especially me.

I was so not wearing the right outfit for garbage picking.

The Morning After

"You like Sean!" I gasped. "And I'm pretty sure he likes you."

"What are you talking about?"

"The waiter guy! You couldn't even talk to him you were so shy."

"Shut up!"

"Freddie's got a boyfriend."

"I do not!"

"Yes you do, and he's really cute."

"He is really cute."

"I know, right?"

"I hope he didn't see me in this fur."

I snorted a laugh. "Yeah, and I hope he didn't see me in this turban."

"Erica, nobody cares if you're wearing a turban."

I blinked. "You're a mean one, Mr. Ng."

Chapter Twenty

"I can't feel my toes."

"Do you normally go around feeling your toes?" Freddie asked, flicking some slush off his galoshes.

I wrapped Freddie's suit jacket more tightly around my torso and hiked up the hem of my dress as I stepped over a minidrift of snow. "No, but it really hurts when you can't feel them." We couldn't figure out where our coats had gotten off to, so Freddie had lent me his tuxedo jacket, and he had *borrowed* the galoshes sitting at the back door. Hopefully this wouldn't take too long.

"All right. All right," Freddie said. "I'm getting a little tired of this myself. We'll just get the glass and give Grady a little heads-up that somebody is trying to kill his girlfriend then I'll let it go."

"*Maybe* trying to kill her. Like *not really*. Like probably *not at all*," I said. "And I'm sure he'll love hearing that from us."

"Why are you so grumpy? I thought you were young and single and at a fancy party. You love New Year's. You should be happy."

"I am. I am. But Stanley's sick, I'm cold, my boots are

back at the snowmobile, and I have slush in my shoes. Not to mention the fact that I nearly broke my neck tripping on that jug of antifreeze back there. And let's not forget that we are about to pick through garbage. That all is kind of tipping the scale."

"That and the twinkly lights," Freddie said, stopping to look at the trees Matthew had shown me earlier. "They are a bit much."

"What? They're beautiful!" I said with probably a little too much enthusiasm, because my back heel almost slipped out from underneath me, making me pinwheel my arms for balance. We were walking a mainly clear path around the side of the house to where Sean had pointed earlier. "They are not too much. They're just right."

"For a *My Little Pony* Christmas special maybe," he muttered. "I betcha the rest of the town is in the dark with all this wattage."

"Wow, you are not doing well," I muttered. I felt bad, though. Freddie was really starting to look kind of down. I mean, first there was Stanley, then there was the insult to his tuxedo, and *then* there was the whole thing with Sean. He was having a pretty rough time of it. "So are we going to talk about what happened in the kitchen back there?"

Freddie looked at me. "What are you talking about?"

"That whole business where you walked away midsentence from an extremely handsome man who seemed to be interested in both you and your dog?"

"Who? Sean?" Freddie puffed some air through his lips. "Sean. What a ridiculous name."

"Again with the names. What's the matter with Sean?"

Freddie's shoulders bounced with a huffed laugh. "Only an *Erica* would ask that."

I swatted at him but missed, nearly spinning myself into the snow.

"Did you see his nametag? He spells it S-E-A-N."

"So?"

"So change the *S* to a *B* and you've got *Bean*! I mean, have some dignity already."

I sighed as I hugged Freddie's too thin jacket to my chest. Okay, this was getting ridiculous. Sure, Freddie did not like to spend time talking about the really personal stuff going on in his head—apparently that's what my life was for—but he couldn't keep all this stuff in. It wasn't healthy. "All I'm saying is that maybe—"

Freddie stopped walking with a jerk. "What are you trying to do right now?"

I stopped to look at him. "I don't know. Just . . . maybe it wouldn't kill you to—"

"I am too busy trying to get our business off the ground for any distractions," Freddie snapped before smoothing down his silk scarf. "Besides, I can't date a server."

"What? Why not?"

"It's bad enough that I have to keep you and Rhonda afloat. I need to be half of a power couple or nothing." He suddenly pointed a finger in the air. "And, you know, while we're on the subject, I think maybe we have been spending too much time together."

"No. No. No. Nice try, but that's not what's going on here. You're just too—"

"Hey!" he shouted with a point. "There's the bin."

"Nice segue," I muttered. Just then my phone rang. I took it out from my pocket and looked at the screen before answering. "Rhonda? What's going on?"

"The target is on the move. I repeat, the target is on the move."

"What are you talking about?" I said, covering my other ear with my hand. Freddie had turned to see what the holdup was. "Who's on the move?"

"Candace! I went to the bathroom for one second and she disappeared. I asked around and someone said they saw her outside headed toward the lake. She's super drunk. We've got to stop her."

I shot Freddie some *uh-oh* eyes. Candace was super drunk? That wasn't going to help stop any of the many rumors floating around tonight. "I thought you weren't going to let her drink anything?"

"Ha! Easier said than done. The girl's determined to get her drink on." And she wasn't the only one by the sound of Rhonda's voice. "I couldn't stop her, so I had to do the next best thing. It was the only way I could keep listening to her go on and on about having the courage to do what needed to be done with Grady."

Freddie walked toward me. I held up a finger for him to wait. "What was the next best thing to stopping Candace from drinking, Rhonda?"

"Well, I've been getting all of her drinks for her and then taste-testing them for poison just to be sure. You know like how they did it in medieval times."

I squeezed my eyes shut and rubbed my temple with my free hand. "That . . . wasn't what we had in mind." Rhonda had brilliant and equally less brilliant ideas in about equal measure.

"Hey, sometimes you have to improvise. But where are you guys? I need help finding her outside. And I can't find my shoes."

I frowned. "You mean your boots?"

"No, I mean my shoes. One minute I was wearing shoes . . . then poof! I'm barefoot."

I took a deep breath. New Year's was supposed to be fun, right? "Okay, you know what? You just stay inside.

Freddie and I will find Candace. We're already out here anyway."

She didn't answer.

"Rhonda?"

"Why are you guys outside?"

"Oh, we're just trying to find the glass Candace dropped."

"So you're evidence gathering? Without me?" Rhonda asked. "You leave me babysitting Candace, so you can go out and collect evidence?"

"Not as fun as it sounds. Especially without shoes."

"You guys suck." And with that she ended the call.

"What's going on?" Freddie asked.

"We gotta find Candace. She's roaming around out here, drunk, and apparently headed for the lake."

"Oh, wow, okay," Freddie said, changing course toward the shoveled path that led down to the water. "So she's doing the killer's job for him. Or her." He stepped over an ice patch. "Candace is always so thoughtful."

I didn't answer. I was too busy trying to walk downhill on an icy path in strappy heels. Seriously, I'd put the difficulty level of that maneuver right up there with brain surgery.

"Okay, but be honest though," Freddie called out with a bit of chuckle. "Tell me that there isn't just a teeny, tiny part of you that has dreamed of a scenario like this."

I held my hands out to my sides as I slid unexpectedly a couple of inches. "What are you talking about?"

"You know, the competition for Grady just tragically slipping into a frozen lake? Through no fault of your own?"

"No, I can honestly say I have never dreamed of that."

"Never?" Freddie needled.

"No!"

Just then a woman screamed.

Freddie's widened eyes met mine. "It looks like you got your wish after all." He then took off in the direction it had come from.

"How many times do I have to say it? I don't want—" I cut myself off when I realized Freddie wasn't listening and hurried after him. "Never mind."

Chapter Twenty-one

"Oh, this is sad," Freddie said.

I nodded. "It really is."

"One of us should go down there."

"One of us should."

"It's funny," Freddie said. "I wouldn't have taken Candace for a drunk-crier. But then again maybe that's why she doesn't drink."

Candace, by the looks of it, had been heading toward the lake, but somewhere along the path, she'd lost her way, and had rolled about halfway down the hill that led to frozen water. Now she was sitting cross-legged in the snow. Weeping. At least she had a warm coat by the looks of it and maybe a blanket?

"I'll go," I muttered. "But give me your galoshes. I can't walk in these heels anymore."

"You sure you don't want me to do it?" Freddie asked, unzipping one of the rubber covers and handing it to me. "My poor shoes," he muttered before finishing with, "I don't think Candace really likes you, and she likes everyone."

"Yeah," I said, grabbing his shoulder for balance as I

pried off my heel, "but I think she might have some things she needs to say to me." My feet were so going to freeze.

"I don't know if they're going to be nice things."

I inhaled deeply and nodded.

"Okay, well, I'll go get some blankets or something while you two talk."

"Get my socks and boots from the snowmobile too," I said, slipping the other cover over my foot and zipping it up. It was not a good fit. I would probably end up rolling down the hill too. "And maybe ask Sean if they have any hot chocolate in the kitchen?"

"Oh my God! What is the matter with you?" He turned and took a backward step toward the house. "Let it go. Bean is not happening."

"Methinks the Freddie doth protest too m—"

"Shut up!" he shouted over his shoulder. "We are so on a break!"

I smiled, but it faded quickly. I looked back to the figure plopped in the snow. This was one conversation I did not want to have, but Candace's weeping wasn't getting any quieter. I sighed then flopped my way, as carefully as I could, down the path that led to the lake. It wasn't too slippery. Someone had thrown some loose pebbled gravel over the snow. Or maybe it was cat litter? The historical society really had thought of everything— except for maybe security to watch for any drunk party-goers who might wander outside. Oh wait, that was us.

"Hey!" I called out to the blubbering wreck that was Candace. We were parallel on the hill. I really didn't want to step off the cleared path. "You okay over there?"

Candace looked over and when she saw who it was calling her, her crying got even louder. She may have even shouted a little as she let her hands drop to her sides.

"I'll take that as a no," I muttered under my breath.

I hiked up my dress again and took a big step toward her into the calf-deep snow. Yeah, Freddie's galoshes were doing pretty much nothing. They were too big, so all of the snow was falling down into them, and I had to flex my foot in weird angles to make sure I didn't lose them in the drift. I couldn't help but wonder if Jessica, vet extraordinaire, knew how to treat frostbite. Probably. She looked like a know-it-all.

"Hey," I said again more quietly once I had reached Candace. "What do you say we get you back inside where it's warm?"

She didn't say anything, but her crying quieted a little.

"Or do you want me to text Grady?" I offered, reaching for my phone. "Ask him to come get you?"

"No! Please! Don't do that," she said, turning her mascara-smeared eyes up to mine.

"Okay," I said, putting my empty hands up. "No problem. We can't stay out here though."

"I just need a minute," she said, wiping her nose with the back of her hand.

I pinched my lips together and nodded. "Do you want me to wait with you, or . . ." I jabbed a thumb back toward the path.

"You can stay, but I do not want to talk about Grady." She looked out toward the lake. "Not with you."

I inhaled deeply. "I get that. I really do. But before we don't talk about Grady, I think you should know there are some rumors going around that—"

"What's happened to me?" Candace asked, looking around bewildered. "I don't drink. Not since college. And definitely not at work parties." She turned her too wide eyes back to me. "Who am I, Erica?"

I nodded. Alcohol always brings out the really deep

questions. I desperately wanted to get back to the whole Grady misunderstanding, but I was thinking I needed to tread carefully.

"Erica?"

"Oh," I said, bringing a hand to my chest. "I thought that question was rhetorical."

She squinted at me then picked up a champagne bottle I hadn't seen half buried in the snow. "Can I ask you something?"

This couldn't be headed anywhere good. "Um . . . sure?"

She studied me in that overly intense way drunk people do. "Why didn't you just hook up with Matthew? I mean, would you look at this place?" She threw her free hand back toward the house. "He likes you. You know that, right?"

"Oh, I don't know . . ."

"He does," she said, looking out at the trees. She tipped the bottle toward her mouth. "But you're still hung up on Grady." She took a hard gulp.

And here I thought we weren't talking about Grady. I cleared my throat. "About him—"

"You're not right for one another," she said, swinging the bottle around. It then slipped from her hand and landed upright in the snow, sending a good splash onto my dress. She didn't notice though. "You know that, right? You're terrible together."

I wasn't surprised to hear her say that. And not just because of the whole love-triangle thing we had going on. A lot of people wondered what it was that had me so hung up on Grady. See, I was the type of person to play my cards close to my chest, so, as a result, people had only seen the bad parts of our relationship. The aftermath. Nobody knew what it was like when Grady and I were alone . . . away from everything that came with Otter

Lake. Like they had never seen the way Grady had rubbed my feet when we watched movies in my apartment back in Chicago . . . or the face he had made when I forced him to try sushi for the first time. That had been pretty funny. They hadn't seen us skate across the rink at Millennium Park like it was a skate to the death. I'd won. But I think he'd let me. And they definitely hadn't got to listen in on all of our late-night phone conversations we'd had about the future . . . or how I had told Grady that I wanted to have a whole bunch of kids but was scared I wouldn't know how to be a mother . . . or make a family . . . and how he had said that any kid would be lucky to have me as his or her mom because I cared so deeply about the people I loved . . . and how he or she would never be bullied at school because everyone would know that that kid had a crazy uncle Freddie who would take care of business if they did. They also couldn't know that every time I had ever gone to sleep in Grady's arms, I had had a smile on my face, feeling as safe and happy as anyone ever could . . . or that I woke up feeling the exact same way.

I also kind of doubted Candace would want to hear about any of those things right now.

"Maybe we shouldn't—"

"Who am I kidding?" she asked, dropping her hand back into the snow. "You'd never listen to me. You hate me. Everybody hates me."

"Candace, I don't hate you. I never hated—"

"Yes you do," she said. "It's okay. You can be honest. You are like that super-cool chick who solves murders and flashes people at town events."

"I don't flash people at town events!" Often. And certainly not on purpose. "And I don't really solve murders eith—"

"And I'm just boring old Candace. Who does charity

work in her free time, but it doesn't make anybody like her any more. No, it does not."

"Everyone loves you."

"Ha!" she said, slapping the snow. "People tolerate me. My own sister can barely stand being around me. Not that I can blame her. Not after all those times . . . when our parents were all like . . ." She made a gesture with her hands like I'd know what she was talking about, but I had no idea. "But I wanted to show her this visit that I'd changed. That I was a big sister she could look up to." She shook her head with disgust then let out a small hiccup. "Now look at me."

"Candace—"

"No, Erica, it's okay. I know I make people uncomfortable because I don't drink, and I don't swear, and I go to church on Sundays. Everybody thinks I'm judging them, but I'm not."

Wow, she was really on a roll. "Nobody thinks—"

"Then there's you!" She gestured wildly toward me. "Everybody wants to be around you. But you and Freddie . . . you're just too cool for school."

"Candace, we wanted to be friends with you. You blocked our numbers!"

"Because you guys accused me of murder!"

"Well . . . you started dating my ex!"

"Who's Daisy?"

"Who's Daisy?" I blinked. It was hard keeping up with this conversation. "What?"

"You and Grady. Earlier. You were talking about Freddie and Daisy." She bit her lip then added, "Everybody in Otter Lake knows about Daisy." She flung her arms wide. I was a little worried she'd fall back. I almost grabbed her arm. But she righted herself. "But not Candace. Candace is the outsider."

I blew out some air. I guess I did owe her one for that.

It's no fun feeling left out. I knew that feeling well. That being said, talking about Freddie's traumatic childhood experiences didn't exactly seem like party fodder.

"Daisy doesn't have anything to do with Grady and me. I promise you."

"Then tell me!" Oh God, there were fresh tears in her eyes. "Do you have any idea how hard it is to fit into a town where everybody knows everything about everyone?"

I sighed. "You really want to know?"

She opened up the blanket she was sitting on to make a spot for me to sit beside her in the snow.

Freddie was going to kill me. For so many reasons. Not the least of which was the fact that I was about to get his jacket wet.

"Okay," I said, hiking up my skirt once again and dropping myself down beside her. "I'll tell you about Daisy, but I doubt it's going to make you feel any better."

Chapter Twenty-two

I was going to have to make this long story quick. The snow was actually kind of insulating, but it wouldn't take long for the dampness to get through.

"Okay, so how much do you know about how Freddie grew up?"

Candace frowned. Wow, her face was close to mine. Champagne breath. "I know his parents traveled a lot. And that he had a whole bunch of nannies."

I nodded. Freddie's parents were real estate speculators. They traveled the world checking out properties and developing them for resale. The rest of his family lived in Hong Kong. It wasn't like they were gone all the time, but certainly more than people around here thought appropriate. And it wasn't like Freddie didn't love them, or like they didn't love him—he was on the phone with his mother and his poppo all the time—but it was just a different kind of family relationship. I suspected Freddie harbored some resentment, but that made him feel guilty because he *did* love them. It was complicated. "Yeah, Freddie and I didn't become best friends until high school. Before that we were both kind of on our own in the friend department. Freddie maybe a little more than me." When Freddie's family first bought the property and built their gorgeous lake home, they were the only visible minorities in town. So that was complicated too.

"Poor Freddie," Candace said.

"Yeah, well, save your poor Freddies. You're going to need them later on." I looked up at the stars. "Anyway, Freddie wasn't the personality he is now back then. He was pretty shy, so while the other kids didn't exactly pick on him, nobody really included him either. Until Daisy."

Candace made an excited noise and clapped her hands.

"I don't know if it was Freddie's parents' idea to help keep him company when they were away, or the nanny's—or maybe it was Freddie's idea—but all of a sudden here was this shy little kid showing up all over town with the most adorable golden retriever puppy you have ever seen."

Candace's head dropped on to my shoulder.

"Um, are you going to sleep?"

"No," she said. "Just looking at the stars while you tell the story." Her voice was slurry though.

"So anyway because the dog was so adorable and friendly and lovable, everybody in town started talking to Freddie. Kids wanted to play with him at the park. Adults wanted to talk to him on the street. It was like in an instant Freddie had gone from being this strange little outsider kid to a full-on Otter Lake citizen."

"That's nice."

"It was nice." I took a deep breath. "Then Daisy got sick. She was only two or three. Cancer, I think."

"Oh no."

I sighed. "Yeah, it was awful. For a while there everyone thought she'd make it. Rumor was Freddie's family spent thousands and thousands trying to treat her. And

Freddie would still take her for walks—pulling her in a wagon and then later on a sled. But in the end, all the attention and treatment couldn't save her. She was suffering, and they had to put her down."

Heavy silence fell around us.

Well, not exactly silence. Candace was sniffing back tears. Truth be told, I had to blink away a few of my own. "Freddie's parents were away at the time, but his nanny put together a funeral—and a good part of the town came. They buried Daisy in a little patch in a far corner of his property."

"That is so sad," Candace said, taking a shuddering breath.

"Yeah." I nodded, remembering how serious little kid Freddie had looked in the suit he wore to the funeral. "He refuses to talk about Daisy to this day." I had the bruised foot to prove it.

"Wow."

I caught Candace wiping a tear from her cheek.

"Yeah."

"I can see why you and Grady didn't think this was a party story."

"Yeah."

We sat in silence for a good long while just looking at the stars. Finally Candace said, "Thank you for telling me."

"We were being rude before." I cringed. I shouldn't have used the couple *we*.

I felt her nod. "I wish we could have found a way to be friends."

I hugged my knees to my chest. "We've got a lot of strikes against us."

"Grady."

"Not just Grady. Your working for MRG does make things complicated."

"For us?" she asked, sounding confused. "I mean, I get that you're a local—"

"First generation," I said, interrupting her. "So, yeah, I'm a local, but I'm not like all the way in."

"That's what I mean. I didn't think you'd be as bothered about all the changes MRG's making."

"It's still my town." I was kind of annoyed, but I got where she was coming from. Not only was I first generation, but I had left Otter Lake for years—that was pretty unusual for people in this town. But that had more to do with trying to find my own identity separate from my mother. I was happy to be back. "I'm probably more okay with *progress* than a lot of other people here." Although I had just said *progress* like it was a dirty word. "But there are some practical concerns too. It's hard to bond with someone who can outbid you on every place you want to live in."

Candace lifted her head from my shoulder. "What places were you looking at?"

"Um, all of them. I love the Wilsons' place, but you guys bought that before it even made it to market. Then there was the Daleys'. And the Arthurs'. Their place would have been perfect for me, but you've already made an offer."

"You know I'm just doing my job."

I could feel her wanting to make eye contact, but I resisted the pull. I didn't want to say anything to ruin what was actually kind of a nice moment. I mean, I couldn't be sure that Candace would remember any of it after tonight, but *que sera sera*. Just then I remembered I should be using this bonding opportunity to find out what was really going on. "Candace . . . I heard something about someone sending you threatening notes?"

She sighed. "I told you everyone hates me. But it was just one note."

"Are you worried? Was it serious?"

"I don't know. I doubt it." She shook her head. "People don't like change. At least that's what Grady thinks." She rubbed her forehead then said, "So you really want that place? The Arthurs' place, I mean."

"I'm living on an island with my mother and the twins. You can't imagine how much I want that place."

She straightened up. "Well, maybe I can get MRG to back off."

"What?"

"Seriously."

"Oh," I said, shaking my head. "I don't think Gerald and Nanette would like that."

"Well, the property is worth what the property's worth," she said. "Yes, we could take you down in a bidding war, but we never start at that price. You would still have to come up with the money, but I promise I won't bid against you. I don't think they want to sell to us anyway. They hate me too." She laughed a little. "I think they'd accept a fair offer."

"Why would you do that? I haven't always been . . . great to you."

"Erica, I'm sitting in the snow, crying on New Year's Eve." She took another drink. "Forget about Grady. I don't exactly like who I have become. It's not easy being the bad guy all the time."

"You're not the bad guy. You're—"

"Truth is, I've been thinking about leaving MRG. I want to do more to help people. I'm not cut out for this kind of work. Bryson can have it. He's been landing most of the sales lately anyway. He should get the credit."

I wasn't exactly surprised. Candace had done well for herself in that she was good with people. And people *did* like her. But she obviously had a tough time with the more cutthroat aspects of the job. "I get it, but I don't think you should make any decisions tonight. I—"

"Hang on," she said. "Someone keeps texting me." She rolled into the snow to take her phone out from her pocket. When she looked at the screen, her face went still.

"Everything okay?"

"It's Grady."

"Oh." I was dying to know what the text said, but Candace and I had just made major inroads . . . and it was none of my business.

"I guess someone told him I was outside," she said, eyes glassy. "He wants me to meet him at the boathouse, so we can talk."

"The boathouse?" I asked, looking down to the small structure seemingly hovering over the ice. Sure, it looked pretty—someone had hung a lighted wreath on the half-opened door and lined the eaves with more twinkly lights—but it was original to the estate. It would be both cold and rickety in there. A small, dark corner of my mind was trying to bring up the rumor the twins had told me about Candace wanting to do their breakup in public, and the boathouse definitely wasn't public, but Candace certainly didn't look scared. More resigned. "Why down there?"

"I guess there's not much privacy inside."

"Why don't you guys just leave the party early, so you can talk about . . . whatever it might be that you need to talk about?"

"Erica," Candace said, looking away quickly, I think maybe to hide another tear. "I meant it when I said I would like for us to be friends, but this is one area we can't talk about, okay?"

"Oh, yeah, of course. I understand."

She picked up the champagne bottle and took an extra

long sip before passing it to me. "Okay, I'm done." I reached out to accept the bottle, but she snatched it back quickly. "Maybe I'll just hang on to it for a little bit longer." She then tried to push herself to her feet, but I'd say her balance had left her about half a bottle ago.

"Let me help you," I said, grabbing her arm. "Do you want me to walk you down there?"

"No." She flopped a hand at me. "I'm fine, and I would kind of prefer it if Grady didn't see you. Then again, you have been in our relationship the whole time." She laughed before glancing up at my face. "Oh, you don't have to look so horrified. I knew what I was getting into. It's not like you can live in this town and not know about *Grady and Erica*. I still decided to date him."

"Candace, I—"

"Nope. Do not apologize. I've already left my self-respect back there," she said, spinning too quickly to point at where we had picnicked in the snow. I had to steady her, so she didn't end up doing a face-plant. "But I stand by what I said about you and Grady not belonging together."

I frowned. We were doing so well. Still not the right time to plead my case though.

"And can I tell you one other thing?"

I smiled politely.

"Next guy I date is going to be all about me." She swirled her finger around her face. "Only me."

I nodded.

She brushed herself off and took a deep breath as she looked down the path toward the boathouse. "Wish me luck."

"Luck," I said halfheartedly, not knowing at all exactly what kind of luck I was wishing her.

As Candace shuffled her way down the path, I felt Freddie rush up behind me. "What are you doing? You didn't talk Candace into seeing the futileness of it all, did you?"

I backslapped him lightly on the belly.

"Hey! Watch the hot chocolate." He passed me a mug then a blanket he had slung over his shoulder. He even had my boots pinned under his armpit. "So what's going on? Why *is* Candace teetering her way dangerously toward the icy water while you watch on?"

"She's meeting Grady at the boathouse. He texted her." Freddie looked around. "So where is he?"

I shrugged. "He hasn't shown up yet. I'm just making sure Candace gets there okay."

"Aw," Freddie said. "So your heart isn't two sizes too small."

"For the last time, I never wanted Candace to fall into an icy lake!" Hmm, that came out louder than I had intended it on this still winter night. Candace turned and waved at us from the threshold of the boathouse. I waved back. She went inside and closed the door.

I grabbed Freddie's elbow to lead him back up the path. "She, uh, doesn't want Grady to see me."

"So, we're going back inside?"

"No, we're hiding."

"Excellent," he said, moving toward a small cluster of trees. "I don't want to miss this."

"I meant we're hiding because we don't want to leave the drunk woman alone by the icy lake, but we want to respect her privacy."

"Right. Right. By the way, what have you been getting into? You smell like Baby New Year's spit up on you."

I shot him a look before turning my attention back to the boathouse. I then took a sip from the mug Freddie had passed me. "Mmm, this is good. Did you get it from—"

"I thought I made it clear we would not be discussing Bean."

"I wasn't going to say anything about *Sean*," I said, taking another sip. I totally was though.

A few more minutes passed. No sign of Grady.

Finally I said, "Do you think we should—"

"Hey, guys! I found my shoes!"

Both Freddie and I jumped, sending hot chocolate splashing everywhere.

"Rhonda? Where the hell did you come from?" For a brief moment, I almost enjoyed the warmth of the hot chocolate on my hands. Might as well, they'd be icy cold in minutes.

"Sorry." She chuckled. "I didn't mean to scare you." She snickered some more. "Okay. Okay. Actually I did. You two were just huddled there looking all suspicious, I couldn't help myself."

"Hilarious," Freddie said, voice completely devoid of humor.

"Where's Candace?" she asked. "I thought we were supposed to be babysitting her."

"We still are. She's in the boathouse waiting for Grady. He texted her saying to meet him there."

"They need to *talk*," Freddie said.

Rhonda nodded knowingly back at him before she looked at me. "I get it. You're waiting to pounce." She curled her hands into claws and thrust them at me.

"No. I'm just keeping an eye on Candace until Grady gets here. She's a little drunk, you see."

"Aren't we all," Rhonda said, nodding again. "But aren't we also still worried someone's trying to poison her?"

"No," I said, meeting Freddie's eye. "We agreed that that whole theory was probably just a case of imagination running wild."

Freddie let out a huff but didn't say anything. I took that to mean we were finally on the same page.

"I see," Rhonda said, still nodding big. "Just a little New Year's game of Clue."

"Something like that," I muttered.

We all looked back to the boathouse.

I took another sip of hot chocolate. "The water would be frozen at the edge there, right?"

"Yeah," Rhonda said. "It should be pretty safe."

"Right."

Freddie sighed. "Grady sure is taking his sweet time."

I nodded.

"How long do we wait before we go get her?" Rhonda asked.

"I think we should give it a few more minutes," I said. "This isn't exactly our business."

"Right. Right."

We all set our attention back on the lake.

Nothing.

"It's pretty out here," Rhonda said, looking up at the stars. She had to throw a hand out to balance herself.

"So quiet too," I said, grabbing her elbow to help steady her. "I can't believe you were able to sneak up on us like that."

"That's why they call me the Snow Ninja."

"Nobody calls you that," Freddie said.

She laughed. "You're right. I totally just made that up."

I laughed, too, then we sank back into our silent observation of the boathouse—occasionally looking back up to see if Grady was coming.

"It was pretty good, though," Rhonda said, "the way I snuck up on you two. I mean, it *is* a quiet night. You can barely even hear the party. Just the trees cracking with ice and . . . what is that? A generator?"

I could hear the faint hum and rattle of a generator too. Somewhere. "Hey, Matthew said he has a surprise planned for later. Maybe it has something to do with that."

"Surprise?" Freddie asked. "What kind of surprise?"

"No idea," I said, trying to pinpoint the noise. "It almost sounds like it's coming from the boathouse."

We all stopped to listen.

"Yeah," Rhonda said slowly. "It does."

"Maybe it's powering a heater?"

Rhonda and I looked at each other. "Isn't that dangerous? From the—"

"Carbon monoxide!"

All three of us dashed through the snow for the path.

"We are the worst babysitters ever!"

The Morning After

"That was not our finest moment," I said with a weak cough.

"Sadly, not our worst though either."

"But it's not like anything bad happened, right? Candace is okay?"

"Yeah," Freddie said slowly then, "wait . . . actually, I think that was just the beginning of Candace's troubles."

I frowned. "Really?"

"Oh no!" Freddie said with a gasp. "Don't you remember what happened next? The toast? Oh crap! And then there was the—"

"Okay, slow down, you've lost me. I remember we ran down the hill, and—"

Chapter Twenty-three

"Candace!" I shouted as I hopped, skipped, and slid down the path.

"Open the door!" Freddie shouted after me.

Rhonda, however, wasn't yelling. She had opted to take a shortcut, and now she was falling and . . . oh God . . . somersaulting down the hill.

"Rhonda!" both Freddie and I shouted.

Once she hit the bottom, she popped up to her feet. "I'm okay!" She shot us a big thumbs-up. She then trudged toward the boathouse door as we scrambled to catch up.

"I can't get it open!" Rhonda yelled back at us. "It's stuck!" She banged on the wood. "Candace! Open the door!"

Freddie and I finally made it over. We yanked at the handle with Rhonda. The door wouldn't budge.

"Candace?" I yelled again.

Nothing.

"Do you think she locked herself in there?"

Rhonda and Freddie didn't answer, just shot me worried eyes.

I banged on the door again with the side of my fist. "Candace! Answer me!"

I thought I heard a moan.

"What did you two talk about?" Freddie asked. "Was she depressed?"

"Well . . . yeah," I said. "But not that depressed. I mean, she was talking about the future."

"Why . . . won't . . . this . . . door . . . budge?" Rhonda grunted while really giving the handle a good pull. She then kicked at the snow around the bottom of the frame before looking up. "Oh shoot! There's a latch!"

There was too! One of those old-fashioned levers that swings down into a metal envelope at the top of the door.

Freddie jumped up and smacked it out of place. We swung the door open.

"Candace!"

She actually looked quite comfy. She was sitting on a workbench with her coat curled up around her, arms wrapped around the champagne bottle pinned at her chest.

I ran toward her as Rhonda hustled over the outside planks of the boathouse—around the frozen water where the boat normally sat—to get to the generator on the far side of the room.

"Candace," I said again, giving her shoulders a little shake. She moaned some more but didn't open her eyes. "We need to get her out of here."

Freddie threw one of her arms over his shoulders, causing the empty champagne bottle to drop to the wood planks with a heavy thunk. I moved to her other side. We lifted her off the bench and dragged her toward the door.

Once we got outside, Candace coughed then blinked her eyes open. "Hey, guys. What's going on? Where's Grady?"

Freddie and I exchanged looks.

"Did we break up?" She laughed and her head rolled back onto her shoulders. "Or did we make up?"

"Let's get her to Jessica," Rhonda said. "I think Dr. Reynolds is here too."

"I'll call 911," Freddie said, reaching for his phone. "I mean, she wasn't in there that long, but—"

Candace swatted it out of his hand.

"Hey," he shouted.

"Nine-one-one?" Candace asked thickly. "Why are you calling 911? I feel great. I just had a few too many drinks with Rhonda and a little too much champagne with Erica. Where is Erica?"

"I'm right here."

Candace's head whipped around. When she saw me, she snorted. "Hey girl! Where did you come from?"

I smiled.

"Steal my boyfriend yet?" She laughed again and turned back to Freddie. "She's always trying to do that."

"I know," he whispered back conspiratorially.

I shot him a look over Candace's head.

What? he mouthed back.

"Right," I said. "Let's at least get Dr. Reynolds to check her out. Let him make the call about the hospital."

"Hospital?" Candace said. "No hospital. It's New Year's!"

Freddie and I dragged her toward the hill. Rhonda followed behind just in case Candace fell back. Minutes later, we had her in Matthew's room lying on the bed with Stanley as Jessica checked her over. Rhonda was searching for Dr. Reynolds. We had opted to use the porch to get inside, as opposed to going through the party. I didn't think Candace wanted the entire town seeing her this way. Who knew if she had actually meant it when she said she wanted to quit—stumbling drunkenly through a party wasn't exactly great PR.

And then there were all the other rumors to think about.

All the other rumors that were suddenly taking on new weight.

I mean, the door could have locked itself shut when Candace had closed it, but why was a generator going in an empty boathouse?

And where the hell was Grady?

"Her vitals are good," Jessica said, pulling her stethoscope from her ears. "You said she had a lot to drink?"

"Yeah. She did."

"And how long was she in the boathouse?"

"Not that long. Five? Ten minutes?" I said.

"Could have been fifteen," Freddie said. "But fifteen at most."

"I think she probably should go to the hospital just in case."

Right then Dr. Reynolds came through the door and headed directly over to Candace. He then got to work doing whatever it was that doctors do.

"Maybe we should wait outside," I said to Freddie.

He nodded.

We headed out into the hallway. A few people had gathered in the conservatory, so we searched for another private room. We ended up in what I was guessing was Matthew's office.

"So?" Freddie asked as soon as I shut the door.

"So what?"

"So what do you make of all of this?"

I walked over to the desk shaking my head. "I don't know, okay? It could've been an accident. Maybe Candace read the text from Grady wrong and—"

"She didn't."

I whipped my head back around to face Freddie. He

was holding a phone. A phone that I was pretty sure wasn't his.

"I swiped it from her coat pocket after she tried to check her messages. There's definitely a text here from Grady saying, *Meet me in the boathouse. We need to talk.*"

"I don't like this," I said, folding my arms over my waist. "I don't like this one bit. There has to be some sort of explanation."

"Listen, I'm not saying it was Grady—even though the text is from his phone—but *someone* sent Candace into a building with a running generator and a door that locks itself shut. I think you finally have to admit . . ."

I raised an eyebrow at Freddie.

". . . that it's possible that someone is trying to kill Candace. And in the process they poisoned my dog."

I chewed the corner of my thumbnail.

"The question now is, what are we going to do about it?"

"Grady didn't send that text," I said quickly. "He wouldn't do that. If he knew Candace was drunk and outside by herself, he would be out there trying to find her."

"Exactly."

"Which means someone is trying to set him up. He didn't—"

"I know Grady isn't behind all this. Just relax," Freddie said, spreading his hands out. "He doesn't have the imagination to be a murderer."

"He does too. You cut him some slack."

"And that's the problem, right there. Other people are going to think he's capable of murder too. So, again, what are we going to do about it?"

"I know exactly what we're going to do."

"You do?"

I nodded. "Freddie, there are many things I *cannot* do."

He nodded. "I know this to be true."

"I can't find a place to live," I said, holding up a finger.

"You have had trouble." He was still nodding.

I added another finger. "No matter how hard I try, I can't seem to have the relationship I want."

He tilted his head from side to side. "Probably because you don't know what that is."

"I definitely can't figure out how to handle men like Bryson," I said and added another finger.

"Sweetie, nobody can figure that one out."

I threw all my counting fingers out toward him. "I certainly can't make you figure out your love life."

"Are we seriously going back to the whole Bean thing again?" Freddie asked. "Because—"

"But you know what *we* can do, Freddie?"

"Uh-oh, it's *we* now."

I looked over to the clock above Matthew's desk. "For the next . . . two hours and forty-five minutes we can keep Candace alive."

Freddie's eyes darted over my face. "Um . . . okay."

Yes, this was a bit of a reversal. I couldn't quite believe it myself. But it was looking, more and more, like someone *was* trying to hurt Candace. And after the conversation I'd had with her outside, I'd be damned if I let anything bad happen to her. She really was a nice person. The way she offered to back off the Arthurs' place? I'm not sure I would have been able to be that generous if our roles were reversed.

"So . . . just so I'm clear," Freddie said. "Are we letting her die after midnight?"

"No! But everyone will go home after that, and we'll make sure Grady knows what's going on. Stop nitpicking."

"And how exactly are we going to keep Candace alive? I mean, we've already got people watching her."

I raised my eyebrows and shot him a satisfied smile.

"We're going to do better than that. We're going to find out who is trying to kill her."

Freddie smiled back at me. "Are you sure? Like, I mean, you're completely onboard?"

"I am." I pointed another finger in the air. "So help me, Freddie, for whatever is left of this godforsaken year—"

"Well, that's a little dramatic, don't you think? I mean, there were some good things about this year. You moved home. We—"

"Godforsaken!"

"Okay. Okay. Sheesh."

I moved my point from the air to Freddie's face. "Two hours and forty-five minutes, Freddie. For two hours and forty-five minutes we are going to make good decisions, keep Candace safe, and use everything we have in us not to suck. And if we're lucky, we might even catch a killer." I nodded. "We will have justice for Stanley."

"Okay," Freddie said, nodding back. "I'm with you. You know that. *I* was with you before *you* were with *you*. I say let's do this. And let's do it right. I am so tired of the murderers always being in control. High five."

I slapped Freddie's palm. "Let's see if we can ask Candace a few questions before she goes to the hospital. You know, like if she has any enemies—aside from whoever sent her that note. That kind of thing."

"Oh, look at you being the detective," Freddie said, holding the door open for me. "But you know that thing you said about this year being godforsaken?"

"I didn't mean us, Freddie."

"BFFs forever?"

"BFFs forever."

The Morning After

"I did not say BFFs forever."

"Yes you did."

"I never would have said that. Best friends forever-forever? It's redundant."

"You have intimacy problems."

"I have intimacy problems? I have intimacy problems?" I might have gone for a third indignant repetition, but the volume of the second nearly killed me. I lowered my voice. "Should we return to the topic of Sean? Or is it still Bean?"

"Whatever," Freddie grumbled. "And for the record, your little speech wasn't as inspirational as you made it sound just now. You weren't all resolved and Napoleonic-like."

"Napoleonic-like?"

"You know what I mean. You were still all *I don't know if we should be doing this, Freddie.*" He used his girliest voice for that. "*You know, like you always are.*"

"That's not how I remember it. I think you're just jealous."

"Jealous? I was the one who was right all along that someone was trying to kill Candace while you were all like Freddie, *you're just upset about your dog." Again with the voice.*

"I really don't sound like that."

"Whatever. The point is I told you so."

"You just love saying that, don't you?"

"Told you so."

"Are you done?"

"Told you so."

I just looked at him.

"Okay, I'm done."

Chapter Twenty-four

Unfortunately, right when our investigation was getting off the ground—like for real, not like earlier—we found Candace had passed out in Matthew's bed, curled up beside Stanley, with an oxygen mask on her face. She had adamantly refused to go to the hospital, and Dr. Reynolds felt there wasn't much of a risk seeing as her exposure hadn't been that long and her vitals were good. As an added bonus Mr. Greer, our old high school custodian, had a spare oxygen tank in his van. He had emphysema. Jessica and Dr. Reynolds were taking turns watching her. So far the official story was that the latch on the door had fallen into the locked position by accident. Freddie and I thought it best to stick to that story until we could talk to Grady. While Grady was skeptical of pretty much every theory Freddie and I had ever come up with, he had also once grudgingly admitted that we had a way of shaking evidence free. Plus he would be more likely to know about any enemies he and Candace might share. Oh! Plus, plus he was sheriff. Couldn't forget that.

"You know," Freddie said as we headed back toward

the party. "This disappearing act of Grady's really isn't helping his alibi."

"Well, he's got to be here somewhere," I said, scanning the crowd. It wasn't normally difficult to spot Grady. It was like spotting a supermodel dressed in couture at a mall. He kind of stood out. It was really starting to worry me.

Freddie took his phone from his pocket. "I'll get Tyler and his friends on it too, but in the meantime, I'll search the west side of the house. You take the east."

"Got it."

We fist-bumped.

"Go team."

Freddie disappeared in the crowd as I scanned the room again. Hmm. Before I left for the less crowded rooms of the house, maybe it wasn't a bad idea to do some asking around. No better people to start with than the twins. They were right where I had left them at the blackjack table. Poor Carl looked kind of worn out. His hair was a bit mussed and his collar was open. Unfortunately for him, I doubted the twins would be vacating their seats any time soon. They were the types that once they had found a comfy spot, they were likely to settle in for a good long time.

"Hey!" Tweety said when she spotted me. "Finally. Again, we've been looking everywhere for you." She turned to Carl. "Go get yourself a coffee, kid. We're just getting warmed up." She then turned back to me. "So there's a new rumor going around that you and Candace were wrestling in the snow and then you locked her in a shed."

"And by the looks of you," Kit Kat said, jumping in, "I'm guessing at least part of it is true."

I looked down. The hem of my dress was a little worse

for wear. The boots didn't exactly add anything to my outfit either. I had dumped my shoes in Matthew's room. They were pretty much unwearable. The snow had stretched out all the faux leather.

"Yes, I was wrestling with Candace in the snow. That's exactly what happened. Have you two seen Grady?"

Kit Kat squinted at her sister. "Not in a little while."

"He was looking for Candace earlier," Tweety said. "And he was muttering something about being sent on a wild-goose chase."

I sighed. "Look, I need to ask you guys something before I go track him down."

They waited.

I took a quick look around to see if anyone was watching us. Great, now I was turning into Freddie. "Who told you the Candace and Grady rumor? You know, that they were breaking up, and Candace was worried Grady might . . ." I shook my head. "It's too ridiculous to even say."

They looked at each other again, probably sharing a telepathic moment.

"Alma, wasn't it?" Tweety asked.

"Or was it Marg?"

"Marg," I said, chin dropping to my chest. "You were gossiping with the woman who accused you of adultery and murder two falls ago?"

Kit Kat straightened, looking mildly offended. "Yeah, what's the big deal?"

"Life is too short not to forgive your neighbors," Tweety said before taking a sip of . . . something. It was fluorescent blue.

"Especially when they own the only salon in town and have all the best gossip," Kit Kat added, lifting her own neon-pink drink. They clinked glasses.

I guess they spotted the look of horror on my face because Tweety held hers up to me and said, "These frou-frou drinks aren't bad. Mine's an Aqua Blue Cruise."

"Pink Passion," Kit Kat offered, copying the gesture. "That Mrs. Watson sure knows how to run a martini bar."

I shook my head. Amid the worry of the twins dying of liver disease, I couldn't help but wonder how the would-be murderer managed to get the poisoned drink into Candace's hand—if that was indeed what had happened. I'd have to add that to the list of questions to ask her when she came to. "Right," I said. "So you're more forgiving of people than I am, but it's really important that you remember who you heard the rumor from. Marg? Or Alma?"

They exchanged another look.

"I think that's the thing," Kit Kat answered while her sister nodded. "They'd both heard the rumor."

"From who?"

Tweety stroked the ends of her loose bow tie as she leaned back in her chair. "Neither said."

"Well, do you think you could find out?"

"Maybe." Kit Kat scratched her chin while giving me a considering look. "What's going on? Is this about that whole poison thing earlier? Is someone really after Candace?"

I sighed. "Are all the details really that important?"

Tweety's eyes narrowed. "Oh, I think so, yes."

"Here's the thing," I said, running my hands over my face. I couldn't help but wonder if I had any makeup left on, and if so, how badly was it smeared? Oh well, at least the look would match my snowmobiling boots. "I am concerned that if I tell you what Freddie and I think we know, you'll tell everyone here, and that could . . ." I didn't quite know how to finish that sentence. It might actually be a good thing if I had Kit Kat and Tweety spread the news that someone was trying to frame Grady for Candace's murder—like a counterrumor to the original rumor—but I was also pretty sure it could backfire in all sorts of ways. It was hard to articulate those ways other than to say that most of Freddie's and my plans did backfire, but—Oh! Maybe it would tip the murderer off to our investigation and get us killed. At least that's what they were always saying on TV. Sounded . . . possible. My head hurt. "If you tell everyone," I tried again, "that could be . . . bad . . . or not. I'm really not sure."

"Did Candace hit you in the head while you were wrestling, honey?" Tweety asked. "You're not making much sense."

"No, she did not hit me on the head. We actually had a really nice talk." Again, hopefully, a really nice talk that she would remember when sober—I really wanted to make an offer on the Arthurs' place. And plus, you know, it was nice to have a new friend.

"Well, I'm not sure we can really be of much help unless we know what's going on," Tweety said.

"She's right." Kit Kat dragged her bottom lip through her teeth while shaking her head. "The gossip industry is all about fair trade. You want us to get the good stuff, you got to be willing to give the good stuff."

I stared at them both in turn. They had totally just made that rule up because they wanted to know what was going on, but maybe if they did, they'd be extra motivated to help. Unlike my mother, they liked Grady. And more importantly, they had a really solid old-school sense of justice. "Okay, here's the deal, while I can't say anything for certain, it is looking more and more possible that maybe—"

"You want some trimmers for that hedge?" Tweety asked, making her sister cackle.

"Someone might be trying to kill Candace. And it is

possible they're trying to set Grady up to take the fall for it."

Kit Kat's laughter died.

"And, I'm willing to bet that whoever has been spreading all the rumors is the would-be murderer."

The sisters lifted their glasses in identical motions and took identical sips while staring at me with an intensity that was almost creepy.

"So . . . ?" I asked. "Will you help me?"

"Oh, we'll help you," Kit Kat said.

Tweety jabbed a finger down on the table. "Nobody uses the gossip mill for true evil."

"The mill is for slightly evil entertainment-type purposes only."

"Right," I said slowly.

"Plus, I'm glad that we get to be part of an investigation again," Kit Kat said.

Tweety nodded. "Yeah, you've been freezing us out lately."

"Okay, well, good."

The twins didn't move.

"Can you do it like now?" I asked.

Tweety frowned. "Like right now?"

"Yes."

"But we were just getting comfortable," Kit Kat added. "And it takes a while to break a new dealer in."

"Do you want to be part of this investigation or not?"

Tweety groaned as she lifted herself off her stool. "Fine. Fine. We're going."

"And don't say anything to anybody about why you're asking. We still don't know what we don't know." It suddenly occurred to me that if I wasn't careful with this information, Grady could end up spending New Year's in his own department's jail cell. Yup, that was probably the best reason for keeping all suspicions on the down low.

"Sure. Sure," Tweety said. "But in this kind of information swap I wasn't lying about needing to give the wheels a little grease in return, so what's your official story for what happened between you and Candace on the back lawn out there?"

"Say whatever you need to about me to get the information. I don't care."

"Got it," Kit Kat said.

"Ooh!" Tweety whacked her sister on the arm. "Maybe we can say they're thinking of entering one of those polyamorous relationships and—"

"No," I said, holding up a hand. "No. Do not say that."

"But you just said—"

"I know what I just said, but I didn't mean . . ." I took a deep breath. "You know what? Just get the information. And maybe don't tell me how you're going to do it."

Kit Kat popped a new cigar in her mouth. "I think that's best." She linked arms with her sister. "Let's roll."

"Keep an eye out for Grady too," I called after them.

They shot me an identical thumbs-up.

I looked around the sparkling room filled with happy people in glittering clothes, but there was only one person I wanted to see.

Where are you, Grady?

Chapter Twenty-five

I tried texting Grady again, but he still wasn't answering. I was almost certain someone had taken his phone. He never would have sent that text to Candace. Sure, whoever took it would have to know his password . . . but he might not even have one. Grady didn't use his phone all that much and he certainly didn't keep any personal information on it. He didn't trust the security. It was more than a little creepy to think someone else could be sending texts pretending to be him.

So after spending a minute or two figuring out which way was east, I headed off to search that wing. And yes, it felt pretty presumptuous to go searching Matthew's house without his permission, but Matthew had to be the most understanding, forgiving, rational man alive. I was pretty sure he wouldn't hold it against me. Besides, I didn't have time to try to find both him and Grady. And I was also pretty sure no one was trying to frame him for murder.

Scary thing was, the more time that passed, being framed for murder wasn't the worst thing I was imagining anymore. It wasn't like Grady to just disappear. I had a bad feeling about what it could all mean. Actually, it wasn't so much a bad feeling. It was more like horrible, morbid scenarios kept running through my head . . . like I would open a door to find the love of my life sprawled dead across a bearskin rug. Not that Matthew would ever own such a thing, but—

"Get it together, Erica," I mumbled in a harsh whisper as I reached for yet another door handle—how many freaking rooms did this estate have? This door was open just a crack, and I was just about to go in when I heard a voice.

"I'm sorry! How many times do I have to say it?"

I peeked through the sliver of space into the room. Bethanny, Candace's sister, was pacing the far side of what I was guessing was the library, judging by the old books that looked like they might dissolve into a pile of dust if you actually touched them. It was pretty dark. Only one small lamp was on.

She stopped walking in front of the leaded beveled-glass windows on the far side of the room. The dim light from outside cast strange shadows on her face. "It's not like this is how I wanted to spend New Year's either, okay?"

And here I was eavesdropping again. I couldn't just leave though. I needed to tell Bethanny about Candace. Actually, we kind of sucked for forgetting about that earlier, but now seemed like an awkward time to interrupt. And more importantly, it definitely sounded like she was having a conversation with her boyfriend . . . and wasn't she supposed to be broken up with her boyfriend?

"I know," I heard Bethanny say. She had her hand on her forehead. "I know!"

Oh wow, it was one of those arguments. You know, the

kind you have over and over again, come to an agreement, then totally do the same thing that pissed your partner off again in the first place? I knew all about those.

"It's not that easy, okay? They're my parents."

I held my breath as I waited for her to go on.

"Oh nice. That's really nice. So what do you think I should do? Just cut them all out of my life? How would I even pay for school?"

Whoa. Granted, I couldn't hear the other side of this conversation but most people were usually more concerned with the emotional aspects of cutting off their family than the financial. Then again, *most* people probably weren't eavesdroppers either.

"Just . . . don't say that, okay? It's going to get better. I promise. I know what I have to do."

Maybe it was just the murderous circumstances, but that sounded ominous.

"I love you."

Another moment of silence passed.

"What? You're not going to say it back?"

I waited.

Bethanny let out a small shriek as she whipped the phone away from her face.

My cue.

I counted backward from ten and knocked softly on the door. She didn't answer, so I peeked around the frame and said, "Oh, there you are. I thought I heard someone in here."

Bethanny quickly swiped her cheeks. "It's Erica, right? Sorry. I'm not sure if I should be in here. I just needed some privacy to make a call."

I walked into the dimly lit room. "Listen, I'm glad I found you. There's something I need to tell you."

Bethanny's eyes locked onto mine.

"First, let me say she's all right," I said, holding up my

reassuring *no cause for alarm* hands. "But Candace has sort of been in an . . . accident."

Candace's sister stared at me. Then the strangest thing happened. A small sound escaped her lips. It almost sounded like a huff of . . . laughter? It was quickly followed by another one. And then another. Yup, she was laughing. Really, truly laughing.

Huh, well, that wasn't exactly the reaction I had been expecting.

Bethanny continued to laugh as she threw a hand over her face and collapsed into a green velvet armchair. "I'm sorry," she said, waving her other hand out. "I'm sorry. I just need a minute."

I couldn't stop my brow from furrowing into a really judgmental crease.

"It's terrible," she said, taking a shaky breath. "I know. I shouldn't be laughing. What kind of accident?"

I gave her the lowdown on what had happened outside. I decided to keep the poisoning suspicions to myself though. Not entirely sure why. Probably had something to do with all the unexpected chortling. When I was done, Bethanny just shook her head. "Yup, sounds like Candace."

"Okay," I said, sitting across from her, "I get that sibling relationships can be complicated, but . . ."

"I should have a little more compassion?" Bethanny asked with a humorless smile. "You sound just like my mother."

I pressed my lips together. Well, I hadn't actually said that, but I *was* thinking it. What the heck was going on here? I hadn't considered Candace's sister as a suspect in her attempted murder, but right now it was looking like Miss Bethanny did it in the library with a . . . book? Okay, that wasn't quite right. Freddie was better at the Clue thing.

Bethanny looked over to the fireplace, seemingly studying the blue tiled pattern of the hearth.

"Is there something you want to talk about?"

I hadn't really expected an answer, but suddenly the young woman looked at me and said, "I can't do it anymore. I can't take care of her."

"Who? Candace?"

"Yes," she said nearly in a shout. "My whole life it's been, *Bethanny, can you go up to Candy's room and see if she's okay? Bethanny, can you make Candy something to eat, you know she's not good at taking care of herself. Bethanny, could you maybe skip that sleepover—just this once—and watch a movie with your sister? She's had a hard day.*" A tear slipped down her cheek. She quickly swiped it away. "I am the younger sister! But, nope, we all had to take care of Candace. I thought it would be better when she went off to school, but that just made my parents worry more."

"I thought . . . I thought Candace was looking out for you tonight?" I said carefully. "You know, your bad breakup?"

"Ha! My boyfriend and I aren't broken up. We're fine. Well, we would be if . . ." She didn't finish the thought.

"Well, why tell Candace that . . ." I paused, trying to figure out what exactly it was that I was asking. "Why get her to take care of you if you're not really broken up?"

"I'm taking care of her!" Bethanny said lightly, slapping her chest. "She's the one who's getting dumped!"

Chapter Twenty-six

"You've lost me."

"My mother got the feeling that Candace was about to get dumped," Bethanny said, shaking her head. "So she sent me here, like always, to make sure she's okay. Didn't matter that I had plans. We gotta make sure Candy is okay. And make up some ridiculous story in the process, so she doesn't know that's what we're doing."

"So, this is a bit of a pattern?"

"Yeah, you could say that," she said, getting to her feet and walking back to the window. "How well do you know Candace?"

I shrugged. "Um, well enough, I guess? She's always struck me as a really sweet person."

"Oh yeah, she's sweet." Bethanny crossed her arms over her chest. "And kind. And full of sunshine and lemon drops."

I waited for her to go on. I wasn't exactly sure what to make of this speech, but the emotions were real. And kind of scary.

"What Candace is not—at least according to my

mother—is able to take care of herself. It's like she believes my sister is just too precious for this world."

I waited again as Bethanny resumed her pacing. Suddenly she whirled around and asked, "Did you know Candy was seriously overweight when she was younger?"

I blinked.

"My parents would kill me if they heard me say that. But it's true. She didn't exactly have an easy time making friends." She wiped her nose with the back of her hand. "I'm pretty sure that's why my parents adopted me. So there would always be someone to look after Candace. They wanted to make sure that she'd never be alone."

"Wow." It was all I could think of to say.

"So yeah, now it turns out I may be getting dumped by a really great guy because once again my parents demanded I take care of my sister."

"I'm sorry about your boyfriend, but I don't think . . . I mean, Candace doesn't strike me as the type of person who needs a round-the-clock babysitter." You know, except for when she did. "She has a lot going for her."

"Tell my parents that." Bethanny took a deep breath. "Growing up I tried so hard to be perfect. To make my parents proud. But it didn't matter how spectacular a report card I brought home, or what event I won in track and field, the question around the dinner table was, *How was your day, Candace?* And you know what's crazy?" She shook her head. "I got it. I mean, like you said, she's a nice person. For so long I did my best, but . . ."

"But?"

"I have to start taking care of me."

Again with the ominous tone. "I get that. I mean it sounds fair." As long as *taking care of me* didn't include *taking care of her sister.* I was going to leave it at that—it wasn't my business—but I kind of felt that I had to say something to defend Candace. When she was doing all that weeping in the snow, she genuinely seemed upset about not being there for Bethanny . . . among all the other things she was upset about. I really got the impression that she did want to do better by her sister. Be that big sister. The timing was just bad. "Look, I get where you're coming from. I have a similar relationship with my mother. I always thought she needed taking care of . . . but it turns out she's doing just fine on her own. Candace has done pretty well for herself in Otter Lake. A lot of people care about her. Your parents may think you all need to take care of Candace, but I think she's doing a pretty good job taking care of herself." Again, crying in the snow aside. But who among us hasn't been there once or twice? "I really think she'd like to have a different sort of relationship with you. She was just saying earlier that she wanted to—"

Suddenly the door burst open.

"Freddie?"

He rushed in with Tyler . . . and Bean?

"What's going on?"

"We gotta go."

"Why?" I asked, rising to my feet.

"I'll explain outside." Freddie's eyes darted to Bethanny. "Good thing we found you. Now you can take care of Candace."

I winced and shot a look over my shoulder. Ouch.

"Why is Candace's sister laughing?" Freddie asked lowly.

"It's a long story."

"Okay, well, come on. We've got to go."

I heard Bethanny get to her feet behind me. "Where is Candace?" she asked. "I probably should go check on her."

Freddie snapped his fingers in the air. "Tyler, take Bethanny to Candace."

"Oh, um." Hmm, this was awkward. Okay, it's not like I was thinking Bethanny was the one behind Candace's so-called accidents, but I couldn't exactly ignore the fact that she did have motive and Candace was incapacitated.

"What?" Freddie asked.

I shot him my best, most intense, panicked eyes.

"I don't understand," he said with a little shake of his head.

I put even more intensity into my gaze.

"Timmy's in the well?"

"Um . . ." Think fast, Erica. "Bethanny, here, has kind of had a rough night. I think maybe it's better if she takes some time to have some fun?"

Freddie looked at me sideways. "Except that would be really weird because her sister was just in an *accident,* and she's probably worried about her."

"It's okay," Bethanny said, walking past me. "Thanks for the advice, Erica, but I know my job."

She left with Tyler, and I whipped out my phone.

"Who are you texting?" Freddie asked.

"Rhonda," I muttered, quickly typing the words *Do not leave Candace alone with anyone. Even her sister.*

"Why?"

"Because I just had a long talk with Bethanny, and her and Candace are not exactly on the best of terms, so I need to give Rhonda a heads-up."

"Seriously?" Freddie asked. "You think she's the killer and you just let her walk off with my charge?"

"No, I don't really think she's the killer, but—"

My phone buzzed. I looked at the screen.

Ack.

That was Rhonda's short form for *acknowledged.* The woman really did know how to take an order.

I looked back up at Freddie then quickly back down and started typing.

And don't tell her I told you that.

I almost added, *And don't ask any suspicious questions,* but quickly thought better of it. Telling Rhonda not to ask any suspicious questions might guarantee that she did.

"Now," I said, looking up. "What's your lead?"

Freddie blinked. "It seems kind of anticlimactic now."

"Seriously?"

"No." He grabbed my elbow. "It's awesome. Let's go!"

Chapter Twenty-seven

"Where are we going?"

"Coat room," Freddie said, speeding down the hallway ahead of me, Sean at his side.

"Why?"

"We need to get our coats."

I should have seen that one coming. "*Why* are we getting our coats?"

"Because we are going outside again."

Dammit. That one too.

"Freddie, just tell me what's going on."

"I will, but we need to hurry."

Sean at least had the decency to look back at me with an apologetic smile. He also looked kind of happy too. Excited. I knew that expression. Freddie had him drinking the *chasing a hot lead* Kool-Aid.

Once we were back in the main foyer, a number of people lobbed questions about Stanley to Freddie, but he batted them all away without so much as a glance. This lead had to be a pretty good one.

A moment later we were inside a room with beautiful dark wood paneling—but no furniture—just long metal racks heavy with coats. Freddie planted his hands on his hips. "Now how the hell did Tyler and his friends organize all these coats?" He spun a plastic disk with a *W* on it clipped around the top bar. "Is it by last name?" It looked like some of the coats had number tags, but others were filed alphabetically—maybe for the locals that the kids knew? That didn't make much sense. Then again stealing a boat and launching into a bunch of trees didn't make a whole lot of sense either. They were probably doing the best they could.

I headed over to where I thought I might find the *B* section. "Seriously, Freddie, talk. What's going on?"

He flicked his eyes over to Sean. "Bean here came through for us."

I cleared my throat. "You mean Sean?"

"Of course, I mean Sean," Freddie muttered, whipping through coats like nobody's business. "You see any other *Beans* around here?"

My turn to shoot Sean an apologetic smile, but he didn't look upset. Actually, he looked kind of amused. Huh, he was extremely good-natured. Freddie needed someone who was extremely good-natured.

"Bean," Freddie went on, making my ears cringe, "tell her what you told me."

"Well, I knew how worried you both were about Freddie's dog," he began. "So I started asking the other servers if anyone remembered getting the pretty blond lady a drink with any peanuts in it or chocolate—because chocolate can be bad for dogs too."

"You are so sweet." I made eye contact with Freddie through some coats and smiled. Freddie's return expression sliced down my smile like a warrior on horseback.

"Anyway, nobody remembered anything like that, but Chloe had a funny thing happen."

Uh-oh. Chloe? Why did I suddenly have the feeling

that Freddie was gathering us for a witch hunt? "When you say a funny thing happened, do you mean, funny ha-ha?"

"No," he said, a little gleam coming to his eye. "Funny, odd."

"Okay," I said slowly then let out an excited yip. "Found my coat!" It was in the *B* section right where I had expected to find it. Of course it also had a sticky note with *Blome* written on it. Maybe Freddie could tackle Tyler's spelling next . . . once he stopped growling with frustration.

I slipped on my jacket. "Okay, so tell me Chloe's funny, odd story."

"Actually," Sean said, pushing up his glasses. "I shouldn't have said funny at all. Chloe's pretty upset."

"Why?"

A pained expression crossed his face. "I think I should let her tell you."

"We're headed to find her next," Freddie shouted. "Once I can find my stupid coat! How hard is it to file a coat under the name Ng? It's two letters, *N-G*!"

"Can you at least tell me what it's about?"

Sean picked up one of the coats that had slipped off its hanger in Freddie's rampage. "Chloe thinks she's the one who gave Candace the drink."

"What? Seriously?" I don't know what I was expecting, but it wasn't that.

He nodded, returning the coat to its place.

I whipped my head around. "Would you hurry up already!"

"It's not under *F* either!"

"Wait," I said, looking at Sean—Freddie was beyond reaching. "Why do we even need our coats?"

"Chloe is outside going through the trash. She feels terrible. She's trying to find the glass."

"Or she's destroying evidence!" Freddie shouted.

Sean shook his head in a little motion and mouthed the words *I don't think she's destroying evidence.*

I nodded.

"You know what? Forget it!" Some metal hangers jangled to the floor as Freddie yanked a fur coat off the rack.

"Um . . . what are you doing?"

"I am taking this one."

I frowned. "I don't know if taking someone's fur is such a good idea."

"Oh please," Freddie muttered angrily. "It's Mrs. Applebaum's. She won't care if I borrow it. I lent her husband my backhoe to . . . do whatever it is that people actually do with backhoes."

Freddie had bought a backhoe a couple of years ago to dig out his own pool. He'd abandoned the project once the dirty lake water seeped up into the hole—and he realized he needed permits. More trouble than it was worth. He decided to keep the machine as a recreational backhoe, though, because he couldn't return it for full price.

Sean shot me a bemused look.

"It's a long story."

He picked up another coat from the floor. "Freddie is a really interesting person, isn't he?"

"Yes. Yes, he is."

"Let's go," Freddie said, his fur-covered shoulder brushing past me.

"Should I come along?" Sean asked with feigned lightness.

"As long as you don't slow us down," Freddie said.

"Great," I said, smiling at Sean before hurrying after Freddie. Once I made it to his back, I hissed into his ear, "You know, you need to be a little bit nicer to Sean."

"Why?"

"Because if you're not careful, you're going to end up dying alone."

"Oh thank God," Freddie muttered. "And here I was worried I was going to die with you."

The Morning After

"*That was not very nice.*"

Freddie patted Stanley's belly. "*Hey, you're the one who doesn't want to be BFFs forever.*"

"*It's just BFFs! The last* F *is the* forever*!*" I sighed. "*And I think you're just nervous around Sean, and it makes you snarky.*"

"*Oh really? Well, I think you're—*" He cut himself off with a disgusted scoff. "*I don't have the energy to go into all of the things that you are.*" He looked down at the coat he was wearing. "*I'd better get this dry-cleaned. Do you dry-clean furs?*"

"*No idea.*"

"*Besides, who are we kidding? We're both going to die alone.*"

"*Alone, but probably together.*" Huh, a wave of déjà vu washed over me.

Freddie sighed. "*You were right all along, New Year's is depressing.*"

"*I never said it was depressing! I love New Y—*"

"*Are you sure you never said that, Erica? Like really, really sure?*"

I frowned. New strange images flashed through my mind. One of them . . . blinding? "What . . . happened next?"

Chapter Twenty-eight

"Would somebody please get this girl a tissue?" Freddie put his hand over his eyes and shook his head.

Turned out we didn't have to go all the way outside. We ran into Chloe in the kitchen. She hadn't had any luck finding the glass either. Now she was sitting on a stool, weeping.

Freddie accepted a tissue from another server and passed it to Chloe. She blew her nose, which made him roll his eyes.

I leaned over to whisper to Sean, "Just so you know, Freddie's not always so . . ." Hmm, what was the word I was looking for? Unsympathetic? Rude? Impatient? "It's just . . ." What was I doing? They couldn't start a relationship based on a lie. "Never mind."

Sean smiled. His nose wrinkled when he smiled. It was adorable. I was really hoping Freddie wouldn't mess this up for us.

I took a step toward Chloe and put my hand on hers. "Can you tell us what happened?"

"Am I in trouble?"

"No, we just want to help."

"I didn't think I was doing anything wrong," Chloe said, turning her puffy eyes to mine.

I gave her a small smile. "I believe you."

I thought I heard Freddie scoff again, but I didn't think Chloe had heard it over her catching breath.

"I mean, this guy came up to me and asked if I would mind giving this drink he was holding to someone." Her hands flopped into her lap. "I asked who, and he pointed at Candace. She and Sheriff Forrester had just finished talking to you." She met my eye. "And they were headed down that hallway off the foyer."

I strained my memory to see if I could remember anything that might help, but I'd been so wrapped up in my own stuff. An alien could have landed, and I wouldn't have noticed. "What did this man look like?"

"He was really, really tall and good-looking for an older guy." She shrugged. "You know, kind of like Sherriff Forrester. Dark hair. Light eyes. Bigger maybe."

"What kind of drink was it?"

"I don't know," she said, shaking her head. "It was like fluorescent green and smelled fruity."

"Appletini, maybe?" I asked, looking at Freddie.

He stroked the end of his chin. "Mrs. Watson." His eyes narrowed. "I should have known the dragon was involved."

I shot him a warning look before turning back to Chloe.

She pointed at me, tissue clutched in her hand. "He also asked me to give Candace a message."

I went still. "What kind of message?"

She sniffed. "He said to tell her *Happy New Year from a friend.*"

Whoa. I folded my arms over my chest and took a step back.

"Here's the thing though," Sean said, jumping in. "Chloe wasn't able to give her the message."

"What?"

Chloe shrugged. "I mean, I caught Candace in the hallway, and she took the drink, but she was in the middle of some sort of *thing* with Sherriff Forrester. I didn't want to interrupt. They were in that room with all the plants like a second later."

Sean and I exchanged a look.

"So I went back to find the man to tell him that I couldn't deliver the message, but . . ."

"But?"

She gave another shaky shrug. "He had disappeared. That's when I started to worry that maybe I shouldn't have taken that drink to Candace. I mean, I've heard about roofies and stuff. But at the time I didn't think about anything like that. I mean, she was with Sherriff Forrester."

I squeezed her hand. "I get it."

"Was there something in that drink? Does this have something to do with Freddie's dog being sick?"

"I don't know," I said. That was kind of partially true. "But I think you might have to make a statement to the police." If we could find the freaking sheriff, that is! Where the heck was Grady?

Chloe started to cry anew.

"Oh for the love of . . ." Freddie whirled away.

"Hey!" I hissed, hurrying over to him. He was hovering angrily over a cheese platter. "You be nice. She just made a mistake."

"She's a crying menace," Freddie hissed. He popped a spicy-looking cube into his mouth. "First she's mean to Tyler then—"

"Mean to Tyler?" Chloe called out. "When was I mean to Tyler?"

Freddie pushed past me. "Oh, so you're going to sit there and tell me that you didn't say you were out of his league and his tux . . ." Freddie closed his eyes. "His tux was *cheap*."

"Oh my God. I was so kidding!" she shouted. "I was just surprised to see him dressed in a tux. I actually thought he looked pretty good."

"Oh, pretty good," Freddie said, folding his arms over his chest. "But not good enough to be in your league."

"No! I would never say . . ." Chloe's cheeks flushed. "Oh no. That wasn't supposed to get back to him." She closed her eyes. "I didn't want to hurt Tyler's feelings. I didn't mean that I was out of his league. I just meant that he's a year younger, and I've just always seen him as . . . younger." She looked at me with pleading eyes. "Does that make any sense?"

"It does." It's funny how a year can make such a difference in high school. "I get it. And for the record you don't have to apologize for not returning someone's feelings. Right, Freddie?"

We warred eyes for a bit.

Finally Freddie said, "Right, Erica." Then added, "But you remember this moment when you have your own child."

Just then another server with his hair slicked back into a man-bun came up. "Hey guys, I don't mean to interrupt . . ."

"Josh," Sean said. "What's up?"

"Well, it's not like I was purposely eavesdropping, but . . ."

"Don't worry," I muttered. "I do it all the time. Do you know something about this?"

"I think I might have seen the guy you were talking about."

Freddie and I cocked our heads to the side like dogs hearing the same whistle. We were definitely spending too much time together.

Man-bun pointed to the foyer. "I spotted someone walking around the front porch through one of the windows. I thought it was kind of weird. I mean, he wasn't smoking or anything."

"Why do you think it was the same guy?" Freddie asked.

"Because he was a *really* big, good-looking dude," Josh said with a slow nod. "And I don't know how exactly to describe it, but it kind of seemed like he was skulking."

That didn't sound good. The porch wrapped all the way around the house, meaning he could get to Matthew's room . . . and Candace. "When was this?"

"Not very long ago. Five, ten minutes maybe?"

Freddie and I exchanged another look.

"We'd better go."

Chapter Twenty-nine

"I don't like this," I said, stamping my feet in the spot I had made in the snow. "We're wasting time, and I can't feel my toes again."

"Nobody said surveillance was easy."

About fifteen minutes later, Freddie and I were huddled behind some bushes just near the tree line watching the door to Matthew's room. Occasionally Rhonda's silhouette moved past the curtains. We had already walked the entire porch and checked on Candace. We didn't find anyone or anything suspicious and Candace was fine, so we opted for a stakeout. As per usual, we didn't really have a plan, but Freddie felt it was our best lead. We were hoping to spot a big, handsome man skulking around outside.

"Maybe we should split up," I suggested. "You can stay out here while I go back to looking for Grady."

"Tyler and his friends are on it," Freddie said. "Cool your loins."

"My loins are cool. Freezing actually. Every part of my body is freezing." I stamped my feet again. "And it's not like Grady to just disappear." This standing outside doing nothing was giving my imagination free rein again. It's amazing how many awful scenarios you can dream up when you're worried about someone you care about. And that worry was growing with every passing second.

"No way you're leaving me out here with all these creepy lights," Freddie muttered, looking suspiciously at a twinkling reindeer decoration. "I might get attacked by elves. Besides, for all we know Grady could be the big, handsome man skulking around outside."

"That doesn't make any sense." I blew some air onto my thinly gloved hands.

"The description did sound a lot like Grady."

"It wasn't Grady. Chloe knows what Grady looks like." I shoved my hands back into my pockets. "And Grady was with Candace when the mystery man asked Chloe to give Candace the drink."

"But man-bun Josh doesn't know what Grady looks like. And doesn't it seem weird that there are *two* big handsome men with dark hair and blue eyes hanging over Candace?" Freddie suddenly chuckled. "Maybe it's Grady's evil twin."

I huffed a laugh, but I wasn't feeling very funny. Sure, when we first couldn't find Grady, it'd seemed likely that he was just in another part of the party and we weren't crossing paths, but, again, with every second that ticked by . . . I didn't know what I'd do if something happened to Grady.

My mind was spinning with everything that had happened tonight. I had gone from believing I was over Grady, to hoping that I might get my second chance with him, to hearing him say we weren't meant to be together . . .

Now I just wanted him to be safe. I'd give anything for him to be okay.

I exhaled a rough breath and shook my head.

No. Everything was fine. It had to be.

He had to be.

"What are you thinking?" Freddie asked.

"Honestly?"

He didn't deign to answer.

I took a deep breath. "I'm freaking out. I feel like any minute we're going to stumble across Grady . . . hurt . . . or worse. Like see that fallen tree over there?" I said, pointing back into the woods.

Freddie's brow furrowed as he darted a glance over his shoulder.

"Doesn't that look like Grady collapsed on the ground?"

He didn't answer.

"Or . . . or . . . maybe he *did* go down to the boathouse to meet Candace and he fell into the lake. Or maybe he fell down some cellar stairs and broke his leg, and he's been yelling for help, but nobody can hear him. Or maybe—*maybe*—he confronted Candace's *friend* and the friend shot him with a crossbow, pinning him to a wall in a creepy old bedroom—*or to the inside of a door!*—and, and by the time somebody finally swings that door open, it will be too late! He'll have bled out!"

Silence fell over us.

Maybe I shouldn't have let out everything I had going on upstairs. "So . . . what were you thinking?"

Freddie turned his face to mine. "Same thing."

"Really?"

"No, you psycho! What's the matter with you?"

"I told you I'm freaking out!"

"Well, stop it," Freddie said, looking back at the estate. "You're freaking me out, and we need to be smart about this. The mystery man is our best lead to figuring out what's happening tonight."

I wrapped my arms around my waist. "But he's not the only suspect. We still can't rule out Bethanny."

"A minority has been in town, what? A couple of hours? And you're already accusing her of murder?"

I backhanded him on the arm.

"So what's the deal between her and Candace anyway?"

I told him all that Bethanny had told me, and what Candace said earlier.

When I was finished, Freddie said, "Whoa. That's heavy."

"I know. Bethanny has some serious issues with her sister, but Candace really does want to make it right."

"And I never would have guessed that Candace was a social outcast like us back in the day," he went on. "But I guess it makes sense. She was always trying just a little bit too hard. Nobody's that nice all the time. It's weird." He sighed then squinted back at the house. "Can you see anything? I think I need a new prescription for my contacts. Maybe we can go into town next—"

I let out a small shout of frustration.

"What now?"

"I can't just stand here talking about prescriptions while Grady's missing!"

"You have the patience of a two-year-old," Freddie said, keeping his eyes on Matthew's bedroom door. "For all we know, Grady is just brooding by himself, and—"

"During the exact time period when somebody is trying to frame him for murder?"

"I wouldn't underestimate Grady's capacity to brood," Freddie said.

"Yeah, but what if our mystery man does come back?" I asked, gesturing wildly at nothing. "What are we going to do then? Make a citizen's arrest?"

"Um, no. Especially not if he's as big and muscular as everyone seems to think he is."

"Well, then?"

"We," he said, drawing the word out into nonexistent syllables, "are going to take his picture."

My jaw dropped, but its effect was wasted as Freddie had already gone back to watching the house. "And how exactly are *we* going to do that? I know for a fact that your smartphone does not take pictures in the dark." He had been complaining about it just last week.

Freddie chuckled again in that way that sounded like *Erica, Erica, Erica*—but, you know, in laugh form. "I'm not going to take the picture with just my smartphone."

I frowned. This couldn't be going anywhere good. "So what are you going to take it with?"

"This!"

Freddie pulled a black metal tube from his pocket.

I frowned. "And that is what exactly?"

"The Blinder 3000. It's a tactical-grade flashlight. It can light up this here entire woods with just the flick of a switch," Freddie said. "I'd give you a demonstration, but it would totally give away our position. I thought it might come in handy when we were working security."

I rubbed my arms. "You bought that off an infomercial, didn't you?"

"So what if I did?"

"No, it's nothing."

"Tell that to all the judgment in your voice," Freddie muttered. "But you'll be impressed once our mystery stalker reveals himself. Not only will I get my picture, but I will blind the sucker in the process. If you flick it on and off really fast, I think it can even induce seizures."

"Oh, for the love of—" I put my hands over my face. Wow, my nose was cold. "This is so not a good use of our time! For all we know the guy has taken off. Maybe we should call the sheriff's department. Amos is probably there or . . . or what's the name of that other deputy they hired?"

"Greg?"

"Yeah, Greg."

"Not Greg," Freddie whined. "He's zero fun."

"This isn't about fun!"

Freddie pointed his flashlight at me. I almost put my hands up. "What are we going to do? Report Grady missing? He's a grown man. At a party. In a fight with his girlfriend. He's probably drinking in a corner somewhere with high school buddies. "

I forced Freddie's shooting hand down. "That's not Grady, and you know it."

"What I know is that we've only been out here for fifteen minutes tops, and that stakeouts typically take— Did you hear that?" Freddie hissed, slapping me on the arm.

I froze. "Hear what?"

"The sound of the universe proving me right?"

"Nope." I shook my head. "Pretty sure I've never heard that sound before."

"Shush!" Freddie waved a hand in front of my face. "There it is again!"

I listened as hard as I could which really just meant I froze and moved my eyes side to side. Oh! Crap! I did hear something. It sounded like someone walking slowly through crunchy snow.

"It's coming from the drive," I said, pointing to the cars. A lot of people must have carpooled to the party, and I had seen at least one bus. But all that aside, there was still a ton of cars parked alongside Hemlock Estate's long drive through the woods. They probably went all the way to the road. Maybe even beyond that.

"It could be anyone," I whispered. "Maybe someone forgot something. Or they're just late."

Freddie gasped. "Someone big and handsome." He pointed to a man emerging between the bumpers of two parked cars.

My heart thudded in my chest. "You can't tell if he's handsome from here."

"But he sure is big," Freddie hissed. "And why isn't he sticking to the path that leads to the front door?"

He was right. Freddie was right. The man wasn't following the cleared path that led to the front doors. He was veering off onto the lawn. The snow-covered lawn that led around the side of the house to the same view that Freddie and I had. The view into Matthew's bedroom.

"That's gotta be him," Freddie whispered.

Oh boy. Oh boy. Oh boy.

"What do we do? What do we do?"

Freddie fumbled with his flashlight. "We stick to the plan." He handed me the Blinder 3000. "You should work the light while I take the picture."

"What? Me?" It's not like I wanted to be the one to take the picture either, but . . . but . . . this was all just happening too fast! "Are we just going to run out there and ambush the man? What if he has a perfectly good explanation for—"

"For peeping into Matthew's bedroom?" Freddie asked, fiddling with his phone. "If he does, then we'll apologize."

It certainly did look like the man was peeping. "I don't like this. Maybe we could just ask for his picture?"

"'Cause would-be murderers are so cool with having their photos taken?" Freddie shook my arm. "Come on, I thought Candace was your new best friend. Stop being such a chicken and do this for her. Do this for Stanley!"

My eyes snapped back to Freddie. "Oh my God! Are

you tweeting right now?" I could hardly believe my eyes, but Freddie's face was washed aglow with the light of his phone as his thumb flew over the screen.

"There are thousands of people around the world following hashtag justice for Stanley. They're going to want to know what's happening." He pressed his phone one last time. "There. I've got my camera set to rapid-fire. Now put your big-girl panties on and let's do this thing!"

I gulped down a breath. "So we're really going to just run out there and snap this guy's picture?"

"We really are."

"Okay," I said shakily. "But, for the record, this is exactly the kind of thing we are not doing in the Year of the Adult."

Freddie widened his stance and crouched. "And that's why I say *forever young!*" And with that he took off, breaking free from the shelter of the trees.

Chapter Thirty

"Erica!" Freddie shouted. "The light!"

I scrambled to catch up, but it was hard to move quickly in a dress and snow boots. Freddie was having no trouble whatsoever. He was speeding across the lawn with his camera outstretched in front of him like a jousting lance. In fact he had almost made it to the startled man.

"Come on! Hurry! The light!"

I felt my dress rip up the side as I pumped my legs harder through the snow.

Almost there.

The enormous man had spun round at the sound of our approach, his hands out to his sides like he couldn't quite decide which way to bolt. I pointed the flashlight out in front of me and hit the switch.

It was like . . . like . . . a brand-new baby sun had erupted from my hand.

The giant let out a surprised yell. His hands flew up to block the light.

I was so focused on trying to keep the light on him that I lost my footing on the uneven ground. I hit the snow hard enough to make my teeth snap shut, but I managed to keep my arm outstretched.

"Erica!" I heard Freddie shout, then, "Oh God! My eyes!"

I spun the flashlight away from where I thought Freddie was as I struggled to my feet, but I dropped the light in the process. The Blinder 3000 toppled in the air, the blast of light hitting me twice in the face before it hit the ground. Suddenly I could really see how this thing might cause seizures.

I fumbled blindly for it in the snow.

"Turn it off!" Freddie shouted.

"I'm trying!" I yelled back, patting ground.

"Seriously, turn it off," Freddie called out again, quieter this time. "I think . . . I think he's gone."

Finally, my fingers hit the metal tube. Once I had it in my grip, I clicked it off then blinked, trying to restart my burned-out retinas.

"Erica?" Freddie called out again. "Where are you?"

"Over here."

I heard more than saw him approach.

We took a moment to catch our breath.

"Did you get it?"

"I don't know," he said, still puffing. "Maybe. We'll have to go through the pictures."

I pressed my fingers against my closed lids. "Where did he go?"

"I just saw him take off. I went blind after that."

I hauled myself to my feet and looked down at my dress. Wow, the side seam had split almost to my hip. I was also pretty sure that my knee was bleeding.

I tried to smooth my hair back from my face, but my gloved fingers kept getting tangled in the product-drenched clumps. "Let's just go back inside."

We trudged our way back toward the house in silence.

When we reached the back porch Freddie said, "You know, next time I'm not going to cheap out."

"Huh?"

"For ten more bucks, I could've gotten us two Blinders."

I didn't answer.

"What do you think?"

I still didn't answer.

"Nah," he said a moment later. "Maybe not. You, me, *and* two Blinders? The world's not ready for that kind of power."

The Morning After

"That . . . that was horribly done."

Freddie snickered.

"What's so funny?"

"Well, I was just replaying the whole thing in my mind and suddenly the thought popped in my head, Hey, good thing I didn't give her a gun."

A snort escaped me before I slapped a hand over my mouth.

"It's funny because"—Freddie's laughter was growing—"you would have shot my face off!"

Strangely that made me laugh even harder.

"And your own!"

"Twice!" I added.

We laughed for a good solid couple of minutes then Freddie wiped at the hysterical tears escaping the corners of his eyes. "I don't think I've ever been this hungover."

My laughter settled and I coughed out, "Yeah, you'd think we'd been drinking all night."

With that thought our mood settled back down into something much darker.

"Something's not right. I mean, obviously so much is not right. But the whole drinking thing? We would have had to have started super early to be this hungover."

"Yeah," Freddie said, shaking his head no. "And I don't remember visiting any of the bars."

I rubbed my face. My cheeks were all pins and needles from the laughing. "I think I might have gone to the martini bar to see Mrs. Watson . . . but I'm pretty sure I didn't drink anything."

"It doesn't make sense. We were being pretty responsible for us. Competent. Like even with the whole Blinder 3000 mishap, we still got the picture."

"We did?"

Chapter Thirty-one

"No. No. NO!" Freddie must have taken a couple hundred pictures in under a minute with his rapid-fire.

"Lovely shot of a tree," I said dryly.

"Well, you take the pictures next time."

We were standing on the terrace outside Matthew's room. Freddie was swiping furiously through the photos. We were going to go inside, but Candace was still passed out, and we didn't want to wake her if we didn't have the shot. There was still no word from the twins or Tyler . . . or Grady.

I was feeling both exhausted and on edge all at the same time. After that last adrenaline rush, it was hard to think straight.

"Snow blur," I said as Freddie flicked to the next shot. "That one looks like there might be a Yeti hidden in it."

Freddie swiped back and brought the photo closer to his face. "Nah, it's just a snowman." His thumb slid across the screen again. "Wait! What's that?"

I leaned toward the screen, squinting. It was hard to say for sure, but it did kind of look like . . . an elbow? "Keep swiping! Keep swiping!" More and more of the man appeared, moving in slow motion, as Freddie swiped at warp speed.

"Gah!" he shouted. "He's got his hands over his face!"

"Just keep swiping!"

"I'm trying. My thumb is tired."

"Give it to me." I grabbed Freddie's phone and starting swiping with my fresh thumb. Photos whipped across the screen. *Almost there. Almost there.* Wait . . . wait . . . his hands were dropping . . .

"Bam!"

Freddie grabbed my hand to bring the phone closer to his face. "Whoa," was all he said when he caught sight of the image.

I nodded. "I know. Candace's killer is—"

"Super hot," he finished.

I yanked the phone back and shot him a withering look. "I was going to say that he *does* kind of look like Grady."

"Actually, no," Freddie said, snapping his fingers. "You know who he looks like?"

Our eyes met.

"Who?"

"That werewolf from the vampire show."

I frowned. Now what was Freddie going on about? "Werewolf? Which one? The one with the teenage vampires?"

"No, no," he said, grabbing his phone back. "The other one. From a while back. It was set in the South and had all that nudity?"

"Oh, I know who you mean," I said, wagging an excited finger at him. "You mean the actor who married that actress on that funny show from Colombia."

Freddie frowned as his eyes darted over my face. "I don't watch Colombian shows."

"No," I said, swatting his shoulder. "She's from Colombia. The show's American."

"They're married?" Freddie asked, looking back down at his phone.

"I think so."

"Oh wait," Freddie said. "Didn't she have some sort of lawsuit with some other guy about frozen embryos?"

"Yeah, yeah," I said with an excited nod. "I think you're right."

Freddie sniffed. "That's why I'm not freezing my embryos."

I gave him the side-eye. "Yeah, that's why."

We exchanged challenging looks then went back to looking at the screen.

"He is hot. I'm surprised I didn't notice him earlier," I said again, huddling in by Freddie's shoulder to get another look. Well, to get a better look and to try to stop myself from freezing to death. His fur coat was radiating warmth.

Freddie let out a slow breath and frowned. "Why would someone this hot want to kill Candace?"

I threw him yet another look. "I can't help but think that maybe those two things don't have anything to do with each other."

"Of course they do. Nobody this handsome should have to resort to a life of crime."

I huffed a laugh. "Tell that to hot mug shot guy."

"Hot mug shot guy?" Freddie asked.

"You know," I said, searching his face. "That guy whose mug shot went viral?"

Freddie's expression didn't change. "That explanation supplied me with no further information."

"You know the guy with the ice-blue eyes—"

"Oh yeah! I totally forgot about—"

"Oh my God! What is wrong with us! Why are we standing out here? Let's go wake up Candace!"

"Yeah, Grady could be bleeding out as we speak."

"I'm going to regret telling you that, aren't I?"

"Probably."

"Do you recognize this man?"

Freddie and I offered Dr. Reynolds and Rhonda a break from their bedside duties. Rhonda didn't seem too keen to leave, probably because she knew we were going to question Candace, but she really had to use the restroom. There was no sign of Jessica. She was off probably falling in love with Matthew, like in the ballroom scene from Cinderella. Not that I cared. Much. I totally wished them well. Stanley was sleeping on a pillow near the fireplace. He looked so painfully cute with the IV bandaged to his little paw and his oversized cone of shame. We heard secondhand that Jessica didn't want him gnawing at the needle, and she had one of the plastic contraptions in her van what with her moving offices. Unfortunately, it wasn't the right size. But still, he did look adorable. In a miserable kind of way.

No word on Grady.

We had Candace propped up on pillows and somewhat awake. She was holding the phone up to her face, but if her hand wasn't swaying then her face was. Finally she was able to lock onto her target. "Hey! I know him. That's Joey."

"Isn't that the name of the werewolf guy in real life?" Freddie said with an amused smile. "You don't think—"

I cut him off with a look. "That he really is a werewolf? No." We had no more time for tangents. "Candace, how do you know this guy?"

She collapsed back against the pillow with a contented smile. It must be nice to be in that place where your troubles can't reach you. Of course, they'd probably get her with a vengeance in the morning. "We're pen pals."

"Pen pals?" Freddie and I exchanged a look. Who had pen pals anymore?

"For over a year now," she said, leaning over and grabbing my wrist to get me to sit down on the bed beside her.

"Would he . . ." It looked like Freddie was struggling to find a delicate way to phrase his next words. "Have any reason to want you dead?" *And* he failed.

"Joey?" Candace said with a laugh. "Joey would never do something like that. He's found God."

Well, this was getting *curiouser* and *curiouser*.

Candace didn't seem to think her *accident* in the boathouse was anything more than an accident. I thought about trying to explain it to her—I mean, she certainly had the right to know—but it seemed kind of like a fool's errand given her current state. Not to mention it *did* also seem kind of mean given our whole conversation earlier about everyone hating her. And she was so happy right now.

"Hey, so where exactly did he find God?" Freddie asked.

"Oh, in jail."

I found myself blinking rapidly. Freddie was too. "I'm sorry, did you say jail?"

Candace nodded. "He just got out yesterday. I remember thinking it would be nice for him to get out in time for New Year's. He wanted to come visit me," she added with a cute deepening of her dimples, "but I didn't think Grady would like that, and we have enough problems." For just a second, she looked quite sad. Then she laughed and jabbed me in the ribs with her elbow. "Erica knows what I mean."

I chuckled awkwardly. "So you and Joey were close, I take it? How did you meet?"

She flashed me another smile again. "Through the church. Our pastor thought if we exchanged letters with inmates, it would help with their . . ." She paused, looking very confused. "Rehabilitation," she said suddenly. "That's the word. But we've never met in person. I've seen pictures though. He credits me with saving his life. You know, because of the support of my letters. I think he had a little crush." She pinched a *little* air between her fingers. "But I told him we couldn't be together." She shook her head no in a big side-to-side movement. "That I had a boyfriend."

"And how did he take that news?"

"I don't know." She squinted and looked off at nothing. "I never got another letter after that."

Freddie and I exchanged looks again.

I cleared my throat. "Do you know what he was in prison for?"

"I never asked," she said with a thoughtful-sounding sigh. "I didn't want him to feel judged." Suddenly she slapped the mattress. "I think I'm ready to go back to the party now. I feel much better."

"Whoa. Whoa. Whoa." I pinned her hand to the bed. "What do you say we hold off on that until we get Dr. Reynolds to check you over one last time?" Keeping an eye on Candace, while finding Grady, and being on guard for the werewolf, would really tax our resources— especially if Rhonda started testing all of Candace's drinks for poison again.

"Really, Erica, I'm fine. And I need to talk to Grady."

I'd be happy just to know he was all right. "I get that. I really do. Just hang on a sec—"

"Erica, can I talk to you?" Freddie asked, jerking his head for me to follow him to the far side of the room. He then held up some placating hands to Candace and mouthed the words, *I got this.*

As I walked toward him I mumbled, "You're not seriously thinking she should go back to the party, are you?"

"Of course not," he whispered. "I just wanted to be able to talk about her in the same room without her worrying that we are talking about how we are going to keep her in this room."

I nodded. "Right. Right. I think I get that. Good plan." Just then I noticed a large plastic box at my feet filled with medical equipment. That must be Jessica's stuff. There was also a sharp astringent smell in the air. I looked in the garbage can beside the box. Broken glass. "What happened there?" I asked, pointing at the can while looking over my shoulder at Candace.

She frowned. "I think I heard that pretty vet saying some kid dropped her stuff?"

Freddie sighed. "Tyler. He's got butterfingers." He then threw a smile over my shoulder at Candace and whispered out of the corner of his mouth, "So what are we thinking here? That this is some kind of *if I can't have her, no one can*–type scenario?"

"All I'm thinking is that we need to find Grady. Now."

"Yeah, that hasn't really been a successful strategy so far."

"It's time to call the station." I reached into my jacket pocket for my phone. "Maybe Amos has some special way of getting a hold of Grady."

"What? Like a bat signal?"

I swiped at the screen. "Yes, exactly like that."

"Okay, but I really doubt Amos is going to be of any use."

"It's worth a shot. Maybe he can get other officers over here to help with the search for Grady."

"Again, yes, let's organize a search team for the adult man who has been missing for less than two hours at a large party on an estate."

"Well, do you have a better idea?"

He nodded. "I think that it's time we take this investigation to the next level."

"It terrifies me when you say stuff like that."

"You call Amos. I'm going to gather everyone else for a team meet—" Freddie suddenly bounced up onto his toes. "Just as soon as we find out where Candace has got off to."

I whipped my head around again to the empty bed. "Frick!"

She hadn't made it far, just out into the hallway. Rhonda was on her way back from the guest bathroom and cut her off at the pass. She actually had to bring Candace back into the room by lifting her in a giant bear hug, which Candace found hilarious. She was such a happy drunk. And a sleepy one. Once Rhonda had dropped her back on the bed, she curled up, closed her eyes, and started snoring.

Ten minutes later Freddie had everyone else—Tweety, Kit Kat, Tyler, Bethanny, and Sean—gathered in Matthew's bedroom. That's right. Sean. Very telling that Freddie thought to invite him. We had debated bringing Bethanny into the mix, but she had already made friends with Tyler, and it didn't seem like a half-bad idea to keep her close, just in case. She looked confused—I picked that up from her *I'm surrounded by crazy people* face— but I couldn't worry about that right now. Also, I *had* called Amos, but Freddie was right, it didn't get me very far. Every time I asked him about getting some help to find Grady, he would get caught up on the fact that it wasn't procedure to start a missing person's investigation so soon for a nonvulnerable adult, and he'd have to ask Grady first.

"Okay," I said, clapping my hands together. "Let's get this meeting going."

I could see Freddie's horrified expression at my taking charge of his investigation, but we couldn't waste any more time. Freddie might still believe that Grady was off brooding, but I didn't. "Kit Kat, Tweety, what have you two found out about the origin of the rumors?"

"We're circling in," Kit Kat said, "a lot of the same names keep coming up, but we can't say anything for certain as of yet."

"Okay, well, we're abandoning local suspects at the moment," Freddie said, pushing past me with a cutting look. "You're being reassigned. In fact, everybody is now being reassigned to the task of finding Grady Forrester."

"Nobody's found him yet?" Tweety asked. Then she let out a cackle and backhanded her sister lightly on the arm. "Hey, don't all these old houses have secret passageways? Maybe he got caught—"

"Behind one of those swirling bookshelves!" Kit Kat, said finishing the thought.

I sighed.

"What?" Tweety asked. "You don't know that he didn't."

"Yeah," Kit Kat added. "For all you know, somebody has him chained up in the basement."

Tweety nodded with a disturbingly lecherous look on her face. "Wouldn't that be a sight?"

"Shirt off," Kit Kat went on. "Manacles around his wrists and ankles—"

"Oh my God! Knock it off, you two." I would have said something more, but the visual of that had just caught up to my consciousness. Their imaginations were way better than mine.

"She's seeing it," Kit Kat said.

Tweety nodded knowingly.

"Ladies!" Freddie snapped. "Please control your ovaries. We need to break up into teams and search this estate from top to bottom."

"I could go with you," Sean offered with a little shrug. "I can get Josh to cover for me."

I could have sworn Freddie's cheeks flushed just a little. "No, Bethanny's coming with me."

At which point Tyler jumped in. "But I thought Bethanny and I could maybe go together."

"Yeah, not when you're under my care. Your mother would not approve." Freddie caught Bethanny's confused expression. "I have my reasons. His body spray is overpowering anyway. You'll thank me later."

Tyler's eyes widened in horror.

"We need to focus," Freddie ordered. "The twins will of course go together. Bean, you go with Tyler. Bethanny and me. Rhonda, you're still on Candace and Stanley duty. Oh, and if you could get that vet to check in on my dog once in a while, I would appreciate it."

"What's the big deal with finding Sheriff Forrester anyway?" Tyler asked.

"That's need to know. Need. To. Know."

"What about me?" I asked. "I don't have a partner."

He sighed. "You don't need a partner. You have Graydar."

Freddie gave a few more instructions on staying together, being careful of good-looking werewolf-type men, and staying in contact via text. He then assigned different sections of the house to search. I wasn't given any particular area. My instructions were to just follow my nose. We all took off in our various directions.

I headed back out to the main ballroom. I was getting more than a few looks seeing as I was still wearing my boots and my coat, and my dress had an obvious tear in it, but that was the least of my concerns.

I scanned the room.

Grady. Grady. Grady. Gr—

"Matthew."

Not the handsome man I was looking for.

"Erica, are you okay?" he asked, looking me over.

"I'm fine," I said quickly, eyes moving back to scan the room. "I just fell in the snow."

"And what's this about Candace getting locked in the boathouse with the generator on?" He took a step toward me. "And who are you looking for?"

"Grady. Have you seen him?"

"Not in a while. Last I saw him he was looking for Candace. Is she okay? I was just about to go check on her. Jessica said Dr. Reynolds is with her in my room?"

"Yeah, but she's sleeping." I brushed my hair back away from my face. Where was he? "Hey," I said suddenly. "Is there any way the latch on the boathouse could have fallen shut when Candace closed the door?" I wasn't sure why I was asking. All the other pieces fit. But I guess I still wanted there to be some logical explanation that didn't involve murder.

"Yeah, I was actually at the hardware store just last week looking for a new handle. I was going to replace that latch." The muscles at his jaw flexed. "I feel terrible."

"Did you talk to anyone about it?"

Matthew shrugged. "Shane."

He owned the store. "Anyone else? Did anyone overhear you?"

"Probably. The store was pretty full."

It usually was. A lot of the people liked to hang out there. Anyone could have heard Matthew talking, which meant anyone could have planned for Candace to get trapped in there.

"What about the generator? Do you know why it was on? Does it have something to do with your surprise?"

"No, not at all. I assumed Candace turned it on, maybe thinking it was a heater? I heard she was drinking pretty heavily. What's going on, Erica? It was an accident, right?"

"I think we should let Grady decide that one. Where did you last see him?"

"Here, in the ballroom, but he said someone told him Candace and a couple of other guests were trying to find all the secret passageways in the house and he had lost her."

My eyes snapped to his. "Who told him that?"

"He didn't say."

I cursed under my breath. "So does this house actually have a secret passageway?"

"Just one," he replied. "But it's not a big deal. It's actually just a semihidden staircase by the fireplace in the old billiards room. It leads to the attic. Used to be the servants' quarters. I offered to show him, but he said he could find it, and I was on my way to get Jessica some food. She hadn't eaten since her earlier call."

I looked behind me. I thought the billiards room was back that way. "That Jessica sure is a trouper."

He chuckled, but it was short-lived. "Erica, can I help in any way?"

"I'm sure everything's fine." I didn't have time to explain everything. Besides, if he went to check on Candace, Rhonda could give him more of the details.

"You seemed freaked out, and there's some strange rumors going around that Grady and Candace are breaking up?"

I nodded with my head still turned. I needed to go check that staircase out.

"I mean, it sounds wrong to say, but I thought you'd be . . . happy?"

That made me look back at him. "Yeah," I said. "It feels kind of wrong for me to think it too."

"Do you want me to show you that staircase I was talking about?"

Just then it sounded like a tray of drinks smashed in the other room. Matthew's head whipped around.

"It's okay. I can manage," I said. "You go. But which room is it exactly?"

"It's the third door on the right down the main hall-way to your left when you first come in." Matthew then leaned in and kissed me on the cheek. "Good luck."

He probably thought I was trying to finding Grady to make my move.

"Thanks."

I watched him walk away back through the crowd for just a half second longer than I had to waste. It suddenly occurred to me that I was always a little sad when Matthew walked away.

Chapter Thirty-two

"Third door on the right," I muttered as I wound my way through the crowd, still ignoring all of the interested slash concerned looks I was getting. I didn't want to waste any more time. "Third door on the right."

I trucked down the near identical hall to the one on the opposite side of the estate.

Bingo!

I'm not sure why Matthew had called it the old billiard room. There was a new-looking pool table in it, and the room itself had a pretty modern man-cave feel. But that was a question I was sure could wait for his engagement party.

Now the secret door.

I walked up to the cold fireplace and checked out the wood panels on either side. You wouldn't be able to see the outline of the hidden door if you weren't looking for it, but I was, so it didn't take long. I gave it a little push, and that was enough to release the spring mechanism keeping it shut. It popped right open.

Well, that was easy.

I took a step into the darkened space and looked up.

Yup, totally easy.

All I needed to do now was climb up the very dark, very narrow, claustrophobic stairs to the closed door at the top without spontaneously screaming. Seriously, if I half straightened my arms out, I could touch both walls. It was like they were hugging me . . . until I could no longer breathe.

I turned on the light on my phone, gulped, and took the first step.

Wow, old wood sure knew how to groan.

I almost thought about shouting out Grady's name but quickly decided against it. The thought of hearing my own voice yelling at me in this confined space might set off that screaming I was thinking about earlier.

This was probably silly. Grady wouldn't still be up here.

Thump!

Great. It had come from the room at the top of the stairs. But no, it was totally good. I was looking for a live, moving person after all. Then again, given all of the experience I had had with murderers lately, it wasn't unreasonable that I was just a little bit freaked out. But not, you know, freaked out enough to stop investigating. I wasn't that much of a chicken. And I *was* looking for a man, who I had been told was looking for a woman, who had gone up these stairs and—

Thump!

Okay, that thump sounded exactly like a body hitting the floor.

Maybe I was that much of a chicken.

I couldn't do this alone . . .

. . . but I couldn't wait either!

What if Grady needed my help?

I tapped the first number on my phone, waiting on the stairs as it rang.

"I said text messages only."

"Yeah, but I'm climbing up a hidden staircase in real time," I said, taking a step, "and I want you to hear it if someone jumps out of nowhere and kills me."

"What?" Freddie snapped. "You're exploring a secret passageway without me?"

"Hey," I said, swiping at a phantom cobweb by my head. I think it was probably just my hair. "You're the one who wanted to partner up with Bethanny."

"True," he said. "Oh, and by the way, she's really kind of offended that you thought she might be the one trying to kill her sister."

I froze mid-step. "You told her? Why would you tell her?"

"We're bonding," Freddie said, voice rising a pitch. "And I had to explain what we were doing. Where is this secret staircase?"

I resumed my climb. "In the old billiards room."

"Wait for us. We'll come. We're on the other side—"

"Whoa . . ."

"What? What?" my phone asked.

Now that I could see the foot of the door, I realized something was blocking it. A pipe maybe? It was pretty big for a pipe. And heavy by the looks of it. Maybe the iron chimney of an old stove? It was wedged between the wall and the door. So . . . maybe somebody was trapped inside?

"Something's blocking the door at the top of the stairs." I crept up another step. "Maybe Grady's trapped inside."

"Or maybe someone else! Who's about to kill you!"

This whole situation was suddenly feeling a little Jane Eyre-y. Matthew didn't seem the type to lock up family members, and or insane wives, in the attic, but then again the creepiness of the situation was making it hard to be rational. *And* another spiderweb, a real one this time, had just brushed over my shoulder, so, you know, I was pretty sure I was going to die.

"Erica?"

"Hang on a second," I whispered.

I looked over my shoulder. Maybe I should wait for them.

Nah, it was silly. I was being silly. Grady might need me . . . and if it was someone else trapped in there, well, they were trapped. As long as they didn't have a gun to shoot me in the face with through the closed door, I was pretty safe.

I snorted a nervous laugh.

"Are you laughing? What is wrong with you?"

"Just stay on the line, okay?" I whispered. "I'm going to knock on the door."

"What? You're going to knock!" I think Freddie went on muttering some knock-knock joke that ended with me being dead, but I was too scared to appreciate his punch line.

I climbed the remaining steps up to the last two. You know, silly or not, I didn't want to be at shooting height, so I stretched my belly over the landing and knocked softly at the very bottom of the door. "Grady?"

Chapter Thirty-three

"Erica?"

Quick footsteps crossed the floor.

"It's Grady! I'll call you back." I ended the call with Freddie.

Oh thank you. Thank you. Thank you. I popped up to my feet and climbed the last two steps, brushing the dust off my dress. "Hey!" I called out. "Thank God you're not bleeding out. Everyone's looking for you! What are you doing in there?"

"Bleeding out? What?" Grady rattled the door handle. "Can you see what's blocking the door?"

"Just give me a second." I bent down, jiggled then slid the heavy piece of iron a few inches away from the door before I tried the handle. It opened just enough for Grady to pop his head out. He then pushed the door with enough force to get it most of the way open.

I rushed toward him then stopped myself short. I had been super close to throwing my arms around him.

"Finally. Thank you," he said, eyes meeting mine. "How did you know I was up here?"

"I didn't, exactly." Hot chills of relief rushed down my body. "But Matthew told me you might be looking for Candace in the hidden staircase." I took a couple of steps toward Grady. My nerves couldn't take having a conversation at the top of a flight of stairs. He backed away to make room.

"Yup," he said, looking around. "She's not here. I guess I didn't see the pipe leaning against the wall out there. It must have fallen, locking me in."

I frowned. Somehow I didn't think so.

Grady shot me a sideways look. "Why do you look so freaked out?"

"There's a lot going on," I said, stepping farther into the room—which really felt like more of a loft than an attic. Exposed beams. Big windows. There were lots of storage items though. "I don't even know where to start." I turned to face him. "What was all that thumping? And why haven't you been answering your phone?"

"I lost it somewhere," Grady said, slapping his jacket pockets. "And I was just moving some boxes so I'd have a better place to sit than the floor."

I nodded. That made sense. About the phone I mean. I knew Grady had never sent that message to Candace to meet him in the boathouse.

Grady looked me over. "Erica, are you okay? Did you fall?"

"Why didn't you yell for help?"

"I did a bit," Grady said, eyeing me. "Nobody came. So I figured I'd give it a little while before I resorted to destruction of property." He held up a book. "Besides, I found a copy of *The History of Otter Lake*. Did you know that the town has had fifty-three official mascots? One was a weasel. It bit into the hand of a town official at a parade in the 1890s." His eyes dropped to the book as he gave the cover a pat. "I think I just needed some time away from the party to think." He frowned. "Why all the questions?"

Grady knew me well. He knew I wasn't asking just to make conversation. Well, that *and* I probably looked like a survivor of a natural disaster. I chewed the corner of my lip. "There's been an accident."

"What are you talking about?"

I filled Grady in on as much as I could as quickly as I could and ended with, "So, I initially thought Freddie's poisoned-drink theory was nuts, but then there was the thing with Candace in the boathouse, her prison pen pal, Joey, and now you being locked in the attic. Plus there's all these crazy rumors."

"Are you sure Candace is okay? Is she safe?"

"Rhonda's with her."

Grady planted his hands on his hips. He didn't look all that reassured. "Did you contact the sheriff's department? Amos? Any kind of authorities?"

"That's kind of what I'm doing right now, big guy," I said, punching his shoulder. Ow . . . yup, just as hard as I remembered. "But yeah, I tried the other things too."

"I can't be lead investigator on this." He rubbed his forehead then peeked at me from under his hand. "You realize that I'm a suspect. I'm Candace's . . ."

"Yeah, boyfriend. I am well aware of that fact. But *I* know you didn't do it," I said, resisting the urge to squeeze his arm this time. I mean, a friendly punch was one thing, but I definitely didn't have arm-squeezing privileges. "Besides, I doubt you locked yourself in the attic."

"Right. Except the person who discovered me just happens to be my ex-girlfriend."

I threw my hands in the air. "Well, next time I could just leave you in the attic until someone less involved finds you."

"I didn't mean that," he said, shaking his head. "I'm just processing all this. It doesn't make any sense."

"Do you know anything about this Joey? Or anyone else who might have motive for killing Candace?"

"Not really," he said, scratching his jaw. "I knew she was part of a pen-pal program through her church . . . and then there's Bryson. He'd like his job back, I'm sure."

"Murder seems a bit extreme though."

Grady nodded. "Agreed. But, otherwise, I can't think of anyone. Despite the fact that she's the face of MRG, everybody loves Candace."

It took every micromuscle in my face not to betray any kind of emotion. *Everybody loves Candace.* Breakup rumors aside, I couldn't help but wonder if *he* was included in that *everybody*.

I guess Grady noticed my unnaturally rigid posture because he looked like he was about to say something to try to smooth it over . . . but didn't. Probably because he also knew there was nothing really to say. I mean, he could say, *Well, maybe not everybody.* And then I would say, *What about you, Grady? Do you love Candace?* And then he could be all like, *You know there's only one woman I've ever loved, Erica.* And then he could throw me to the floor for some hot attic sex . . . but that didn't really seem likely.

"Well, maybe not everybody," Grady suddenly said.

My eyes snapped up to his.

He stepped toward me. "I know you were never really a fan."

"So not true," I said with a loud scoff. "In fact, we are practically besties now—"

"Just like I'm not really a fan of Matthew's."

"Oh," I said, dropping my eyes to the floor. I prodded at a raised plank of wood with the toe of my boot. "Right."

Grady stepped toward me again . . . and wow, there

were not that many steps left to take. "I should probably make some calls. I mean, these still all could be bizarre accidents, but it's worth looking into. Finding the glass is a good place to start."

Huh, that had almost sounded like a compliment.

I didn't say thank you though. Just nodded. It had been a long, long time since I had stood this close to Grady. It was like every cell in my body was waking up after having slept for way too long.

"But before I do . . ."

I swallowed hard. I needed to play this cool. With the look on Grady's face, the way he was so carefully picking his words . . . something was happening right now. Something I needed to let happen. Freddie may have been a little right earlier. I didn't always handle strong emotions well. But not anymore. I could do this. I would not screw this up.

"I have to know something. I've been sitting up here thinking—"

"About the weasels?" Frick! Weasels?

"Not just about the weasels," he said with a smile. "I have to know. All these months . . . why didn't . . ." He scratched his forehead. "I kind of thought you and Matthew would get together."

"I . . ." I stopped to clear my throat. "I, uh, couldn't do that to him."

Grady smiled again. It was different this time though. It held a shadow of that sexy smirk he always had back in high school. "Come on, you're not that bad."

I felt myself smiling too, but I couldn't meet his eye. Too dangerous.

Suddenly he was even closer to me.

Like so close, if I sneezed, I'd bonk my head on his chest. That close!

I finally looked up at him. There was a whole lot going on behind those eyes.

Be cool, Erica. Be cool.

Grady picked a small twig from my hair. I could feel the warmth of his hand on my cheek.

I swallowed hard. Oh yes, it was very difficult to talk . . . and yet I couldn't seem to stop myself either. "My hair was better before the snowmobile. You would have been impressed," I mumbled, then snorted an awkward laugh. "Before we got here, my finger waves were perfect. Freddie kept trying to drive this little toy car he had over the bumps." Why? Why was I talking about Freddie right now? Maybe because it felt like I might die if Grady didn't kiss me soon. I swallowed hard. "Freddie always thought he could be a hairstylist, but, you know, he doesn't really like hair." Gah! Yeah, no, I don't have intimacy problems.

Another smile touched the corner of Grady's mouth as he stepped back from me. It felt like a cloud had moved in front of the sun. "I've hurt Candace. And she really is a good person."

I thought again about her offer to get MRG to back off the Arthurs' property. "I know. She really is. Is that . . . is all this why she's breaking up with you?"

He did a small double take. "She's breaking up with me?"

I felt my eyes widen. "Oh . . . you didn't . . . ?"

"I . . . I was going to break up with her."

"Oh." That was good. Just *oh*. Like *I heard you. Please go on.* Very calm.

"I've been so unfair." He closed his eyes. "I've let so much get in the way of . . . everything."

"What do you mean by *everything*?"

He shook his head. "I shouldn't have started dating

Candace so soon after we . . ." He let the thought trail off. "It wasn't fair to her."

I nodded. Part of me wanted to blurt out everything I was feeling . . . everything I had been *thinking* for months but not saying. How I really, truly believed in the pit of my soul that if we just gave it one more chance, I knew we could make it work. But Grady was building up to something, and I needed to hear what that something was. For almost a year now, more than anything, I'd just wanted to hear what was going on in Grady's head.

"It wasn't fair to you either. To either of us."

I couldn't breathe. My lungs had completely shut down. My heart was doing a pretty good job at thumping though.

"We should have talked things through. I was just so afraid that if we did talk, we'd fall back into whatever it was that we were doing and—"

"I totally get it, Grady," I said quickly. "You had every reason to break up with me."

For so long I had gone back and forth with the question of whether or not I would move home. Then last Christmas just when Grady was leaving for his flight back to New Hampshire, he had told me that he loved me. He said that I didn't need to say anything back because he knew I needed more time. But I hadn't. I knew I loved him then, but my stupid insecurities got in the way. That had been the moment when it all started to go wrong. He said he understood, but he had put himself out there, and I had just left him hanging.

"Then that weekend of the storm when I found out you nearly died, and you didn't tell me . . ." He shook his head. "It felt like that was really, truly *it* for me. I was done. It was too hard to be with you . . . to wait for you. And I believed you would never be ready. Like the only way you'd ever tell me you loved me was if you knew you were going to die, and you didn't have to live with the consequences."

I could see why he would take it that way. I had written a letter to Grady telling him that I loved him when I thought I might be spending my last night on earth. I couldn't take the chance that there would be things left unsaid between us. But it had taken that do-or-die moment to get me to that point. Would I have said it otherwise? I'd like to think I would have, but I did have a remarkable ability to sabotage my own happiness. "You know that wasn't it," I said, trying to choose my words carefully. "That wasn't why I wrote you that letter."

Grady met my eye for a second before looking away. "But it's what I believed."

"Grady, listen, I get it. I understand why you're telling me all this. But you have nothing you need to explain. Everything that happened . . . it was my fault. And I am so, so sorry." He didn't answer. We were so close. So close to getting it all back. This was it. My moment. I could feel it. I just needed to say everything I needed to say without screwing it up . . . without bailing at the last moment. "And do you want to know what I believe? What I know?"

He didn't answer.

"That Christmas you spent with me in Chicago," I said, gripping my hands to stop them from shaking, "those were the best five days of my life. And . . . I think it might have been that way for you too. We were so happy in like . . . our own little snow globe. I want that again. I want it all the time."

Grady saw my hands and took them in his. "Erica, please stop. I don't need you to say all of this. That's not what I need from y—"

"Maybe, but I need to say this. I'm here, Grady. In Otter Lake. I'm not leaving. This is our chance. I—"

Just then my phone buzzed. No. No. No!

"You'd better take that," Grady said, letting go of my hands. "We shouldn't have stayed up here so long."

I met his eye to see if he really meant it. It certainly looked like he did.

Seriously?

My nerves bubbled into frustration.

Don't scream, Erica. Don't scream.

Okay, sure, fine, someone was trying to kill Candace and frame him for murder, but we were in the middle of a really productive talk! I looked down at the text on my phone.

"What?" Grady asked.

"It's from Rhonda. About Candace."

He stepped toward me to get a look at my phone. "Is she okay? I thought she was watching her."

"She was, but Candace was asleep, so she took Stanley out for a bathroom break and . . ."

"And what?"

"Candace is missing."

Chapter Thirty-four

Grady and I decided it would probably be best if we didn't look for Candace together. Neither one of us wanted to hurt her any more than we already had. Not that Grady and I had actually decided on anything about us. We agreed to talk later . . . which was kind of brutal because we had been so close! But you know, Candace might be in mortal danger, so I guess I could let her have him for a little longer. She could have me, too, for that matter. I was serious about not letting her die on my watch.

On our way back downstairs, Grady put a call in to Amos to get a couple of uniforms out to Hemlock Estate to start a proper investigation. He also tasked Amos with finding out everything he could about Candace's pen pal. If he was just out of prison, there was a good chance he was on parole. And if he was on parole, there was also a good chance that he had violated some of the conditions of his parole. If that was the case, Grady could bring him in for questioning.

Just before we made it back to the ballroom, Grady touched my elbow to get me to stop. "Does Rhonda have any idea where she might have been headed?"

"Not really, but Candace did say earlier that she wanted to go back to the party. Freddie and Rhonda are checking outside just to be sure she didn't decide to go to the boathouse again trying to find you. She's pretty out of it."

"Okay, let's split up and cover this room first. Tell everyone you can that we're looking for her."

"But won't that tip off the murderer? What if it makes him or her panic?"

"It's the best shot we have with Candace missing," he said. "The more people looking for her the better. Maybe the murderer will run, and we'll have time to get Candace safe."

"Got it."

I pushed my way through the crowd. The jazz band was really swinging now. It had to be getting close to midnight. The guests were louder too. There had to be a couple hundred people here now, all laughing, singing, dancing. Nobody seemed to have a clue what was going on. It didn't help that someone had passed out noisemakers. Everything was feeling just a little bit surreal. Or maybe this is just what it was like being at a New Year's party completely sober. Weird.

I tried spreading the word that I was looking for Candace, but I doubted that the message was really sinking in. Everyone was having too good of a time.

I had a bad feeling about this.

"Erica!"

I spun around.

Kit Kat and Tweety were elbowing their way through the crowd like a pair of white-haired juggernauts.

"What's happening?"

Tweety swallowed hard, trying to catch her breath. "We know . . ."

"You know what?" I asked. "You know who started the rumors?"

"No," Kit Kat said, shaking her head. "But we know . . . someone who does."

"What? Who?"

Tweety grabbed my elbow, leading me toward the far side of the room. "We followed all the trails." She paused to swallow. "They all lead back to the same person."

"Tell me."

"Betty Johnson," she said, still struggling with her breath. "All the trails lead back to her."

"But," Kit Kat added, "she said someone else told her. And when we talked to that person—"

"Who? Where are you taking me?"

"To the bar," Tweety said. She was the head of our awkward snake making its way through the crowd. "She wouldn't tell us who started this whole mess. She said she wanted to tell you herself."

"What? Who? Why?"

"Who knows?" Kit Kat said, hands on my back, pushing me forward.

Tweety yanked on my arm. "I think she just doesn't want to be left out of the mix."

When we finally got through the crowd, I spotted our destination.

The martini bar . . . although it kind of felt like it should be called the Dragon's Den.

It was the nicest pop-up bartending station I had ever seen. I hadn't really noticed it earlier because it was tucked far back into a corner—mainly because it needed a lot of room—but it was worth noticing.

Blue, red, green, yellow, and orange bottles glittered on the glass shelves. There was even a purple drink in a martini glass sitting on the counter. I had never seen so many colorful types of alcohol in my life.

Mrs. Watson was instructing a young man behind the

counter on his stir-stick technique. He looked equal parts scared and confused.

I thought about stopping to text Freddie to tell him what was going on, but there wasn't time. Not with Candace missing.

"Erica," Mrs. Watson said as I approached. She gave my outfit a concerned once-over but was kind enough not to mention it. "I wanted to thank you for taking care of things earlier in the smoking room. Your mother's fortune-telling has been a hit. Despite all obstacles."

"She means Freddie," Kit Kat whispered too loudly in my ear.

"She's still mad he denied her grandbaby the crown," Tweety added. Also too loudly.

I simultaneously elbowed both of them in the sides, launching myself a few steps closer to the bar.

"Can I offer you a drink?" Mrs. Watson asked. "I'm teaching Harold here how to make a beetini."

"A *beet*ini?"

"Don't let the beets scare you. They're wonderful for your health and very sweet."

The thought of a beet martini did scare me though. It scared me very much. "Um, maybe a bit later." I thought a moment about what to ask her first. Before we tackled all the rumors, I should probably check out the details of Chloe's story. "Mrs. Watson, I know you were with my mother earlier, but have you been keeping an eye on the martini bar tonight?"

"Of course. I was just getting your mother settled. You know, making sure there wasn't any trouble." She arched a knowing eyebrow as she pinned me in her gaze. "Harold, be a dear and pass me the sweet vermouth and the agave nectar."

The young man hopped to attention.

I placed my hands on the counter. "I know this is a

long shot, but was there a really big, handsome man here earlier—someone from out of town—who might have ordered an apple martini or some other green drink?"

"No, but it's funny that you should mention that," she answered, dragging her attention completely away from the beetini.

"Funny how?"

"Well, let me start by saying, I've only made one apple martini tonight." She looked over to Harold. "Have you made any green drinks?"

He shook his head quickly no.

"And Kit Kat and Tweety here were telling me that you wanted to know who started the rumors about Grady and Candace breaking up."

I nodded.

"Well, it just so happens that the apple martini I made was for the same person who told me all about Candace's concerns over Grady."

I could feel my heart pulsing at my throat. "Who?"

When she told me, I immediately said, "That . . . that doesn't make any sense. Why?" But even as I asked the question, thoughts were turning in my head, pieces were fitting together. I could see . . . I could see the why. Maybe . . .

But there were still so many things that didn't make sense. Like how did Candace's prison pen pal fit into this? Was he in on it? Or did he even know what he was doing when he gave her that drink?

Maybe . . .

No . . .

I suddenly remembered Jessica asking Freddie if Stanley had spent any time in the garage . . . and I had tripped on a container of antifreeze right outside the door of the kitchen! I knew windshield-wiper fluid was particularly dangerous around pets and children because of its sweet smell. Could someone have poisoned the drink that way? Mixed with alcohol the taste might not be noticeable. And Candace wasn't a drinker. She wouldn't know what it was supposed to taste like. There were so many people coming and going from the kitchen it was possible no one noticed. And the same person could have taken the glass from the garbage . . .

. . . the boathouse must have been Plan B after the poisoning failed.

And if the killer had been thorough enough to make a Plan B then there might still be a Plan C . . .

I quickly thanked Mrs. Watson for the information and left. I think she called after me, but my head was too full of thoughts to hear properly. I also didn't know exactly where I was headed, but my feet seemed to have an idea. Kit Kat and Tweety hurried to follow.

"So what are you going to do?" Kit Kat asked, panting in her effort to keep up. "I mean it doesn't necessarily mean anything. They're just rumors."

"Yeah, I've been holding on to the belief that none of the things that have been happening tonight mean anything, but I have a horrible feeling that sticking to that belief is going to leave Candace dead."

Tweety grabbed my wrist. Forcing me to a stop. By the look of concern on her face, I was guessing I was coming off a little weird. I couldn't help it. I couldn't think all of this through and still look normal. "But Candace is safe, right?" she asked. "Rhonda's with her."

"And what about Grady?" Kit Kat chimed in.

"Yeah, I found him, but—" I got up on my toes trying to spot him in the crowd. "But no. Candace is missing. I'll call Grady and—Frick! He lost his phone." Or it was stolen. His phone was stolen to set him up for murder.

"What do you want us to do?"

"Find Candace. Fast."

"We should split up," Kit Kat said.

I nodded. "But don't do anything else. We're not confronting anyone. Find her. Then call me. That's it."

"Got it."

"Just whatever you do, don't leave her alone. And be safe."

"Got it." The twins hurried off.

Just then my phone buzzed. Freddie.

Any sign?

No.

She's not outside. We're coming in.

Right, but—

Just then someone caught my eye.

I didn't finish the text.

I had spent so much of the night trying to track people down . . . and there, headed for the smoking room with my mother, was the very person I needed to have a word with. Someone who—if I was right—was the key to figuring out everything that had happened tonight.

I had to be sure.

Chapter Thirty-five

I shoved my way through the crowd. Angry shouts followed me as I cut my path. Really, what was the matter with people? Given the way I looked right now, I know I would move out of my way. There was no lineup outside of the pocket doors of the smoking room anymore. It had to be really close to midnight. People were in full-on party mode. My boots slapped against the marble floor as I broke into a run. I slowed only when I got to the half-shut door.

I took a breath and slid it open.

The room was empty except for my mom and Bryson. The fire had burned down to embers. He sat at the table, head collapsed over his arms. My mother stood patting his shoulder, looking bewildered. Then again she always looked a little bit bewildered.

"Erica? Honey, I'm glad you're here. I think this young fellow could use our support."

Bryson looked up. "Erica?" He moaned, dropping his head back on his forearms. "No. Not Erica. I am so tired of Erica!"

"Erica, honey, what did you do?" My mother's blue eyes had grown even wider.

"Nothing," I said quickly. "He's just mad because I didn't want to be his girlfriend. Then he was mad because I wouldn't sleep with him."

My mother threw her hand away from Bryson's back and rubbed her fingers together as though he had left a sticky residue.

"And you were really mean about it," Bryson's muffled voice called out.

"Hey, it's not my fault you don't hear nice."

My mother made a weird flexing motion with her arm and mumbled, "Do you want me to . . . ?" It kind of looked like she was acting out snapping his neck with her bicep. Or maybe just choking him out?

"Nope, I've got something else in mind." I rushed forward and plucked the turban off her head. I plopped it down on my own and hurried over to the chair across from Bryson, dropping myself into it.

"What are you doing?" a miserable Bryson asked, peering up at me.

I picked up the tarot cards and began shuffling. "I'm going to tell your future, Bryson."

His eyes jumped from me to my mother. "Are you psychic too?"

"Absolutely." I flipped cards over on the table, giving each one a good smack.

A spark flickered in Bryson's eye. He had been deep into the Scotch, but even so, he knew something was up.

"Hmm," I said, catching his gaze with my own. "These cards tell a very interesting story."

His brow furrowed. "You haven't even looked at them."

"I don't need to." I tapped the side of my head. "Psychic, you know."

"Erica, I had no idea you were so interested in—"

"Not now, Mom."

She didn't say anything more, just eased herself into a seat halfway between Bryson and me at the side of the table.

"Do you want to know how the story starts, Bryson?"

He studied my face. "Sure."

"Great." I folded my hands on the table. "Once upon a time there was a weasely man who thought he was entitled to everything his little heart desired."

Bryson's face went from being comically sad to something much harder.

"So in order to make a name for himself at the development company he worked for, he resorted to less than legal means to *encourage* seniors to leave their homes before they really wanted to in order to make room for this company's luxury cottages."

"This is an old story," Bryson said. "I've done my time."

"No. No you haven't," I said, losing my grip on the stony tone I had going on. I took a deep breath. "No, this man didn't do any time for his crimes. In fact, he didn't even lose his job."

"I have paid though," he said, collapsing hard against the back of his chair. "I'm Candace's assistant."

"Right. A job you don't like very much. It's beneath you."

"I want to agree with you right now," Bryson said, pointing at me with the hand that was holding his Scotch. "But I'm sensing it's a trap."

"No, seriously," I said, shaking my head. "A guy with your charm, charisma, lust for power . . . answering Candace's e-mails? Managing her social med—"

"What are you getting at?" Bryson asked, disgust forming on his pouty face. "You're right. I don't like doing those things. It's a waste of my talent."

"You want your old job back."

"I want more than just my old job back. I want—"

"Exactly," I said. "You're a man with unbridled ambition."

Bryson's eyes darted up to my turban. "I'm having a hard time remembering why I wanted to date you."

"Yeah, and this card right here," I said, tapping randomly at the table, "says you're a douchebag, but—"

"Actually," my mother said, jumping in, "that is the High Priestess card. It—"

"Mom!"

"Right," she said, holding up some apologetic hands. "You weren't done with your strange little story. Go on."

"That's right," I said, looking back to Bryson. "I'm just getting started." I pinned him in my gaze. "You see, my guess is that this man was so desperate to get his position back, he was willing to do just about anything to get it. Even resort to some of his old tricks. Like blackmail."

"I don't have to listen to this," Bryson said.

"Yes you do!" I slapped the table. "Candace's life might depend on it."

His brow furrowed with confusion. But I couldn't tell if it was real confusion or just lying-liar confusion.

"Now," I said, dropping my voice back down. "This man knew if he was going to climb his way back up to the top, he had to be more careful this time. Do a better job of covering his tracks. Find a way to do it so that he would win no matter what."

Bryson looked away again to the embers dying in the fireplace.

"You see, I spoke to Candace. She said that you had been doing most of the sales lately. That you've been able to buy up more properties than MRG thought possible." I tapped the edge of the table with my index finger. "In fact, Candace was going to give you all the credit. And how do you thank her for that?"

Bryson sighed and took a sip of his drink. "I have no idea what you're getting at. It's not a crime to work hard."

"Yeah, I guess in a weird way you were working hard."

My mother shot me a look of confusion. Hers was definitely real.

I tightened my eyes into a reassuring *I've got this* face.

"But tell me, Bryson, was it just the Arthurs you blackmailed or are there others?"

The Morning After

"Whoa. Whoa. Whoa," Freddie said, pushing himself up from the small carpet at the hearth into a seated position. "There's no way that's how it all went down."

"What do you mean?"

"You've never been that cool and badass under pressure."

"Sure I have."

Freddie snorted a laugh. "Your investigative questioning style is awkward at best."

"Hey! Not true."

"And you gave your mother an I've got this face?" Freddie asked with another snort. "What does that even look like?"

I pushed myself up on the bed. "You know what I think?"

"What?" Freddie asked, lying back down and staring at the ceiling.

"You're just jealous."

"Ha! That'll be the day."

"No, you are. You are totally jealous that I was the

one who figured out that Bryson was blackmailing the Arthurs."

Freddie laughed.

"And that I thought of the antifreeze."

"Yeah, when it didn't matter anymore." Freddie shook his head against the floor before letting out a frustrated shout. "Okay, fine! You're right. You are totally right! How could you have done all that without me? You wouldn't have even been at this stupid New Year's party if it wasn't for me. I got us this job!"

"I'm sorry. I didn't plan it that way. It just kind of happened." I slouched back into the bed. "And it may not have happened exactly like that, but it was pretty close."

"Hey, I just thought of something," Freddie said, voice suddenly dropping in intensity to something much more careful. "You don't think we got killed, do you?"

"What?"

"Yeah. Yeah," Freddie said. "What if you, me, and Stanley, we all died . . . and this room is like some sort of limbo?"

"No."

"You could have at least taken a minute to consider it."

"No."

"Fine. What happened next?"

Chapter Thirty-six

"I'm not blackmailing the Arthurs. That's ridiculous."

"Oh, of course not," I said, keeping my eyes on Bryson. He was still looking away, but I knew he could feel the accusation in my voice. "No, you would never blackmail the Arthurs. But Candace is, isn't she?"

My mother gasped. "What? Not Candace." She leaned across the table and grabbed my hand. "Erica, I know you have feelings for Grady, but really, this is taking it too far."

I squeezed my eyes shut with my whole face. "Mom, I know Candace is not blackmailing the Arthurs. Bryson is. I was just going for a little dramatic impact here to throw Bryson off and—" I waved my hands in the air. "Doesn't matter."

My mother leaned back in her chair. "Well, *phew,* I was really worried there for a second. Go on."

I rubbed my forehead. I couldn't remember where I had left off . . . oh yeah! "Yes, Candace is blackmailing the Arthurs. Or at least, that's how you wanted to make it look if ever there was an investigation." I threw my hands up in a *fait accompli* gesture. I was feeling very

Poirot—but a very angry Poirot who might smash Bryson's smug bearded face into the tabletop if he didn't cooperate with me. "You win either way. Either you get the credit for the sales or Candace goes down for blackmail. And I'm willing to bet your rich uncle wouldn't help sweep those charges under the carpet, would he?"

Bryson flashed me an amused smile, but I could have sworn there was just a little too much tension in it to be genuine. "I have no idea what you're talking about."

I slammed my hands on the table again. "Well, you had better figure it out real quick because if you have more people than just the Arthurs thinking they are being blackmailed by Candace, I need to know right now. Because she is in danger." I knew the Arthurs were the most likely suspects because Mrs. Watson had said they were the ones who started the rumors and ordered the apple martini, but I had to be sure. There was still Joey in the mix . . . and so much else I didn't know.

Bryson folded his arms across his chest and shrugged. "I don't know what you want me to say."

"What do you have on them?"

I saw the barest of smiles touch the corner of Bryson's mouth.

"I saw that," I said with a point. That was it. That was all I needed. He *was* blackmailing them. "You're just too proud of yourself to deny it."

"I saw it too!" my mother shouted. "He's got something on the Arthurs!" A moment later she tagged on, "I wish I knew what we were talking about."

"Later," I said, jumping to my feet. "I've got to—"

Just then my phone buzzed. Freddie.

I scanned the text. "Oh no."

"What?"

"They found Candace."

"And that's bad? Is she okay?"

I shook my head no.

"Then what is it?"

"I got to go."

Chapter Thirty-seven

Given all that had happened to Candace tonight, what she was about to do wasn't the worst thing ever, but as her friend, I thought it was pretty bad. Freddie had managed to track her down . . . well, actually, no. It was more like Candace had revealed herself to the entire party.

I hurried out of the smoking room as fast as my snow boots would carry me. I spotted the lights of a police car out a window by the front door. I sent my mother, who was following close behind, to greet Amos and tell him to keep an eye on Bryson.

The crowd thickened as I pushed my way to the part of the foyer under the arch of the dual staircase. It was standing room only. I guess I had been so deep into my questioning of Bryson that I hadn't heard the crowd file in here. Then again, it was pretty quiet. The music had stopped and everyone was murmuring in that low voice people use when they are waiting for something to happen. Was it midnight already? Or was everyone just looking up because Candace was standing on the exposed hallway of the second floor that bridged the two stairways.

Frick. I stared up at her. Yup, she was hanging onto the railing, but definitely swaying.

"Everybody?" she called out. "Are you all listening? I have a little something I want to say." Her words were thick and slurry. She hadn't sobered up much at all.

Suddenly Freddie and Rhonda were at my sides.

"We tried to stop her," Rhonda said, "but she wanted to make a speech."

"There was nothing we could do," Freddie added. "Aside from tackling her on the stairs. And I'm pretty sure that's illegal."

Poor Candace. I knew what public humiliation was like in this town. I mean, don't get me wrong, for the most part nobody would hold this drunken display against her, but they'd never ever let her forget it entirely either. Not to mention what this could mean for her job. Here's hoping she had meant what she had said earlier about wanting a career change. She was having one epically bad night. I mean, on top of all this, she was breaking up with her boyfriend . . . and it looked like the Arthurs were trying to kill her. Oh God, the Arthurs were trying to kill her!

My eyes flashed around the room.

Where were the Arthurs?

"Thank you so much for coming tonight," Candace drawled. "Oh wait . . . it's not my party!" She laughed at that, throwing her balance off enough that she had to grab the railing with both hands. "Whoa . . . I love you guys."

"Hey! Hey!" I hissed, whapping Rhonda and Freddie. "Have either of you seen the Arthurs?"

"Um, I don't know," Freddie asked. "Why?"

"Bryson has been blackmailing them to buy their property, but he's been making them think it was Candace doing it."

"What?" Rhonda shouted, causing a few people to turn away from whatever it was Candace was saying.

"But what about her prison pen pal?" Freddie asked. "I thought he was our main suspect? He's the one who gave Candace the drink."

"I don't know. I don't know! Maybe they're working together?" That didn't make sense. "Maybe there are two sets of people trying to kill Candace?"

"Don't forget her sister," Rhonda added. "We haven't cleared her yet."

"Yes we have," Freddie said with total certainty.

I let out a small shout of frustration. "We've got to get her down from there."

"Calm down," Freddie said. "I don't think anyone's going to kill her with the entire town watching."

"I don't think we can say we know anything for sure."

All three of us turned our attention back up to Candace.

"It's okay," she said loudly. "I get why you hate me. I hate me too." She pounded her chest then wobbled on her heels.

"Nope, we have to do something," I said. "It's too dangerous for her to be up there."

"Yeah and there are some train wrecks just too painful to watch," Freddie added.

We again pushed our way through the thick crowd as Candace called out, "But I want you to know that I love all of—Stop right there, Grady Forrester!"

We froze and whipped our heads around to the opposite staircase from the one we were headed for. Grady stood halfway up the stairs, hand outreached to Candace.

I couldn't quite hear what he was saying even though it seemed like the entire room had stopped breathing. If I had to guess it was something like, *Let's talk about this.*

"Oh no," Candace shouted, trying to plant a hand on

her hip but missing. "Let's just do it in front of everybody. Everybody knows everything about everyone anyway." Her eyes swept the room. "Is Erica here? Erica should be here."

Oh crap. Maybe if I stayed really still, I could just blink myself out of existence. I squeezed my eyes shut.

"Erica?" she called out again. Louder this time. "Where are you?"

I peeked one eye open. Well, there was no point in trying to hide with all these heads turning round to look at me.

I raised my hand in the air.

"Hey! There you are!" Candace let out a happy-sounding laugh. "You're going to want to be here for this."

I smiled in return, but I was pretty sure I looked like I might be sick. I certainly felt that way.

"Now," she said, swinging her attention wildly back to Grady's side of the room. It took a second for her gaze to land on him. "Where were we?"

"Please, Candace," he said, holding his hand out again. "I am so sorry. Let's just go find somewhere private to talk about this."

"Nope. Nope. Nope," she said, swinging her head side to side. "I'm tired of all the gossip. You know, this town has a real problem with gossip. And I'm in PR," she said, whacking her chest. "I am the medium. I am the message." She frowned. "Or something like that."

Grady climbed another step.

"No!" Candace shouted, walking toward his staircase. "I'm doing this."

Grady held his hands up in surrender. "Okay. Okay. You're doing this. But could you step back from the top of the stair—"

Suddenly a phone rang. Loudly.

Grady reached into his pocket and pulled it out. By

the look on his face, I was guessing it was his. The Arthurs must have slipped it back into his pocket when he was making his way through the crowd! Son of a . . . they were still trying to frame him!

He turned the phone off and looked back up at Candace. I could tell he was thinking the same thing. "Okay, I get you don't want me up there, but can someone else . . ."

"No! I need to do this on my own." She took another step toward Grady. "I've been so pathetic. Erica said I needed to take my power back."

Lots of faces turned to look at me again.

Had I said that? Maybe . . . I couldn't remember! Although it did sound like something that might be said in a girl-power type of conversation.

Candace took another shaky step toward the top of the stairs. The crowd gasped. Grady jumped another two steps up.

"I said stay back!"

Murmurs ran wild through the room.

"Okay, okay," Grady said, taking a single step back down. "Just be careful."

"Is he threatening her?" I heard someone ask.

"No," I shouted back. "He's trying to stop her from falling!" This was crazy. I knew that Grady would never hurt Candace. And Candace knew that too. But from an outside perspective this looked bad.

"Candace!" another voice suddenly shouted. "Candace, I'm coming!"

My eyes tracked the voice and landed on a man—a very big man—pushing his way through the partygoers.

Candace squinted and leaned forward on the balcony.

"It's the werewolf!" Freddie shouted.

"Joey?" Candace asked.

The murmur in the crowd rose to something a little

more panicked as Joey stormed his way to the foot of the stairs.

"Who are you?" Grady shouted.

Joey gripped the bannister, one foot on the bottom step. "The lady asked you to step away from her. You need to listen."

"Joey!" Candace shouted. "What are you doing? Don't you have parole?"

"Parole?" Grady yelled. "You're the pen pal."

"Get away from her," Joey said. "I mean it, man."

Grady dropped another step. "What are you doing here? What do you want with Candace?"

Joey didn't answer, just climbed another step.

"Oh no," I moaned. "This is—"

"Going to be the most beautiful man fight ever," Freddie finished.

Just then Joey let out a shout and launched himself up the stairs.

Grady met him head-on.

Screams echoed throughout the towering foyer—my own included—as the two men grappled on the stairs.

Rhonda gripped my arm. "Oh no! They're going to—"

Fall!

Chapter Thirty-eight

Grady and Joey somersaulted down the stairs in a violent tangle.

"No!"

I pushed my way around people, but I couldn't get to the stairs. The crowd had splintered, people dodging in every direction. Thankfully, I saw a couple of big men headed over to the bottom of the steps. Coach Waters, Ted from the marina, and Cam White, a volunteer firefighter. I heard someone else shout, "That's enough!"

"It's okay," Freddie yelled. "They're splitting them up."

He was right. I could see a bunch more men coming to hold Grady and Joey back from one another.

"Holy crap," Rhonda shouted.

"I know?" Freddie yelled. "Can you believe that just happened! I can't—"

"Guys," I said, grabbing both of them by the arm.

The two might have turned to look at me, but I wasn't looking at them. I was too busy looking up at . . .

"What?" Rhonda asked.

. . . the empty landing on the second floor.

"Where's Candace?"

Chapter Thirty-nine

The commotion of the men fighting had distracted us just long enough for Candace to disappear. Freddie, Rhonda, and I pushed our way to the opposite staircase—the crowd was thinner on that side of the room—and charged up the stairs.

Once we got to the top, Rhonda shouted, "I'll go this way!" She pointed to the hall near the far staircase. "You guys go that way!"

We didn't question her. There was no time for that. Besides, Rhonda was an ex-cop. She had training we didn't.

We sprinted into the empty corridor of the upper wing. It was a long dark hallway with way too many doors.

"How many rooms does this freaking house have?" Freddie yelled, grabbing the closest door handle.

I took the other side of the hall. "I don't know. Just look!" I shoved my head into the first room. Empty. No furniture, nothing. Just stripped floors and walls prepped for painting. I slammed the door shut and headed for the next one. "Candace?"

Freddie shouted her name, too, as he opened another door.

The next room on my side had a dresser, but was otherwise empty.

Suddenly Freddie shouted my name.

I pivoted hard in my tracks and ran.

"What?" I shouted, tumbling through the threshold.

"Look!" He stood by the window on the far side of the room near a four-poster bed. This must have been Mr. and Mrs. Masterson's old bedroom. "Hurry!"

I ran to his side.

When I looked out the window, I felt like I had been punched in the gut.

"Oh my God."

Freddie turned his horrified eyes to mine. "What is she doing?"

"I don't know."

We both raced to pry the latches of the antique window open.

No, I had no idea what Candace was doing . . . because there wasn't a single reasonable explanation I could think of for why she would be trying to step out a window from the opposite wing of the house onto an icy roof.

Chapter Forty

Candace stood in the oversized window, her hands clutched to either side of the casement. She was trying to step onto the slippery shingles, but she couldn't find her footing.

Freddie and I yanked at the iron latches on our window till they gave, but snow and ice had the frame frozen in place.

My eyes flicked back over to Candace. She was lowering one knee onto the roof.

We slammed the heels of our hands against the old wood. It only took a few hits before the top of the old frame popped out of the casing. Glass shattered. We hit the bottom of the frame a few more times before the entire piece toppled and slid down the roof, tipping off the edge into nothingness.

"Candace!" I shouted. "What are you doing? Get back inside!"

Her eyes flicked to mine. She had been watching the window fall.

It was hard to tell in the dark, but I could have sworn I saw her mouth the words *Help me.*

"I'll go around," Freddie said quickly. "Find what room she's in."

"Go. Go."

Candace now had one hand and one knee on the roof. It looked like she was trying to ease the other half of her body out.

"Stop! Don't do it! You'll fall!" But the look on her face told me she already knew that. She also looked like she was about to say something more, but something or *someone* caught her attention from inside. She looked back into the room and then back at me saying nothing. My guess was that it wasn't Rhonda behind her. Someone was making her do this. Thoughts raced in my head. Candace was drunk. She was upset. And now she was about to fall off the roof. It might look like an accident, but more likely, it would look like suicide.

"Hang on! Help is coming!"

Candace's head whipped around again. Oh God! The killer had heard me. I clutched the sides of my head. I had to do something! I looked frantically around the room. I needed a rope or—

Just then I heard Candace scream.

"No!"

She slid a foot or two before her feet caught the top of what looked like a wide dam of ice running across the bottom of the roof.

"Come this way," I said, holding out my totally useless hand to her. I say totally useless because she had to make it a good twenty, thirty yards across the span of roof that bridged the two sides of the estate before I would even be close to reaching her.

"I don't think I can make it!"

"Okay . . . just . . . just . . . hang on." My hand dove into my jacket pocket for my phone. Fire truck. We needed a fire truck with a big ladd—

I heard a really disturbing crack.

"Erica!" Candace screamed. "The ice is breaking."

Okay, no time for fire trucks.

"You need to move toward me. I'll . . . I'll find something to pull you in!"

I swung my head around. My eyes landed on the bed. A fully made bed. I yanked the heavy quilt down and starting tearing the sheets off the mattress. I tied two of them together into a knot that was not at all reassuring and ran back to the window. "Candace!"

I flung the sheet toward her.

My throw did nothing. Absolutely nothing. The sheet just flared out and went nowhere.

"Dammit!" I yanked the sheet back in and tied a knot in the bottom end to give it some weight. I tossed the makeshift rope out again. It went farther this time, but nowhere near far enough.

Suddenly I heard a new voice shout, "Oh crap!"

Freddie was leaning out from the window Candace had climbed out of.

"Hang on, Candace!" he shouted. "I'm coming!"

"No!" Candace and I shouted at the same time.

"It's too icy on that side of the roof! Where are the Arthurs?"

"Gone. Not here. I don't know!"

"Fire truck!" I shouted, throwing my sheet rope again, but I knew it was useless. She had shimmied her way closer to my side of the roof, but she was still too far. "We need a fire truck!"

"There's no time for that!" But a moment later I heard Freddie shouting into his phone.

Another deep crack sounded on the roof.

"Erica?" Candace's trembling voice called out.

"Just keep moving this way. I can almost reach you."

She shook her head. "I don't think I can."

"Yes you can! You're almost there!"

"No I can't." Her voice had gone shaky like she might be crying or hyperventilating. "I think I might be sick."

"Candace! Look at me!"

Her too wide eyes met mine.

"You can do this. Keep moving."

"She's right. You can do it!" Freddie shouted.

She eased her way along the edge of ice.

It was working.

She was going to make it. She was—

Just then the loudest crack yet tore into the night.

Candace screamed.

Frick! That sheet of ice, her foothold, was going to slide right off the roof any second.

"The vent!" I shouted. It was one of those old, rusted-out-looking things with the spinning tops. "Grab it! It's by your left knee!"

Candace tilted her head down to see what I was talking about. It looked like she was trying to lift her foot up to step on it, but just then the dam that had been supporting her weight gave out. The enormous field of ice slid off the roof with the roar of an avalanche and crashed below. Candace scrabbled against the shingles but slid after it spread-eagled. Thankfully, the vent caught her under the arm.

"Candace?"

She didn't answer.

"Candace, you need to stay with me, okay?"

"I . . . I don't think this can hold me. The metal's bending."

"Hang on." I grabbed the sheet for another throw.

Please let it reach. Please.

I hefted the rope of sheets down the roof.

"Dammit!"

It was still a couple of feet short.

"Erica? This isn't going to hold! I can feel it going."

I quickly wrapped one of the bedsheets around my waist and tied it in a knot. I tied the other end to an antique radiator by the window. It looked more decorative than anything else, but it felt solidly anchored to the wall. I did not like this idea. In fact, I was pretty sure this was a terrible idea. I'd had a really bad experience with heights not that long ago. In fact, I was pretty certain I was developing a solid phobia.

But I didn't have time to come up with anything better.

"I'm coming!"

I propped my knee up on the sill of the window, grasping the middle divider of the casement that was still intact.

"Erica?" Freddie shouted. "What are you doing?"

I slowly angled my body out onto the roof. Gritty dirt and shingle scraped at my knees, but, on the bright side, soon I'd be too cold to feel it—and after that I'd probably be dead. So there was that.

I shuffled down the sloped roof, my toes bending in my boots at crazy angles to keep me from sliding.

"Hurry!" Candace shouted.

The slope of the roof felt much steeper than it had looked from the ground.

Why . . . why was the roof so steep?

Then it happened.

I knew what would happen as soon as my toe touched the spot, but it was too late to rebalance my weight. Ice. I had stepped on an ice patch.

Once my momentum got going, there was no stopping the slide.

Oh God, please let the knot on the radiator hold. Please let it hold.

I gripped the bedsheet in my hands to lessen the impact on my waist.

Oof!

Okay, that hurt. But I was not dead.

I looked over my shoulder.

And Candace was a lot closer.

"Oh my God! Erica!" Freddie shouted. "Would you be careful!"

"I'm trying!" I yelled back through my clenched teeth.

"I'm coming back around! Don't move!" Freddie ordered. "If you die, so help me . . ."

His voice trailed away as he disappeared from the window.

"Grab my ankle!" I shouted down at Candace.

"What?"

"Grab my ankle! Climb up my body!"

"I don't think I can."

"You don't think you can? You don't think you c—" Huh, okay, she didn't think she could. I kind of wished she had told me that before I came out here! But whatever. "Candace, you have to try!"

I suddenly felt something smack against the heel of my boot. I tilted my head down to see. "That's it! Grab my ankle."

Candace did grab my ankle, but I knew right away it wasn't going to work. The boot was too thick and too heavy. It was going to come right off. "Wait! Stop!"

The boot gave. I heard it bounce down the roof and over the edge.

Thankfully, Candace had enough of a hold on the vent that she didn't go with it.

"I can't do this, Erica."

Oh boy, I did not like the sound of her voice at all. It sounded an awful lot like the voice of someone who was giving up.

Gah! I rotated my body around on the roof in my best

Spider-Man impression so that I could face Candace. "Look at me."

Candace turned her tear-filled eyes up to mine. Smeared makeup and hair covered her face.

She was so at her end.

"You are not alone." I stretched my hand out to her as far as it would go. "We are going to do this together."

She opened her eyes and nodded. I think she even might have moaned something like *okay*.

It was a good thing, too, because next I was going to tell her how I was going to throw her off this roof myself if she didn't listen . . . and I wouldn't have wanted those to be my last words. We were friends.

Candace swung her free hand up to meet mine. Her palm landed on my wrist. Her fingers curled around it.

"Good. Good," I said. "Now use my weight to get your foot up onto that vent."

She did just that and not a moment too soon because I was pretty sure the sheet around my waist was crushing all of my internal organs.

"Okay," I said, taking a breath while trying to inch my way back toward the window. I wrapped both of my hands around her wrist as she brought her other hand up too. "Now, we just have to—"

"Erica!"

I screamed.

"What the hell are you doing?"

Jesus. I squeezed my eyes shut.

Rhonda. It was just Rhonda. Rhonda was in the window I had come from.

"Help," I mumbled. "Help us."

"Oh right." I felt the sheet tighten again around my waist. "Freddie," Rhonda shouted. "Get over here and help me pull them up."

The sheet cut into my waist just above my hips, but it was twisting too. "Easy, guys! Easy! I can feel one of the knots slipping."

They stopped pulling, but I could still feel the slip of the knot giving way. "Guys! Guys! I'm falling. I'm—"

Suddenly I jerked up quickly. The motion caused the knot to give, but just then something cold and hard snapped around my bare ankle. Handcuffs?

"I've got you," Rhonda shouted. "You're not going anywhere unless you take me with you."

Or my foot pops off.

Bad thought, Erica. Bad thought. Not helpful.

"Okay. Okay," I muttered. "Candace, you need to climb up my body."

Candace scraped against the roof, but she was getting nowhere. My hands were slippery with sweat. This was so not good.

"I can't do it! I'm going to fall!"

"Yes you can. Now listen to me. We are *fine*. You're fine! I'm fine! We are both fine."

"What?"

"Actually we are better than fine. We are young. We are single." Some of us more newly single than others. "And we are at a fancy New Year's party!"

"Erica," Freddie said with lots of worry in his voice, "you okay?"

"Haven't you been listening? I'm fine! In fact, I'm freaking great!" I shouted. "You know why?"

"I'm afraid to ask."

I tried to shoot Freddie a look, but Candace caught my attention mumbling something. "What?"

"Why? Why are you great?" she asked weakly.

"Oh. I'll tell you why I'm great. Because you and I are going to get ourselves back inside. We are going to drink some freaking champagne. Well, maybe not you. You've had enough. And we are going to talk about how awe-some this upcoming year is going to be! Okay?"

She was quiet for a moment then finally said, "Okay."

"Okay?"

"Okay."

She let one hand go from my wrist and reached up to grab my jacket higher at the armpit. It had a lot of give, but I was helping to push her up as I hissed, "Ow. Ow. Ow," under my breath. Wow, that handcuff hurt.

"Candace!" a new voice shouted. "Oh my God!"

"Bethanny?" Candace answered.

"What's happening? Help her!"

"We're trying," Freddie grunted.

Candace's feet scrabbled against the roof trying to find purchase. And her right one did. At the back of my head. Mashing my cheek into the shingles. As I lay on the roof like a flattened frog, Candace managed to haul herself up onto my body, wrapping her arms around my thighs. In all the scenarios I had imagined for myself tonight, I never once thought I'd end up in this position. Literally, this position never once crossed my mind.

Suddenly I noticed Candace had stopped moving.

"I'm stuck!"

"Hurry," Rhonda grunted. "I don't know how much longer my arm can hold Erica like this."

What the heck did that mean? I tried to shout *What?* but it came out all wet and muffled with the corner of my mouth pressed against the roof.

"Just a little farther," Freddie shouted. "I'll grab your hand. I can almost reach you."

"I can't," Candace moaned. "I'm barely holding on."

She was slipping too. I tried to grab her feet to give her some leverage, but they were flailing.

"Candace! Come on!" Freddie shouted. "You're almost—whoa! Werewolf!"

And just like that all the weight was gone.

"Joey?" Candace breathed out the name like a woman who had just been rescued in a black-and-white movie . . . a woman safely tucked inside a building . . . while another woman was still lying precariously on a roof!

"Help!' My voice cracked. "Help *me*."

I felt the pull at my ankles. I tried to get up on my elbows to ease my way back so that my face wouldn't get scraped off. Then as my legs tipped in the window, two very large hands gripped me around the waist and eased me all the way in. I went limp. Joey laid me gently on the floor. Rhonda had to go flat on her belly with me, what with her wrist still attached to my ankle.

I lay there, frozen, for a good long while, eyes closed, in that place where time has no meaning.

On some level, I registered Rhonda getting the cuff off her wrist, but the rest of the bracelet was still on my ankle. Guess she didn't want to disturb me.

Suddenly a voice right above my face called my name.

I blinked my eyes open to see Freddie hovering above me.

"Erica? Are you okay?"

I mumbled something.

"What was that?" he asked, tilting his ear toward me.

"I said I freaking hate New Year's!"

"She's fine, everybody," Freddie called out, getting to his feet. "She's fine."

The Morning After

"We should totally high-five right now," Freddie said before adding in a baby voice, "Shouldn't we, Stanley. Yes, we should. Puppy, high paw."

"Please stop," I said, rubbing my head. "This whole situation is weird enough."

"But we totally saved the day! Okay, well, granted, you did most of the work this time, but you wouldn't have come if it weren't for me and Otter Lake Security, and Candace is alive because of us! Think about that. Maybe we're not hungover. Maybe we're sick from wielding the power of life and death."

I belched softly. Oh God, that hurt. I brought my hand to the middle of my chest. "I don't think that's it."

"Seriously," Freddie said, voice rising with excitement. How he could even raise his voice to that level without his head exploding was beyond me. "And we didn't screw up in any major way." He gasped. "Your Year of the Adult curse has come to fruition."

"It's not a curse. It's a resolution . . . or a theme. I can't remember."

"Speak for yourself, witch," Freddie said. "I guess it's

not all bad though. It is kind of nice getting through one of these things without feeling like we have to send out Sorry I nearly got you killed *cards."*

"Did we really get through it though? We saved Candace. But what about the Arthurs? Were they really the ones responsible? Did they get away? Why are we so hungover? And why do I still have handcuffs on my ankle?"

"Wow, I'm really starting to wonder if we have brain damage. You more than me." Then he gasped. "Oh no! I just remembered! My snowmobile! I'm gonna kill that kid!"

"What are you talking about now?"

Freddie turned his horrified face to me. "You really don't remember any of what happened next?"

I threw a pillow at him. "No!"

"Hey! You nearly hit Stanley!"

"Sorry, Stanley," I mumbled. "So last thing I remember . . ."

Chapter Forty-one

As I mentioned, I stayed on the floor a good long while.

I didn't see any real need to move. Besides, the conversation Candace was having with Joey was pretty interesting. I was making it look like I was still staring at the plaster medallion around the old light fixture above me, but I could totally see them from the corner of my eye. They stood a foot or two apart, but each had a hand half raised toward the other, like they might fall into each other's arms. And I wasn't at all thinking that just because I wanted Candace and Grady to be completely done, while still finding a way for Candace to be happy, and for us to remain friends. Nope, not at all.

"I don't understand," she said. "What are you doing here?"

"I wanted to thank you for everything you did for me while I was . . . away," Joey said. Wow, his voice was deep. "You didn't say it outright, but I knew you were worried about what your boyfriend might think, so I just sent you the drink. I hoped you'd know it was from me."

I turned my head just a little to get a better look at Candace's face. Her eyes were all big—like she couldn't quite open them wide enough to see all of him. "That's so sweet."

"Where did you get the drink?" I croaked.

They looked down at me.

"The appletini?"

"Oh," he said, looking back to Candace. "When I first got to town yesterday, I went to your work. I was too nervous to go in, but I met this nice couple outside, and they told me that I should come to the New Year's party to properly thank you. And when I got here, I ran into the man back on the driveway. He said his wife had a great idea. She passed me this drink before I even got in the door. Said it was your favorite."

Boy, the Arthurs had been busy. And it was a good thing Joey was so big. I couldn't see any other way he had survived prison, being this naïve.

"I was going to leave after that, but you seemed upset. I had to know you were okay. Then I saw the doctor treating you . . ." His voice trailed off as though the thought of something happening to her was more than he could bear.

It looked like she was just about to touch him when Bethanny put a hand on her arm, stealing her attention. "And I want you to know that I'm sorry. I know we have our issues, but I could have been more supportive. And I would never want anything bad to happen to you. Despite what some people might think." She near shouted that last part. Over her shoulder. Right in my direction. I wasn't looking at them anymore though. The woodwork was lovely on the dresser by the wall. How the heck was I supposed to know how sibling relationships worked?

I rolled myself onto my hip then and pushed myself up to a standing position by planting my forearms on a chest at the end of the bed. I would have stayed on the floor longer, but my foot was freezing. I padded my way past Candace, her sister, and her werewolf bodyguard toward Rhonda and Freddie, handcuff scraping against the wood floors.

"Rhonda," I said, voice husky. My throat wasn't doing so well after all that yelling. "I need the key for the handcuffs."

They didn't turn, but I heard Freddie say, "I don't see anything."

"They won't get far," Rhonda replied. "I'm telling you. Grady's on it."

"How does Grady even know?"

Rhonda growled in frustration. "I was searching one of the rooms when I heard something. Then I saw the Arthurs were making a run for the far staircase. So I gave chase. I mean, I looked in the room they must have been in, but I didn't see Candace 'cause she must have been on the roof already. So I followed them downstairs, but then they disappeared. I ran to the main hall and told Grady that he needed to find them, and he sent me back up here to get you guys, and there was Erica and Candace on the roof!" She sucked in a deep breath once she got through all that. "I couldn't believe it."

"Rhonda," I called out again, a little louder this time. "The key?"

She looked over her shoulder. "Oh yeah." She reached into the breast pocket of her sailor's uniform. "See? I knew it was a good idea to keep my spares. I was going to return them to the department, but Grady never asked and—" She cut herself off. "Never mind, here you—Oof!"

Freddie had elbowed her in the side. "Hey! Look!"

She dropped the key. I heard it trickle down the shingles.

"Freddie!" I shouted.

"Sorry, but look!" He pointed outside. "All the twinkly lights have gone out!"

"Don't worry," Rhonda muttered. "We'll find it."

I nodded.

Hmm, the lights had gone out.

"Freeze!"

The three of us clutched each other at the shout from the ground below. It was Grady. Definitely Grady.

Candace, Bethanny, and Joey huddled in behind us.

"Who's he shouting at?" I whispered.

"It's gotta be the Arthurs," Rhonda whispered back.

"I don't see them, do you?"

We could hear the distinctive crunch of someone running through the snow. Actually, a couple of people by the sound of it. There was some light shining from the house, but it didn't make it far into the shadows of the lawn.

Suddenly we heard a soft, "Dammit," coming from the ground just to the right of us. Grady again. We couldn't see him though. He was shielded by the slant of the roof. "Chloe! Tyler! Get inside."

"Tyler!" Freddie said with a gasp. "Oh no! I forgot I sent him out there."

"Why would you do that?" I asked, looking at him.

"I told him to get some of his friends to catch you and Candace if you fell."

"We would have flattened them!"

"I told them to use the tarp Matthew had over his firewood at the side of the house. I mean, you probably would have still died, but it was worth a shot."

Another shout came from down below, farther off to the right. "Where . . . are they . . . Sheriff?" By the puffing in between words I was guessing that was Coach Waters. He'd been puffing since high school.

"What did they do?" yet another voice asked. I could

be wrong, but that one sounded like it belonged to Matthew.

"They've been trying to hurt . . . Candace," Coach Waters finished.

"What?" I heard Matthew ask. "Why would anyone want to hurt Candace? That doesn't make any sense. Everybody in town loves Candace."

"I know," Coach Waters said. "She's the sweetest—"

"Quiet," Grady snapped. "We might be able to hear them."

I looked over at Candace. She met my eye. Yeah, she'd heard it.

"We should get down there," Rhonda whispered. "We can help them with the search."

"There's no point," Freddie said.

I had to agree. Hemlock Estate had a lot of property— a lot of property that had vanished in the dark now that someone had cut the lights.

"Erica!"

"What?" I near shouted with a full body jolt. Wow, I still had a lot of adrenaline flowing.

Freddie slapped me on the arm. "The blinder!"

The blinder? What the . . . ? "Oh!" I slapped the pockets of my jacket. "Got it! Got it!" I whipped it out and pointed it at the window.

"That's the wrong end!" Freddie shouted.

I looked down at my hand. Oh crap, I had it pointed at me again. Close one. I righted the sucker and aimed it out toward the lawn below. "Grady! We got you!" I flipped the switch, and the sun once again rose on Hemlock Estate.

"There!" Freddie screamed, pointing toward a cluster of trees. Two figures were sprinting for cover. Too bad that was useless information to all of us currently on the second floor.

"Grady!" Freddie shouted. "By the jingle bell thing!"

The Arthurs—it had to be them—had just ducked behind an old-fashioned horse sleigh the town had been using for rides at the carnival.

Suddenly Grady darted out from underneath the overhang of the roof and across the lawn. Coach Waters and Matthew followed close behind.

"This is so cool," Freddie whispered, shaking my arm. "It's like watching a takedown by satellite! Or . . . or one of those video games where you're hovering above the little pixelated people below."

"No. No," Candace said quickly. "It's not cool. They've got a gun. Grady, they've got a gun!" She shouted the last part out the window.

But we couldn't tell if Grady had heard.

"It's how they got me on the roof," Candace said, coming in close to look over my shoulder. "They've got a gun!" she shouted again. "I don't understand why the Arthurs would want me dead. I've barely talked to them."

"You haven't, but—"

"Bryson!" Freddie yelled.

"Yeah, Bryson has been blackmailing—"

"No! Bryson! He's running too!" Freddie shouted with a frantic point. "Erica, turn the light to the ice sculptures!"

I did . . .

. . . then a gunshot tore through the night.

"No!" I shouted. I turned it back to Grady. They all looked okay. The shot must have missed.

"Erica!" Freddie shouted. "Turn it back on Bryson before he gets away."

"I can't! Then Grady can't see." I threw him a quick look. "You really should have bought the second flashlight!"

"Oh ho ho!" Freddie shouted. "Don't you even!"

"Grady!" I shouted.

If he heard me, he wasn't showing it.

"He can't hear you. They're too far away." All three men were wrestling the Arthurs to the ground. We could hear a lot of grunting and shouting.

"Oh no way," Rhonda said, pushing herself from the window. "No way is Bryson getting away this time. I'm going after him!" She yanked Joey's arm. "And I'm taking the werewolf with me."

Joey didn't budge. "I . . . I just got out of prison. I don't want to go back."

"You don't have to do anything," Rhonda said quickly. "Bryson's the type to be afraid of big men. Besides, he tried to frame Candace for blackmail."

"Let's go!"

"You won't get out there in time," Freddie called after them.

"Just keep sight of him, so I can track him," Rhonda shouted halfway out the door.

Grady, Coach Waters, and Matthew had the Arthurs on the ground. They looked pretty secure. I flipped the beam back to the ice sculptures. "He's on the move!" I looked at Freddie. "We gotta get Grady's attention. Rhonda won't get there in time."

"On the count of three."

I nodded. "One . . . Two . . ."

"Grady!" we both shouted.

"What?" he shouted back.

"Bryson! Get Bryson!"

But I don't think he heard us because just then the distinctive *braap!* of a snowmobile engine tore through the night air.

What the . . . ?

Freddie and I exchanged confused looks.

"Where's that coming from?" Bethanny asked.

"Hey! Hey!" Freddie said, once again slapping my arm frantically. "That's my snowmobile! And . . . and that's Tyler! He's wearing my coat! What . . . what is he doing?"

"Oh no, he must have heard us talking about Bryson! I think he's going after him!"

"Tyler! No!" Freddie shouted. "Stop! Your mother is going to kill me!

We watched as the teen sped the machine across the lawn. Bryson saw him coming and put his hands up, but Tyler didn't let off the gas.

"He's headed right for the . . ."

"Ice slide!"

At the last second, Tyler made a spectacular leap off the snowmobile, tackling Bryson. Maybe the tackle hadn't been completely necessary given that Bryson had had his hands up, but it looked awesome.

The snowmobile kept racing forward right to the ice slide.

Up . . . up . . . flip . . .

. . . crash.

Chapter Forty-two

Not long after, we were all downstairs. I had found an old slipper of Mrs. Masterson's to cover my bare foot. Hopefully Matthew wouldn't mind. Amos and a few other uniforms were trying to clear people out of the house, keeping only the key players behind for questioning. Grady was talking to Joey while Amos was keeping watch over the Arthurs. The other officers had already set about securing all the crime scenes. There were still a few guests hanging around. It was tough getting everybody out, not only because of the logistics, but also the rubbernecking going on by the partygoers. Yup, that's how we *do* in Otter Lake.

After the takedown outside, Freddie had sped off to check on Tyler and investigate the state of his snowmobile. Candace and I headed for the smoking room while Bethany excused herself to call her boyfriend. I put another log on the fire while Candace poked around her phone on the sofa.

"Be careful not to delete anything," I said. "Who knows what Bryson has been up to in your accounts."

"Yeah, actually, I think I'd better stop now. There's an

e-mail here from me to Gerald Arthur. It has a link to an article about a COO embezzling millions of dollars from his company eight years ago. The name of the guy is Brian Williams, but the picture looks a lot like Gerald. I wonder how Bryson made that connection."

"Private detective maybe?"

"Maybe." She sighed. "Wow, my head hurts." Candace's face was worn and sad. Sobering up was never fun.

"Do you want me to see if Matthew has any pain medication?"

"Um . . ." Just then something drew her eyes from me to the door. "Grady's out in the foyer."

"Oh," I said, getting to my feet. "I'll give you guys some privacy."

"Actually, no, I don't think I really want to talk to him right now. This night has already been so . . ." She couldn't seem to find the energy to finish the thought. "Besides, we both know it's over. Neither one of us needs to say it. At least not tonight." Candace pulled a pillow onto her lap and hugged it. "Actually, now that it's done, a part of me is relieved. It's really exhausting trying to keep someone in a relationship who doesn't want to be there."

I pinned my lips together. I wanted to say something that might help, but I didn't think there was anything *I* could say that would accomplish that particular feat.

"You should go talk to him," she said, eyes still on the other room.

I looked at her. I wasn't so much confused at what she had said as I was concerned about whether or not she really meant it. This was a pretty awkward test for our new friendship.

She met my eye. "I'm not going to pretend to understand what it is that you and Grady have together, or if it's healthy, but I also don't think either one of you will be able to move on with anyone else until you figure that out for yourselves."

Okay. I guess we were good. I took a step toward the door.

"Wait! You don't think you're getting off that easy, do you?"

Or not.

Candace got to her feet and walked toward me. "Now, I know this is going to be very hard for you, but . . ."

I looked at her, confused.

"But you did save my life, so . . ." She reached her arms out to me. "We're going to have to hug it out."

Okay, I may have been still getting used to this whole hugging thing, but it was actually kind of nice. Candace smelled like cupcakes. How did she smell like cupcakes? I was pretty sure I smelled like a wet, mildewed newspaper that had just spent an entire winter on the floor of a car. And that was not good. Nobody wanted to smell like that.

"Now, go talk to him. Quick. I don't think I can be this mature for much longer." She sniffed. "I might start drinking again."

"No. No," I said, slicing my hands in the air. "Do not do that. I'm not going back out on that roof." I spun on my heel just as Joey stepped through the door.

"Is it all right if I come in?" he asked.

She nodded. "Erica, seriously, you'd better get going."

I raised an eyebrow.

"Grady's talking to your mother."

I whirled around.

"And take the turban off!"

I whipped the hat off my head. I had completely forgotten it was there. I was also surprised it had stayed on during the roof rescue. I shoved it into my pocket before running out into the foyer, my one snow boot slapping against the tiles.

It looked like my mother and Grady were just finishing up their conversation . . . and she was passing him some sort of package?

"Mom," I said, waving a frantic hand to get her attention. She said one last thing to Grady then walked toward me.

"Do you need more aloe for your scrapes?" she asked, patting the bag at her hip. My mother always carried around her all-natural first-aid kit.

"What did you say to Grady?"

She blinked. "What do you mean, what did I say to Grady?"

"Don't act dumb," I said, pointing a finger at her face.

"Well," she said, rolling her eyes. "If you must know, I was going to give him some much-needed insight into his deplorable behavior last spring, but I didn't."

"Why not?"

She inhaled deeply. "I couldn't do it. He already seems so . . . worn out."

I nodded. "Well, thank you. I appreciate it."

"I am a healer at heart," she said, putting her hands into prayer position.

I nodded. I wanted to go talk to Grady, but not with my mother around, so I said, "Do you have anything in your magic bag that might help Candace with her hangover?"

"*Umeboshi.*"

"I'm sorry?"

"*Umeboshi.* It's a pickled plum. You suck on it."

"Of course you do. That sounds great. She's in the smoking room."

My mother nodded and glided off, coins jangling from her waist. I felt a little bad sending my mother in to break up Candace's conversation with Joey. But, you know, in the big scheme of things, it was probably best that I not worry about Candace's love life. There was no excuse for the plum though.

I hurried over to Grady who by the looks of it was just finishing up another conversation with Amos. They exchanged nods before the deputy walked away.

"Hey."

"Hey."

"I heard you nearly died again," he said, scratching the back of his head. "I really wish you'd lay off the heights."

"Yeah, me too. Soon I'm going to be too scared to climb a flight of stairs." I couldn't tell if it was because of all the danger we had just been in, but Grady didn't look right. I mean, I wasn't expecting him to look happy. We'd all had a pretty rough night. But he looked pale. Maybe even . . . sad? I was just about to ask him if he was okay when he said, "I also heard you saved Candace's life."

I looked down at my hands and shrugged. "She's a good person."

"Have you seen her?

"She's in the smoking room, but, uh," I said, tossing a look over my shoulder, "she's kind of busy at the moment. My mom's making her suck on pickled plums."

Grady frowned then held up the small brown paper bag my mother had given to him. "I guess I was lucky to get off with just the tea."

I smiled.

"Still," he said, "I need to talk to her."

I had to stop him. And it wasn't just because *we* needed to talk. I really got the vibe that Candace had meant earlier when she'd said she wasn't ready to see Grady. "She, uh, doesn't want to talk to you right now."

What looked like more pain crossed Grady's face.

"Yeah, I guess it's not the time to ask her to forgive me. She has every right to be mad."

I touched his elbow. "I think she knows you didn't mean to hurt her."

He nodded. "I hope so."

Something was really wrong here. Obviously he didn't like how things had ended with Candace, but it was more than that.

"I, uh, left her alone with Joey back there," I said, jerking a thumb back at the room. "Was that a mistake?"

Grady's eyes darted from mine. He probably knew I was trying to gauge if he was jealous. "It should be fine. There's nothing violent in his record. He jacked a couple of cars when he was a kid. His family was pretty poor, and he had a sick sister with medical bills. He's not even on parole. He's free and clear."

I nodded. Not that Grady could see it. He was still looking away.

Up in the attic it had felt like we were finally breaking down all the walls between us, but now Grady had his right back up. I didn't want to ask him why though. I was too afraid of what the answer might be. "Um, have the Arthurs said anything? Why were they trying to frame you?"

He shook his head. "My guess is that they were trying to see if they could get away with it—right up until the last minute—so they didn't have to run again. It didn't matter if it looked like Candace committed suicide or I did it. It's early in the investigation though. Maybe they just wanted revenge and getting away with it was bonus. They had a lot of backup plans."

Well, Gerald *had* said they were resourceful. "What about Bryson? Tell me he is going to get nailed with something."

"We'll try, but men like Bryson . . ."

I put up a hand. "I know. I know.

"So . . ." I said, rocking slightly in my boot and slipper.

He looked down at the floor, but I could see the muscles at his jaw clenching. "Erica, I think I may have given you the wrong impression earlier. Up in the attic."

"Okay. You mean, the part about how we broke up because—"

"No. No." He shook his head. "I meant everything I said. I'm talking about why I was saying it."

I waited. Not breathing.

"When I told you I shouldn't have gotten together with Candace so quickly, that I should have talked to you first"—he paused, shaking his head—"I didn't mean . . . we should have just picked up where we left off."

I felt like an icy fist had punched a hole right through my rib cage and pulled out my heart.

"Right. Of course." I was looking at the floor now too.

"It's just we have been on this roller coaster for so long, and I . . . I don't want that anymore."

"I don't either!" I knew there were still people around. People probably watching us, listening to every word, but I didn't care.

"I believe you," he said quietly. "I know on some level we both really want to be together, but it seems like no matter how hard we try—"

"Grady, you know how good it can be between us."

"Erica, Chicago was five days. Five amazing days. But the snow globe thing you were talking about, that wasn't *real* life." His voice had risen too. "My real life is here. In Otter Lake."

"So is mine now."

He shook his head. "I can't keep making the same mistakes over and over again. Especially not with you. It hurts too much."

"Wow," I said, blinking my eyes. "I really didn't

see this coming. I thought if you and Candace broke up that . . ." I blinked my eyes some more. "It doesn't matter what I thought."

"Maybe I'm just not in the right headspace to be dating anyone. I don't like who I'm turning into. Stressed all the time. I need to figure some things out. Then we could maybe—"

"Sheriff?" Amos called out from across the room. "I've got Bryson's uncle's lawyer on the phone? He's demanding to talk to you immediately."

Grady sighed and rubbed his forehead. "We can talk more later, okay?"

"That's, uh . . ." I shook my head quickly. "You know, don't worry about it. I think we're good."

"Erica—"

"No, it's fine. I get it," I said. "You'd better go take that phone call."

He looked like he might say more, but then he just walked away.

I stood in the exact same spot a good few minutes. Then I noticed Freddie standing beside me. Hard to say how long he had been there.

"So . . ." he finally said. "What was that all about? You guys picking a wedding date?"

"Not the time, Freddie," I said, barely keeping my voice from cracking.

"Is there anything I can do?"

I shook my head. "I'm not fine."

"Sorry?"

"I'm not fine."

"I know," he said, nodding. "You never were." Then he quickly tagged on, "I didn't mean that how it sounded."

"Like I'm really not fine. Not at all fine."

He let a moment pass before he added, "You want to talk about it?"

"Oh my God, no!" "

"Right. I understan—"

"You know," I said, feeling the tips of my ears burn, "I'm starting to think Grady has more issues than I do."

Freddie shoved his hands in his pockets. "So you *do* want to talk about it?"

My shoulders slumped. "No."

"You're sure now 'cause it kind of seems like—"

"He needs time?" I threw a hand in Grady's direction. "To do what? To realize that he's screwing this up all over again?"

"I hear y—"

"I don't want to talk about it."

"Right."

We stood there for another two or three minutes, not talking.

Suddenly, I spotted Sean walking out from the far hallway with Stanley in his arms. He was looking at Freddie, but I could tell he wasn't sure if he should come over. Freddie hadn't noticed him.

I cleared my throat. "I think your dog is doing better," I said, tipping my chin in their direction.

"What is Bean still doing here?" Freddie was trying to make it sound like it was all weird that Sean was hanging around, but there was something that sounded an awful lot like pure fear under all his casual disdain.

"He's probably waiting to talk to you."

"What for?"

I sighed. "He likes you, Freddie."

"But why?"

"You know what? I am feeling way too sorry for myself right now to be nice about this." I looked down at my feet. I at least needed to find my other boot before I could feel any pity for anyone else. "Who knows why Bean's interested in you, okay? Maybe it's your dog.

Maybe it's your fashion sense. Maybe it's your somewhat amusing contempt for the world. I don't know. But the fact is he *is* interested in you."

Freddie didn't answer.

"You know what? You *can* do something for me. You can go over there and talk to Sean."

"I don't know if I can do that."

I felt my hands curl into fists. "Freddie, for better or worse, you are my best friend, but if one of us doesn't get better at relationships real soon, we are going to die alone . . . together."

"Oh my God," Freddie said with just the right amount of horror.

"I know."

"I'm going."

I shook my fists out. "Good."

"Wait. Is *good* your new *fine* 'cause—"

"Just go!"

"Okay, but I'll be right back."

"I never doubted it for a second."

The Morning After

"Aww . . . you do love me."

I made a frustrated sound at the back of my throat. "Shut up."

Freddie snickered.

I sat all the way up in bed. "I don't understand, so Grady left . . . but did he come back? When did we start drinking?" I grabbed the turban off the bed. "When did I put this back on? We missed midnight, right? Wait . . . oh boy."

"Now you're remembering," Freddie said with a chuckle.

I closed my eyes, but all I could see were sparkling blooms exploding in the darkness of my mind.

Chapter Forty-three

"Your breath smells like antifreeze."

Stanley managed to lick Freddie's chin despite his cone of shame.

"But I'm glad you're feeling better." Stanley did look like he was feeling better. He also looked quite happy curled up snug in Freddie's arms.

I would've smiled if I could remember how. I was actually kind of numb, but even though I hadn't had time to process everything that had happened tonight, I did know that Freddie having Stanley was undoubtedly a good thing. An hour or so had passed, and Freddie, Sean, Stanley, and I were hanging out in the club chairs Tweety and Kit Kat had occupied earlier. Most everybody had gone home—including my mother. She wanted to whip up some more aloe lotion for my scrapes. The twins had left too. They had a busy day ahead of them tomorrow given that they had at least some of the inside scoop. Freddie and I were still waiting to be questioned, whereas Sean . . . I think he just wasn't ready to say good-bye. Turned out, he was going to med school. The server gig was just to help pay bills over the holiday. I kind of got the impression that this freaked out Freddie even more. I mean, sure he wanted to be half of a power couple, but not the lesser half.

"Hey guys," Matthew said, strolling up to us, bow tie hanging loose. "I was wondering if you all would like to join me outside for a second."

I guess we all looked equally confused because Matthew added, "I know it's been a rough night, and we missed midnight, but there's no sense in wasting the historical society's last surprise."

Best we could figure, midnight had struck right around the time Grady and Joey were tumbling down the stairs, so, yeah, it had kind of been a busy time. We hauled ourselves to our feet and followed Matthew onto the back terrace. Light snow had begun to fall.

There were a few other people waiting outside. Mrs. Watson. A couple of the servers. Rhonda and Bethanny. Tyler. Oh yeah, Tyler had been having a great time celebrating his epic takedown. At one point, his friends were even bouncing him up and down on a chair, parading him around the house. They had waited until Tyler's mom had gone home though. No need for her to know that it had been her son on the snowmobile just yet. She left happy seeing him happy without knowing the reason why. Chloe had gone home too. I couldn't help but wonder if she might see Tyler a little differently now, but Freddie seemed to think that that was beside the point. Tyler could do better. Freddie never had been one to easily forgive. Grady and the other handful of officers weren't outside though. They were still questioning Candace. The Arthurs and Bryson had been taken to the sheriff's department for holding.

"Okay," Matthew called out. "So things didn't entirely go as planned earlier, but I can't see any reason why we shouldn't do the countdown now before it really starts to snow." He then held up a finger for us to wait while he called somebody on his phone. "Is everybody ready?"

A few people mumbled assent. I shrugged.

"All right. All together now. Ten . . . Nine . . . Eight . . ."

Freddie, Rhonda, and I exchanged looks. Rhonda raised a glass. Dammit! I should have gotten myself some champagne. I was so over the not-drinking thing.

"Five . . . Four . . . Three . . . Two . . ."

"One!"

Gold fireworks blew open the night sky.

"Happy New Year!"

We all stared up at the beautiful display. Even Stanley roused himself from Freddie's arms to give the sky a look and then Freddie another lick on the chin. Freddie held him out to Sean, and Stanley obliged to give him a lick too.

"Aw," Matthew said, coming to my side. "The dog gives kisses at midnight? Lucky."

I looked up at him.

"Hey, are you okay?" Matthew asked. "I mean, obviously you're not okay given everything that's happened tonight, but—"

Maybe it sounds a cliché, but all of a sudden, something came over me. For the life of me, I couldn't figure out why I had never kissed Matthew. Here I had spent all of these months waiting for Grady . . . while he dated someone else . . . and for what?

Then, before I even realized what I was doing, I had stretched up and my lips were on Matthew's.

He jolted with the surprise, but then his arms were around me . . . and I was sinking into the warmth of his arms as snowflakes melted on my cheeks.

This . . . this . . . was not what I'd expected. Chills raced up my back as Matthew's hand dropped from my shoulder to my waist, pulling me in just a little bit closer.

A tiny, tiny voice somewhere in my head was screaming something about stopping, but I couldn't really hear it.

Another loud bang exploded overhead. A sizzling crackle followed.

Finally after what felt like both way too long, and yet not nearly long enough, Matthew pulled back. "That was . . ." He shook his head. Sparkles fell behind him like enormous golden snowflakes. "I'm sorry if . . ."

"Oh no . . ."

We stepped apart.

"I should probably, uh . . ." Matthew said, pointing behind him.

"Yeah, you should."

He nodded quickly.

I nodded back.

I whirled around to make my escape and—

"Freddie!"

He shook his head. "Boom go the fireworks."

The Morning After

"Why? Why would I do that?"

"Oh, I think we both know you've been wanting to do that for a while."

"No! Yes. Maybe . . . but not now! I've had plenty of opportunities to kiss Matthew. I've always resisted. And Grady had said something about needing time . . . and I cut him off! I'm so confused."

"Cut yourself some slack. You're human."

I shook my head in disbelief. "How many people saw? Was it really bad? I mean, it didn't look like some big, passionate kiss, right?"

"Oh, it looked exactly like that."

"Do you think anyone told Grady?"

"Knowing this town? I would say that's guaranteed."

I slapped my hands over my face. "No. No. That must be why I started drinking."

"I don't think so," Freddie said, squinting his bright red eyes. He really needed to get those contacts out. "Remember, after you finally broke your lip-lock with Matthew, he suggested a bunch of us use his guest rooms, so *we got Stanley's stuff out of his room, and brought it here."*

"And I was going to go to the other room, but . . ." I wagged a finger in the air. "I remember agreeing to one shot. You wanted to celebrate, and I wanted to forget—"

"The hot passion building between you and Matthew?"

"No!" I frowned. "Maybe . . . I don't know!"

"And there was a tequila bottle! With Jessica's stuff!" Freddie pointed an accusatory finger at the impassive glass bottle sitting on the dresser.

"Oh nutballs," I said with a hard swallow. "Tell me I didn't eat a worm."

"It's not a worm. It's a moth larvae." Freddie army-crawled his way over to the dresser and pulled the bottle off the top. The motion also sent a sticky note fluttering to the floor. "And that's not tequila you're thinking of. It's mescal. Get some class." He squinted at the bottle then picked up the piece of paper. "Uh-oh."

"What uh-oh?"

"Um . . . remember how Jessica had that little accident with her supplies?"

Suddenly I could feel my heartbeat behind my eyeballs. "Yeah."

"Well . . ." Freddie held up the sticky note.

DO NOT DRINK
KETAMINE

"Freddie!"

"I'm sorry! I didn't see it. I guess with all of the excitement—"

"What is ketamine?"

Freddie whipped out his phone. A moment later he chuckled nervously.

"So?"

He scratched the back of his head. "It's a horse tranquilizer. Like an anesthetic."

"What!"

"Yup. Yup. It's a recreational drug too. Its effects include increased heart rate and blood pressure. Vomiting. Hallucinations." He paused. "Amnesia."

Well, that explained a lot.

"It can also cause—"

"Just stop," I said, waving out a hand.

"Death." Freddie nodded. "It can kill you."

A heavy, heavy moment of silence passed. Neither one of us moved.

Finally I said, "I would like one of those I'm sorry I nearly got you killed cards now, please."

"It's not my fault! What kind of vet just leaves horse tranquilizer lying around!"

"With a note! A big ol' sticky n—"

"Quiet," Freddie suddenly said, eyes growing wide. "We've got bigger problems."

"We've got bigger problems than drinking horse tranquilizer? How is that possible?"

Freddie cocked his ear to the door. "Someone's coming. Actually make that someones."

We both heard the heavy footsteps coming down the hallway.

Bang! Bang! Bang!

Freddie planted his hand on his raised knee and hauled himself up to standing position. He shuffled toward the door.

"What are you doing?" I hissed.

"Um, answering the door."

"Why would you do that?"

"Because that's what one normally does when there is a knock?"

I clutched the sheets to my chest.

"Okay, other than indulging in a little Special K, I can't think of anything we did wrong." Freddie reached for the handle. *"You have to stop feeling so guilty all the time."* He then opened the door, blinked a few times, and looked over to me. *"It's for you."*

For me? I mouthed.

Freddie nodded.

I swung my feet to the floor, forgetting about the cuffs. The metal clanked heavily against the wood. I pushed myself up and dragged myself and my chains toward the door.

Grady.

Matthew.

Matthew and Grady standing side by side just on the other side of the threshold.

I looked from one to the other. Then back again.

I dragged my fingers through my hair and cleared my throat. "I—"

Suddenly Rhonda jumped in between the two men.

A noisemaker unfurled from Rhonda's mouth, bopping me on the nose.

"Happy New Year!"

Chapter Forty-four

"Don!" Freddie shouted across the bar to the grizzly bear of a man wiping down the counter. "We're going to need more ice cream over here."

"No. No. No more," I said weakly, waving a hand out. "I'm going to throw up again." I then gently laid my cheek on the cool wood of the table and took shallow breaths in and out of my mouth. Normally I found the grease-and-beer smell of the Dawg comforting, but today was not most days. Why did I think I could handle ice cream?

"Oh, I thought you threw up on purpose earlier to get out of talking to You Know Who 1 and You Know Who 2."

"Nope. Not on purpose. Just lucky, I guess." I lifted my head and slumped back against the faux leather plastic of the booth. "How it is you've recovered already? I feel just as bad as I did this morning." Maybe a little worse.

"Superior genetics," Freddie said, pushing his glasses up his nose. He had finally peeled his contacts off . . . but not without a lot of swearing.

Just then Don ambled over with another bowl of tutti-frutti.

"Oh God," I said, covering my mouth with one hand and waving the other out in front of me. Freddie had thought force-feeding me ice cream was an important first step in dealing with my feelings now that I had finally admitted I was not *fine*.

"Ah, you'd better take that away," Freddie said. "Sorry."

Don did not look impressed, but just when I thought he was going to chew Freddie out, he said, "About time you got another dog, Freddie."

Freddie beamed at the little dog sitting beside him in the booth.

"Daisy would approve."

"Hey," Freddie said, looking back at Don. "Do you think you could bring Stanley something to eat?"

Don nodded.

"Make a good cut of meat, not—"

"You're pushing it, Freddie," he said, but I could see the smile on Don's face as he walked back to the bar.

"We're celebrating, aren't we, Stanley?" Freddie said happily.

"What are we celebrating again?"

"The new year!"

"Of course." I closed my eyes.

"I know what you're thinking . . ."

I didn't answer, just sniffed. Maybe I could fall asleep without Freddie noticing.

"You're thinking, *I'm Erica. I'm so sad—*"

"I don't usually call myself by my first name in my inner monologues." Not unless I needed a really good talking-to.

"I thought I was getting back together with my ex-boyfriend," Freddie went on in his Erica voice, *"but he*

*said he needed time, so I kissed the first available guy I
could, and now he'll never want me back, and I don't
know how I feel about the other guy, but it doesn't matter
because he's moving to New York and maybe marrying
a vet—if she forgives him for being assaulted by a
strange girl who looked like she had fallen off a snowmobile."*

"I'm also thinking I'm going to need to find a new best
friend because I killed my old one."

Freddie chuckled.

"How is your snowmobile by the way?"

"Freaking Tyler's going to be cleaning my rain gutters for the next forty years," Freddie said. "But forget
all that, my point is you need to start looking at the bright
side."

I cracked one eye open.

"I tried to tell you earlier. You're a freaking hero! You
saved Candace's life!"

I closed it again.

I had done that. That was pretty cool. Freddie and I
had spotted Candace and her werewolf sitting in the town
gazebo a little earlier sharing a hot chocolate. It looked
really sweet. Not romantic per se. It was a little soon for
that. But it definitely looked like something. I kind of
liked the idea that my going out onto the roof had made
that moment possible. I'd made the world a happier place.
The pink ball of fluffy sunshiney things that was Candace would live to brighten the world another day.

We also saw online—Candace had unblocked us from
her social media—a pretty cute selfie of Candace and her
sister Bethanny hugging cheek to cheek: #shesgoing-
backtoschool #sosad #missmysisteralready. Sure, things
in real life were usually more complicated than they appeared on social media, but it definitely looked like a step
in the right direction. And speaking of social media—

that was a big part of Freddie's good mood. Stanley already had his own Instagram page and nearly a hundred thousand followers. Freddie felt this could mean big things for Otter Lake Security. #OLS.

But I also couldn't forget the other reason for Freddie's cheerfulness, Bean.

Freddie didn't want to talk about it, and I didn't want to push, but I had seen them exchange contact information.

"You know what else?" Freddie asked.

"What?"

"You are in a much more authentic place than you were twenty-four hours ago."

"Trying not to throw up tutti-frutti ice cream is authentic?"

"*The* most authentic," Freddie said. "But what I mean is that now that you are being honest with your feelings, you can grow." He made a blooming gesture with his hands . . . which kind of made me want to punch him. "And I bet you'll have more luck finding a place now that you and Candace are friends."

I shrugged. Maybe. That would be nice.

"Oh look," Freddie said, stretching up in his seat. "Rhonda's here. Rhonda!"

I grabbed his wrist. "Do not tell her that I kissed Matthew."

"She's going to find out eventually, if she hasn't already."

"Eventually. Not today."

He nodded.

"Hey guys," Rhonda said, coming up to the table. "How are you feeling?"

"Terrific!" Freddie answered.

I groaned and muttered something unpleasant.

Rhonda smiled.

"Where have you been?" I asked.

"I was just helping Jessica move more stuff to her new office. And before that I dropped in at the sheriff's department. The Arthurs have totally clammed up, and Bryson is freaking out! His lawyer's flying in, but he's not here yet."

Okay, that managed to bring a smile to my face.

"Where is your cousin's new office, by the way?" Freddie asked.

"Didn't I tell you? She bought Dr. Lambert's veterinary practice. He wants to retire."

Dr. Lambert was the only vet in town. He had a pretty steady practice.

"Did you hear that, Stanley," Freddie said. "You're going to keep your vet. Hopefully she doesn't poison daddy again."

"Yeah, Jessica feels really bad about the whole Ketamine thing," Rhonda said. "But just between us, while my cousin is super smart, she's always been a bit of a space cadet. You know, absentminded professor?" Rhonda twirled some fingers in the air before darting her eyes in my direction. "I hope we're cool, Erica. I probably should have told you she was coming to the party."

I felt my face go hot. I mean, I was totally cool with Rhonda, but she wasn't going to be cool with me after she found out I kissed Matthew. She was very judgmental when it came to my love life. But I didn't want to lie to her either. "I . . ."

"Hey," Freddie said, jumping in. "I heard Matthew was thinking of moving."

"What?" Rhonda snapped. "Where did you hear that?"

Freddie frowned and shook his head. "Can't remember."

"Well, if that was true," Rhonda said, rocking on her feet, "I'm willing to bet that he's thinking twice after last night."

"Maybe," Freddie said with just the tiniest of smiles.

"I mean you can't get that kind of excitement in New York," she added. "Hey, I'm going to get a coffee from the bar," Rhonda said, jerking a thumb behind her. "You guys want anything?"

"Nope," I said weakly.

"I'm good," Freddie said. "But see what's taking Stanley's steak so long."

She nodded and walked off.

"Thank you," I said, cupping the mug of hot water I had ordered with my ice cream.

"For what?"

"For buying me some more time with Rhonda."

Freddie waved a hand at me. "You can work it out with her later. Nobody wants you to get all upset and start puking again. And Rhonda will understand. Eventually."

I rubbed my hands over my face. "I am a terrible person."

"No you're not. You were hurt. You thought this would finally be your chance with Grady, and he ripped the rug right out from underneath you," he said. "And if you're worried about the architect, don't be. You kissed him. You didn't propose. Besides, he's known all along how you feel about Grady."

I shook my head.

"But speaking of Grady," Freddie said carefully, "do you think you two are finally . . . ?"

"Done?" I asked. "I don't know how Grady feels, but when it comes to me . . ." I shook my head and tapped the table. "Here's the problem. If you asked me, right now, to close my eyes and think about what I want my future to look like . . . I would see Grady and me waking up together, birds singing, sun rising over the lake." I had left out the part about being in his arms and having a smile on my face, but that was there too.

"That sounds really nice," Freddie said a moment later. "I kind of want that. With . . . someone."

My jaw dropped. That was the first time ever Freddie hadn't made a snarky joke when I talked about my feelings for Grady. Maybe this really was a new year.

"I've been meaning to say," Freddie said. "I was really impressed with how you held it together last night."

I squinted at him. "What do you mean?"

"Well, I was giving you a pretty hard time before the party about losing it with all your bottled-up emotions," he said, petting Stanley's head. "But after a rough start, you were like the coolest of us all."

I blinked. I hadn't really felt cool . . .

. . . but I guess I did keep it together. For the most part. Huh. Go me.

"And you got to admit," he went on. "Some parts of last night were pretty fun."

I looked up from the fork I had been spinning on the table. "Exactly what parts are you referring to?"

"You running around in a turban and snow boots? The whole thing with the Blinder 3000—"

"You shouting *werewolf!* every time you saw Joey!"

We laughed.

It felt good . . . and nauseating.

"So," Freddie said once he had regained his composure, "given everything that's happened this past year, do you regret moving back to Otter Lake?"

All that laughing had made me cry a little. I wiped my eyes and looked at Freddie. Aww, if I didn't know better, I'd say that he looked just a little bit worried about what my answer might be. "Nope. Not at all. Not even for a second."

"BFFs forever?"

I sighed. "How many times do I have to say it? The second *f*—"

"BFFs forever?" Freddie repeated at a much louder volume.

I smiled. "BFFs forever."